CATCH AND CRADLE

KATIA ROSE

Copyright © 2021 by Katia Rose

All rights reserved.

No part of this book may be reproduced in any form or by any electronic or mechanical means, including information storage and retrieval systems, without written permission from the author, except for the use of brief quotations in a book review.

The following is a work of fiction. Names, characters, businesses, places, events, locales, and incidents are either the products of the author's imagination or are used in a fictitious manner. Any resemblance to actual persons, living or dead (or lingering between those two states), or actual events is purely coincidental.

This book has been licensed for your personal enjoyment only. Please respect the author's work.

1

Hope

There's a gnome wearing a thong and a pair of lacrosse goggles in our front window.

I pause in the middle of the sidewalk, the clatter of my suitcase wheels on the pavement coming to an abrupt stop. My Uber driver takes off up the darkening street, and I turn to watch the car round the corner before looking back at the gnome.

His name is CJ Junior, and my whole face splits into a grin as I raise two fingers to give him a salute.

"It's good to be back," I mutter as I charge through the little patch of dirt and struggling weeds we call a yard. My suitcase bumps against the wooden stoop as I haul it along behind me up to the front door.

Even if there weren't a gnome dressed in my old lacrosse goggles and a cherry-red thong donated by one of my roommates staring out the window, it wouldn't take a stranger long to realize a bunch of UNS athletes live here. The butter-yellow row house is so narrow it looks like it was squeezed onto the street as an afterthought, but that hasn't stopped us from pimping it out. Besides CJ Junior, the front window is decorated with strings of pink mini lights. We've been told the sultry pink glow makes it look like we're running a gnome brothel, but I kind of like the effect.

The upstairs window is covered with the huge University of Nova Scotia banner Iz, one of my three roommates, uses as a curtain. Our miniscule excuse for a yard has some UNS pinwheels we may or may not have stolen from an orientation event stuck in the ground amidst all the terra cotta pots that house Paulina's perpetually failed attempts to grow an herb garden.

Under my feet is the custom welcome mat Jane had printed when we first moved into the house in our second year. The black block letters spell out 'Welcome to the Babe Cave.'

I remember when we rolled the mat out one August night just like this. The four of us sat on the stoop for hours drinking spiked lemonade in the heat, smacking mosquitoes off our arms and breathing in the faint trace of salty ocean you can usually catch on the breeze in Halifax. I don't know if it's true, but I always think I can smell the ocean more at night.

I fill my lungs up with briny air and take a minute to let the day roll off me: the goodbye with my parents, the rush and roar of the airport, the flight in a tiny tin can of a plane. I let it all go.

One thing at a time. First things first.

Phrases like that have kept me on track for years: little reminders that there's always a next step, and I always have what it takes to get there.

I reach for the tarnished brass doorknob, but before I can grab it, the door is jerked back so hard it slams against the wall inside.

"HOPE IS HERE!"

Jane and Paulina scream and squeal as they throw their arms around me, and I'm screaming and squealing too. The three of us start jumping up and down with our arms woven around each other like a complicated Celtic friendship knot and come dangerously close to falling off the stoop.

"You *guysssss*!" Paulina gushes from above me and Jane. She's six foot one, so she's pretty much always above us. The ends of her long blonde hair are currently in danger of suffocating me. "I'm *sooooo* happy!"

She folds herself nearly in half to lay her head on top of mine and nuzzles into me. We stand there swaying and laughing for long enough one of my arms starts to go numb, but I don't care. We've all been in and out of the house throughout the summer, but this is our first real reunion. Lacrosse training camp starts tomorrow, and the fall semester starts a week after that.

The Babe Cave is officially back in business.

"Hey, wait!" I say, twisting my head so I'm not speaking into Jane's shoulder. My glasses have been knocked out of place, but I can't extract my hand to fix them. "Where's Iz?"

Our fourth roommate normally would have joined the pile by now.

"They're picking up dinner," Jane answers.

"You guys didn't eat yet? It's almost eight!"

Paulina lifts her head off me. "Oh, we had dinner. This is second dinner. We thought you'd be hungry after your flight. Iz is getting pizza!"

My mom made a giant early dinner before I left, but my mouth still waters at the thought of pizza.

"From Davy Jones?" I ask.

I can't really see Jane's face, but I feel her nodding. "Of course."

"Fuck yeah! I've been craving Davy Jones pizza all summer. You guys are the best. You know that?"

"Oh, we know."

I start strategizing about how we're going to get out of this group hug without landing in the yard when Paulina lets out a wail.

"NOOO! My basil!"

She tries to pull away to grieve over what must be a freshly dead herb, but we're all so tangled up that Jane and I get tugged along with her. I stumble off the edge of the stoop, fighting to keep my balance. Jane thuds into my back, which sends me careening forward like a domino to thump against Paulina. She sprawls forward and catches herself against the edge of the house before dropping to her knees to grab one of the plant pots and hoist it in the air.

"WHY CRUEL WORLD?" she shouts loud enough for her voice to echo in the street.

I turn to Jane after we've both righted ourselves from nearly falling on our faces. We have an entire silent conversation as we both bite our lips to keep from laughing at Paulina. We're all close in the Babe Cave, but Jane and I have had our own secret best friend language since pretty much the moment we met.

After making the wordless decision to leave Paulina to her mourning—since she's probably going to be out here for at least half an hour poking around at her plants—I pat her on the shoulder and announce that I'm going to put my stuff in my room.

"You all right?" Jane asks as we kick off our shoes in the narrow entranceway. Everything about the house is narrow. "You must be right tired."

Her words are tinged with a slight Nova Scotian accent that makes her sound like an old fisherman's wife trapped in the body of a twenty year-old university student. Paulina, Iz, and I are all from Ontario, and we call Jane our 'local flavour.' Her accent comes out even stronger when she's angry, and she has a way of putting her hands on her hips and tapping her foot like anyone who pisses her off is a misbehaving husband coming home late from the pub.

At the moment, it's just a subtle lilt. She insists on taking the tote bag I have perched on top of my suitcase so I can start hauling my stuff up the creaky stairs. I can smell something sugary drifting up from the ground floor even when I reach the top of the staircase.

"What's the candle flavor of the day?" I ask Jane as she trudges up behind me.

Her obsession with scented candles is legendary. She uses the converted office downstairs as a bedroom, and she's always got some weird smell filling up the house. I actually like the one she's using today.

"Caramel apple. Isn't it heavenly?" She takes a deep breath and raises her eyes to the ceiling as her mouth goes slack with bliss.

"Okay, okay. Don't have a candlegasm."

I roll my suitcase down the creaky floorboards of the hall. There isn't much in this house that doesn't creak. The door to my room is open, and so are my curtains. Dusk has almost turned to night now, but the annoying streetlight that filters through the leaves of a tree in our backyard casts everything in a greenish-yellow glow.

My bed is stripped, and the top of my desk is clearer than it's ever been during a semester, but other than that, the room looks like I could have woken up here instead of halfway across the country. Lacrosse gear is tucked on shelves and hooks as functional decor. A big UNS flag covers one of my closet doors, and there's a Pride flag tacked to the other. A framed photo of my first lacrosse team back in my hometown hangs over my desk, and the wall behind my headboard is covered by a huge art print of chickadees sitting on a branch. The drawing matches the sleeve tattoo on my left upper arm. There's a stained glass chickadee hanging in the window too, lit up from behind by the streetlamp.

I click the overhead light on and wheel my suitcase inside. I set it down under the display of Polaroid photos I made by clipping them to strings with mini clothespins. Jane comes in behind me, and we stare at the photos together.

"Look at what little babies we were!" I point at a shot of her with her arms around my neck in the campus sports bar, the two of us wearing jerseys and clearly wasted. It was taken after lacrosse season ended in our freshman year.

"Oh my god, my cheeks are right chubby in that. Freshman fifteen much?"

"Jane!" I punch her in the arm. "You are a sexy motherfucker, and you know it."

Jane is one of the most down to earth, breezily confident people I know, but I also know being a curvy athlete has been hard for her.

She stares at the photo for another second and then nods. "Yes. Yes I am. Especially in this one! Oooh, and look at you! This was just after you got your hair dyed."

She points at another photo, this one taken at the start of the summer just after I'd gotten back from a trip to Montreal. I finished exams earlier than most people, so I went to visit my brother and ended up getting the teal ombre of my dreams from his hairstylist girlfriend. In the picture, Jane and I are both wearing smokey eye makeup we tried and failed to copy from a YouTube tutorial. We're not really a makeup household, but we wanted to get all sexy to celebrate the end of term.

Jane steps closer to squint at another photo. "And aww look! It's all of us and—oh."

I can't stop myself from flinching when I spot the reason for the *oh*.

I thought I got rid of all my photos of him. I want to grab the Polaroid and possibly rip it into a million tiny pieces, but my whole body has gone rigid. I can't even turn around to hide the stupid stinging in my eyes from Jane.

"Oh, Hope!" Her face creases when she looks at me. "Come here. Let me give you a Jane hug."

She throws her arms around me and squeezes hard enough to push the air out of my lungs. I flap my hands against her sides since she isn't letting me move enough to pat her on the back.

"Thanks, Jane." I'm grateful my voice isn't shaking. "I'm fine. He's just a fucking asshole."

She pulls back to hold me at arm's length and nods with a fierce gleam in her eyes. "Yeah, that's right. That fucking turd."

I burst out laughing. "Turd is most certainly the word."

She drops my arms, and I unclip the photo before making a dramatic show of ripping it up while she cheers me on. I drop the pieces in the empty trash can by my desk.

"Now that is a good note to start the term on," she says as she applauds. "We should drink to that."

"That would be cutting it close. Dry season starts tomorrow, and isn't training camp at eight?" I wag my eyebrows. "Aren't you supposed to be the responsible one?"

She puts her hands on her hips. "I'll be responsible tomorrow. Tonight I'm busting out the whiskey."

I whoop and lead the way out of the room. I need the

few seconds it will take to get downstairs to pull myself together.

I spent the summer at home doing everything I could to stop the words he said—*screamed*—from playing on a loop in my head, but all it's taken is one stupid Polaroid to hear them again.

You are crazy and selfish and you wasted a year and a half of my life.

I can still remember how the whole room got quiet, like they'd been waiting for a cue. Drake went on singing about one dance over the sound system, but the entire party stopped.

I wish the worst part was that he'd ruined a perfectly good Drake song for me. I wish he'd done something cliché and stupid like break up with me because I'm bi or because he felt weird dating a girl with more muscles than him.

It's hard to write him off as a complete asshole when a lot of what he said made sense.

A few deep breaths of caramel apple help calm me down enough to push the memories away for now. I roll my shoulders back and lift my chin after I've made it off the last stair, the way my mom taught me to do when I feel bad about myself. Jane has only just caught up behind me when the front door swings open and Iz walks in carrying a stack of pizza boxes while Paulina trails in behind them clutching her basil pot.

"SOAP OF HOPE!" Iz shouts. They zoom past me to dump the boxes off in the living room before zooming right back to pull me into a back-slapping hug.

"Iz, that is such a weird nickname." I laugh as I pull them closer.

"No, it's unique and cool," they correct me. "Just like me."

They pull back to smile at me, and I have to agree:

they are very unique and cool. Their shaved head is topped by a backwards UNS baseball cap, and they've paired raggedy cargo shorts and a green plaid shirt over an expensive-looking pair of high-top basketball shoes.

Iz exists almost exclusively in five dollar finds from the thrift store, but their compulsive splurging on designer Jordans is a force to be reckoned with.

When they came out as non-binary last year, Jane, Paulina, and I all chipped in to buy them a pair in the non-binary pride colours to celebrate. For a few weeks after, it was hard to convince them to even take the shoes off for lacrosse practice.

"Jumping Jesus, you think you got enough pizza, Iz?" Jane is shifting through the boxes in the living room. There *is* a lot of pizza there, even for four college athletes.

"It's Davy Jones!" Iz protests. "I had to get all the good flavours."

"I'm hungry enough to eat half of these." I head over to plop down on the squishy royal blue sofa next to Paulina, who's picking the few remaining leaves off the withered basil plant she has sitting in her lap and scattering them on one of the pizzas.

"I killed this plant, but at least I can honor it in death," she says in a forlorn voice without looking up.

The rest of us all exchange looks and struggle to hold back our laughter. I pat Paulina on the shoulder, but I don't trust myself enough to attempt to say something encouraging.

"Okay, wait, before you dig into the pizza, we need to raise a toast!" Jane disappears into the kitchen for a moment, and after some clanking of glasses and banging of cupboards, she comes back with a bottle of whiskey and four shot glasses.

"*Por Dios!*" Iz slaps their thighs. "Hitting the hard stuff already. Can this be our sweet Jane?"

"One shot isn't going to hurt us, and we've got a whole dry season to get through starting tomorrow." She sets the glasses down on the giant coffee table that serves as the Babe Cave's unofficial command station and starts pouring.

Iz gets up to turn the sound system on, and Paulina continues covering our pizza in half-dead basil leaves. I look around at the three of them, and for the second time tonight, heat pricks the corners of my eyes.

This is it. This is our third year. The first semester will fly by like it always does, and before we know it, we'll be in our fourth and final year and on our way out the door. Sometimes it feels like I just went through orientation yesterday, and sometimes it feels like UNS has been my whole life, but it never feels like enough.

I always want more of these moments.

"Hey, you guys." Everyone turns to look at me, and I swallow to keep my voice from shaking. "We should make this a year to remember, yeah? I want...I want it to be special. You guys have been the best two years of my life, and I don't...I don't want to waste...I..."

Paulina squeezes my shoulder, and Jane looks at me like she's close to tears too. I push my glasses up and swipe at my eyes, pissed I can't seem to get myself under control tonight.

"I guess what I'm saying is that we don't have all that much of this left." I gesture around the room filled with UNS memorabilia, photos of us, and a mix of cheap IKEA furniture and second-hand finds. "We should make it count."

I hear Paulina sniff, and a moment of silence passes

before Iz grabs one of the shot glasses and hoists it in the air.

"NO RAGRETS!" they shout, quoting a meme we have stuck to our fridge.

"NO RAGRETS!" we all roar like only sports-obsessed jocks can.

I grab a shot glass for myself and tip the burning liquid into my mouth.

2

Hope

Turns out Jane was right; one shot didn't hurt us, but I'm starting to think the fourth might be doing some damage.

I'm lying on my stomach on the couch, watching Iz and Paulina dance around in the pink glow of our string lights while Jane sits beside me with my feet in her lap. She's scarfing down what has to be her millionth piece of pizza.

Piece of pizza is such a funny phrase.

"Pieccccce a' pizza!" I slur before laughing to myself.

"Whas' at?" Jane says around a mouthful of pepperoni and cheese.

"I said pieccccce a' piiiizza!"

A full-on laugh attack takes over, and Jane calls me crazy before slapping me on the ass.

"Owww!" I yelp, but it only makes me laugh even more. I wait for the hysterics to stop and then realize the room is spinning. "Wow, I am officially drunk."

"No shit." Jane slaps my butt again. "Look at the whiskey."

Catch and Cradle

I work very hard to get my eyes to focus on the whiskey bottle on the table in front of me. "Oh. No whiskey."

After the first toast, everybody started wanting to make toasts of their own, and now I can't feel my toes.

"Are you drunk?" I ask Jane.

"Mhmmm." She grunts as she finishes off her final bite of pizza crust. "I'm not being very responsible. CJ is gonna be pissssssed."

I laugh as I imagine CJ—AKA Coach Jamal, AKA our gnome CJ Junior's namesake—yelling at our sorry hungover asses tomorrow. It really isn't funny; I should be trying to hydrate and get to bed immediately to avoid his wrath, but the whiskey has turned the whole world slow and sticky.

"Not to mention Becca," Jane adds. "She'll probably beat us all with her stick in the locker room before Coach can even get to us."

Jane laughs to herself, but I don't join in. I forgot I'd be seeing Becca tomorrow.

How the fuck did I forget about Becca?

"Need more whiskey," I mumble as I push myself up to a seat.

I grab the bottle even though it's empty and hold it upside down to wait for the final dregs clinging to the glass to trickle into my mouth. I spent the entire day so focused on handling post-breakup feelings about Ethan that I forgot all about handling Becca feelings.

Becca Moore is a force to be reckoned with, both on the lacrosse field and in my thoughts and dreams. This will be her second year as team captain.

Her second year of ordering us around on the field.

Her second year of shouting commands in that smokey, throaty voice of hers.

Her second year of standing on the sidelines to oversee

our warm-up drills with her arms crossed in that specific way that makes her tits look inhumanly perfect.

How one person got blessed with thick, flaming red hair, adorable freckles, the kind of brown eyes guys with guitars write songs about, and the C-cups of the century is beyond me.

I'd probably be jealous if I wasn't so obsessed with thinking about kissing her.

Among other things.

I set the whiskey bottle down and wait for the alcohol to take the edge off my pounding heartbeat.

That's all Becca is: a little obsession. A fun, forbidden fantasy.

Emphasis on the forbidden. Our team takes its unofficial 'no banging your teammates' policy more seriously than some of the codified rules of the sport. The team has always been super queer-friendly, but from tryouts onwards, not dating each other is something of a social contract. Apparently there was some drama in the past, and now that we're the first maritime university to play for the Eastern Canada Lacrosse League, keeping our love lives out of the locker room is essential.

That's still never stopped me from imagining pushing Becca up against a wall in said locker room.

"Yo, Hastings!" Iz snaps me out of my trance and motions for me to join them and Paulina. "Come dance!"

I take advantage of the distraction and push myself to my feet. The room spins again but straightens itself after a second. I stumble on my way past the coffee table, but Paulina catches me and starts spinning me around to the Little Mix song Iz has playing.

It's not enough to chase the images of Becca out of my mind, but it does ease some of the tension that took up residence in my shoulders as soon as Jane said her name. I twirl around, thinking back on the last time I saw her.

After years of struggling with my sexuality in a small town, I finally started coming to terms with being bi after coming to UNS. I also made out with a lot of girls in the dorms, but nobody drove me crazy quite like Becca.

It helped that she didn't seem to notice me at all. She eats, sleeps, and breathes lacrosse, and as a freshman, I doubted I even registered as a human to her off the field. That made it easier to see her as nothing more than an off-limits crush who showed up in my head when I was in bed at night.

Or in the shower in the morning.

Or basically anytime I was alone.

Then I met my ex, Ethan, about halfway through my first year. I clicked with him in a way I never had with anyone else before. I realized I wanted something real, not a fantasy with somebody who knew my lacrosse number better than my name. I'd never even been sure I was the kind of person who could handle a relationship, but Ethan made me feel like it was possible, like we'd figure it out together.

Only I got it wrong. I got it all wrong, and when Becca was the person I bumped into after I ran out of that party so the entire team wouldn't see me sob, she knew way more than my name.

Maybe it was the few beers I'd had or just the emotional turmoil, but when I looked at her after she'd pulled me into a hug, I knew she *saw* me. I knew I saw her.

It knocked all the breath out of my body and arranged new constellations in the sky.

But the term was over. Half the campus was heading home, and one possibly-didn't-even-happen moment with Becca wasn't enough to stitch up every piece of me Ethan had ripped apart, so I went home too. I went home and patched myself up.

One step at a time. First thing's first.

"Eat wasabi! Drink some coffee!" Paulina shouts, totally butchering the words to the song. I let her keep spinning me around until the track ends, and then she, Iz, and I collapse onto the couch in a dog pile that makes Jane give us a disgruntled glare as she goes in for another piece of pizza.

"Aww, you guys, look at our little lobsters!" Paulina wiggles her foot in the air next to mine. We've all got tiny, black ink outlines of lobsters tattooed on our ankles. The whole lacrosse team has matching ones.

Why the founders of the University of Nova Scotia decided to name their athletics department after a crustacean will always be beyond me. They couldn't have picked anything more stereotypical. Seafood was one of the only things I knew about Halifax before coming to school here. The other teams in the league give us a lot of shit about our name—that is, until they get on the field with us.

Then they quickly learn some respect.

"That reminds me of Jim," Iz says. "I miss Jim."

Jim is our team mascot who gets brought out for games and special occasions. He's a six foot long inflatable lobster. Why anyone would need a six foot long inflatable lobster other than to use as a UNS team mascot, I will never know, but apparently he was found on Amazon.

"Oh my god! Jim!" I shout as I wave my foot in the air alongside Paulina's. "We need Jim!"

The whiskey is still making me get very excited about everything.

"We do!" Iz agrees. "I wonder where he lives during the summer."

"In the ocean," Jane deadpans before attacking her pizza again.

Jane is a hungry drunk.

"Probably in the athletics building somewhere," Paulina answers more logically.

"We should free him!" I sit bolt upright, making Iz and Paulina groan as I knock them aside in my sudden moment of clarity. "We must free Jim! CJ won't be mad at us if we rescue Jim and bring him to practice tomorrow."

Even in my current state, I can tell that plan makes absolutely no sense, but it sounds exciting to my whiskey-soaked brain, and it's making it much easier not to think about Becca or Ethan.

"Yes, *chica*!" Iz catches my enthusiasm and sits up too. "Free Jim! Free Jim!"

Jane rolls her eyes as I join in the chant. "Why did I waste my good whiskey on you two?"

"I think it could be fun," Paulina pipes up. "It can't be that hard to find him. He's probably with all the lacrosse stuff."

"He's probably lonely," Iz adds. "He's been by himself all summer. He needs to come home with us, Jane."

Jane is not having it. "How would you even get in the building?"

"It's only nine. I'm sure people are still in there. The gym is open twenty-four seven," Iz insists. "We could head over there now."

"Nuh-uh," Jane shakes her head. "No shenanigans."

"I mean, we *did* toast to this being a year to remember," I cut in. "Triumphantly carrying Jim onto the field for the first day of training camp would be *very* memorable. Everyone would be cheering and clapping, and Coach would be so busy calming them down he probably wouldn't even notice we were drinking last night."

The plan is starting to make more and more sense, which probably says more about my state of intoxication than the plan itself, but whatever.

"Come on!" I jump up off the couch. "Let's do it!"

Paulina and Iz follow me to the entryway so we can start pulling our shoes on, and once Jane realizes she's fully outnumbered, she grumbles her way over and agrees to 'supervise the delinquency.'

Outside, the street has grown completely dark. Patches of sidewalk are lit by the yellow glow of the streetlamps. The temperature has dropped a few degrees, but the cool air feels nice on my arms and face after the heat of the living room.

We're only a couple blocks away from campus, and Paulina freestyles her way through her modified version of Little Mix's 'Wasabi' the whole way there. I've already started to sober up by the time the athletics centre comes into view, and the dopey grin on my face has nothing to do with the whiskey.

This place is home: the grassy lawns, the old heritage buildings covered in vines, the stone pathways winding through it all, and there in front of us, the familiar shape of the glass and red brick athletics centre with a huge lobster mural spray-painted on one of its walls.

I can still remember my first time seeing it on the day of lacrosse tryouts. I've been playing since I was eleven, but as I scanned the outside of the building trying to find the spot where we were supposed to meet for tryouts, my brain kept telling me to run. Thoughts I hadn't had for years bubbled up to the surface like they'd finally reached boiling point again.

You can't take anything seriously.
This is too much for you.

You should be grateful you even got to university. You can't handle school and a sport.

You're stupid, Hope.

Then I spotted another girl carrying a lacrosse stick around at the exact same time she noticed me. She walked over and asked if I was ready to become a lobster.

And that's how I met Jane.

It only took a few minutes of talking before we realized we'd clearly been best friends in another life. It also only took a few minutes before I realized everything was going to be okay.

When I'm here with my team, everything is always okay.

"Free Jim!" Iz shouts, loping along up ahead of us in their prestigious Jordans. "Free Jim!"

I can smell the freshly cut grass of the lawns around us, and I fill my lungs with a deep breath. They must have been mown today to get ready for the start of term. I always love walking around campus at night when it's warm out. It's overcast tonight, but this is my favourite place to see the stars.

We reach the building's dramatic glass foyer and follow Iz inside after they swipe their student ID. Our footsteps echo on the tile floor.

"So, uh, what do we do now?" Paulina asks in a hushed voice.

The stealing Jim plan seems extra stupid now, but it feels good just to be in the building. Everyone else is smiling too. 'It's good to be back' vibes are radiating off us like one of Jane's obscure candle scents.

"Let's walk around." I lead the way forward. "Damn, I missed this place."

I trail one of my fingertips along the wall of the hallway. The whiskey must still be at work; I feel like I can sense the building's heartbeat pumping along with my own. This is where the roar of a thousand crowds have cried out in victory and groaned in defeat. This is where stars have been born, where heroes have risen, where families have been forged with ties stronger than blood.

Yeah, it's definitely the whiskey.

Our shoes squeak on the fresh floor polish that's yet to be worn down by hundreds of students trudging through these halls every day of the semester. I start steering us to the lacrosse closet.

All we get is a closet. They at least gave us a bigger closet when we qualified to play for the Eastern Canada League. UNS is a well-known university, but it's not anywhere near as big or as well-funded as schools in places like Toronto or Montreal.

"Jim! I hear him calling!" Iz rushes past me as soon as the closet door comes into view. They stumble a little but make it down the hall without tripping.

I'm ready for our mission to end in defeat as I watch them reach for the door handle. A gasp bursts out of me when the knob twists and the door swings open. Iz lets out a whoop and starts doing a Backstreet Boys-style happy dance.

"Is he in there?" Paulina's Amazonian legs carry her past Jane and I, getting her to the closet in just a few steps. We jog the rest of the way to catch up.

Iz's voice filters out of the closet. "Jim! *Mi amor*! We are here to rescue you!"

When I make it over, Paulina is in the narrow closet lined with floor to ceiling metal shelves, doing her best to grab the edge of one of Jim's plastic claws where it dangles over the edge of the top shelf.

"Think tall thoughts!" Iz urges.

The tips of Paulina's fingers miss the claw by a good six

inches. "I'm gonna have to climb, you guys."

"NO!" Jane steps past me and grabs Paulina's arm. "No climbing! You do not know how well those shelves are attached to the wall."

"Paulina should boost someone!" I cut in.

"Yes!" Iz raises a hand to high five me. "Teamwork makes the dream work!"

Jane shakes her head and raises her eyes to the ceiling like she's praying for patience. "Did you two really just high five over that? It's not exactly a groundbreaking idea."

Iz and I are too busy trying to measure which one of us has longer arms to answer. I end up winning the contest, and Paulina squats down so I can scramble into a piggyback position.

"This is not where I thought this night was going," Jane grumbles as Paulina straightens up and wobbles a little before securing us both.

"You brought out the whiskey!" I accuse.

I focus my attention on Jim. To be honest, he looks pretty happy chilling up there, but we're too invested to give up now. I push on Paulina's shoulders to lift myself a little higher. She staggers underneath me but catches herself. My fingertips brush the seam of the claw for half a second, but I don't have enough grip to pull him down.

"Fuck," I hiss. "So close."

"Try again! I believe in you!" Iz calls.

A few more attempts end with the same result. I lower myself down and jump off Paulina to give her a break.

"What if you got on my shoulders?" she suggests.

"Jumping Jesus!" Jane's fisherman's wife voice is coming out in full force.

"One more try," I tell her, "and then we'll go home." I turn back to Paulina. "Uh, how do we do this?"

"I think maybe if I like, lean forward, and then Iz helps you climb onto me?"

We try a few variations of that and nearly send me crashing into the shelves, but after a few minutes of struggling, I'm settled on Paulina's shoulders. Now I'm tall enough that my head is in danger of hitting the ceiling.

"This is perfect!" I whoop. "Just move me a little closer to Jim, and we're good."

Balance is precarious up here. Paulina takes a shaky step that radiates up through my body and makes me sway from side to side, but I grab the shelves for support. Once we've righted ourselves, I reach for Jim and start sliding him off the shelf.

"Look out below!"

I yank him out far enough to tip him over and pitch him down to the floor. He really is ridiculously large. Iz catches him by the tail, and one of his claws bonks Jane on the head. She backs out of the closet so she and Iz can start carrying him into the hall.

"Uh, so how do I get down?" I ask Paulina.

"Hmm. I'm not really sure."

The two of us stand there strategizing until Iz comes back in the closet.

"You guys coming?"

"I think we might be trapped in this position forever."

"Hmm." Iz crosses their arms and joins us in strategizing. We settle on a plan that involves Paulina lowering into a squat and me using the shelves and one of Iz's hands to launch myself off her.

We've commenced phase one when the sound of someone clearing their throat by the closet door catches my attention.

"Don't worry, Jane. We're—"

The words die in my throat. My whole body freezes as

the fight or flight chemicals start kicking in right along with the shock.

Becca Moore is standing in the doorway with her arms crossed, and she does not look impressed.

Iz and Paulina haven't noticed her yet, and I only realize they're still trying to get me down when Iz shouts, "One, two, three, go!"

"Wait, what am I—*Ow*! Oh, fuck."

I end up banging my forehead on a shelf, kicking Paulina in the boob, falling backwards onto Iz, and taking all three of us to the ground.

When I look up from all the groaning and limb-rubbing, Becca is still standing there in the exact same position, only now she's pressing her lips together like she's holding back a laugh.

I haven't seen her since April. She looks gorgeous, even under the building's awful fluorescent lights. Her hair is down and fanned out over her shoulders, the thick, wavy red strands making her look like she could be a siren in an Irish Spring commercial. She has a strong nose and jaw that give her a tough and commanding expression, but her perfect almond eyes and all those devastatingly adorable freckles soften them out.

I do my best to keep from doing a totally obvious full body scan, but I can't help noticing her black leggings and dark green plaid button-down. It has to be made by a company with a name like 'Lesbians R Us' or 'Wear These Clothes to Bang All the Women Ever.'

"Hey, guys," she says in a fake casual tone. The rasp in her voice makes me want to close my eyes in rapture and appreciate the sound like it's a holy choir. "How's it going?"

My throat has gone completely dry and I'm not sure

my knees are working, but Iz staggers to their feet and waves at Becca.

"Oh, hey Becca. Fancy meeting you here." They copy Becca's casual tone. "What are you doing here so late at night?"

Becca uncrosses her arms and raises a set of keys in the air, making them jingle. "I'm locking up the lacrosse closet after getting things ready for practice tomorrow. I thought maybe I could leave it unattended for two minutes."

"Ah. Well. Good thing it was us and not, like, a robber." Iz forces a chuckle.

I'm still sitting on the floor glancing between the two of them like an idiot, but Paulina has recovered enough to get to her feet too.

"You guys do know we have our first practice tomorrow at eight, right?" Becca asks.

Iz salutes her. "Aye, aye, Captain. That's, uh, why we're here. We thought it would boost morale to show up on the field with Jim tomorrow. Start training camp off right, you know?"

Becca narrows her eyes and takes a step into the closet. My heart rate climbs another notch.

"You guys are drunk, aren't you?"

To say this isn't how I wanted my first Becca encounter of the year to go is the understatement of the century. I spent a lot of time this summer visualizing how I wanted to start this semester off, thinking about who I wanted to be and how I wanted to feel. Becca usually factored in there, typically in the form of me killing it as a model lacrosse player and her giving me a quiet, almost shy compliment after practice that would lead to the two of us getting dinner and walking around the beautiful, sunset-streaked streets of Halifax like mature, responsible adults.

That's what I wanted to be this year: a mature, responsible, intelligent adult capable of serious things with serious people.

The semester hasn't even started, and I've gotten drunk the day before our first practice and tried to spirit official school property away into the night.

Once again, Ethan's voice starts clanging around in my head.

All you want to do is fuck around and blame it on everything but yourself.

"Hope?"

My eyes have gone out of focus while I stare at the floor. I look back up and find Becca watching me. Her eyes are narrowed again, but this time it's with a trace of concern.

"You okay?"

"Huh?"

She can't know I was thinking about Ethan.

"You fell," she says slowly. "Are you okay?"

"Oh. Yeah." I scramble to my feet and rub my arm. I banged my elbow pretty bad, but Becca's appearance distracted me from the worst of the pain, and it's fading now. "Um, good to...see you?"

Good to see you?

I think the fall knocked away the last of the whiskey's influence, but she's going to think I'm totally trashed if I can't start talking like a normal person.

She squeezes her lips together for a second and lets a breath out of her nose like she's holding back a laugh again. "Good to see you too, Hope. Do you guys mind getting out of the closet now?"

"Oh, I've happily been out of the closet for a while." Iz smirks as they step past me and into the hall. "Hope too. We're still working on getting Paulina over to the dark side. Jane here is a lost cause. Totally cuffed to a dude."

If I could elbow Iz in the stomach without Becca noticing, I would. We do not need to air out our dating histories in front of our captain right now.

We find Jane in the hallway with Jim lying at her feet like an oversized guard dog. She's doing her hands-on-hips, foot-tapping thing and glaring like she wishes she had the whiskey bottle to smash over our heads.

"Uh, should we put Jim back?" I ask.

"You might as well bring him to practice."

I turn around to find Becca locking up the closet door. It really is symbolic; I doubt any woman could go back in the closet with Becca and her plaid shirt around.

"And of course, you'll all be there on time and ready to play, right?"

I can't be expected to keep my crush a secret when she does things like ask if I'm 'ready to play.'

Iz gives another salute. "Yes, oh captain my captain."

Becca nods and crosses her arms. She has to know how good that makes her tits look. "Right. See you then. Goodnight."

Her eyes flick to mine, and she lifts her chin in a nod before turning and heading down the hall.

I exhale for what feels like the first time since she showed up.

"Damn!" Iz shouts once Becca's footsteps have faded. "We did it! We got Jim!"

"Woo!" Paulina raises her hands, and Iz jumps up to clap them in a double high five.

I just stand there staring at the spot where Becca disappeared around the corner while the two of them hoist Jim in the air. Jane comes over and makes a show of looking between my face and the end of the hall.

"So, Hastings, you want to tell me what's going on

there?" she asks in a voice low enough the other two won't hear.

I blink and focus on her. "Huh?"

She raises an eyebrow and waits.

"What do you mean?"

She stays silent for another moment and then shrugs. "Hmm. Guess we better get this lobster home."

The four of us hold Jim over our heads like we're the aquatic version of a Chinese dragon costume in a parade. We only make it to the edge of campus before all our arms start aching and we decide to take turns going two by two. By the time we make it to our place, the combined impact of flying today and doing four and a half shots has me ready to drag myself up to my room and pass out.

I'm about to crawl to bed after we've manoeuvred Jim inside and set him down on the couch when Jane looks up from checking a text.

"Did somebody lose their phone? It's from Becca. She says she had to get something out of the closet after we left and found a phone on the floor."

We all pat our pockets down.

"Not me," says Paulina.

"Me neither," Iz adds.

I've already felt the empty pocket of my joggers.

"That would be me."

Jane looks back down at her phone and starts typing. "I'll ask her where she is. Maybe you can go grab it."

"No, that's okay. I—"

"Whoops! Already sent it."

Great. Not only am I the drunken lobster thief, but I'm now the drunken lobster thief who can't even keep track of her phone.

Iz and Paulina say their goodnights as we wait for Becca to answer. Her text comes in about a minute later.

"Oh, she only lives a couple streets over, or she says she could bring it to practice tomorrow."

It shouldn't thrill me to find out she lives so close. Half the student body lives in this neighbourhood, but that doesn't stop my chest from doing the weird mix of constricting and flooding with warmth it does sometimes when I'm near her.

"I'll just get it tomorrow. Could you tell her thanks?"

I've done enough damage for tonight. Jane is about to send the text when I remember I actually *do* need my phone tonight.

"Oh, shit. Wait. I was supposed to call my mom when I got in. Fuck."

Jane looks up. "I'm sure she's assumed you're fine."

"Yeah..."

I could message her on Jane's phone or my laptop, but then I'd have to tell her I lost my phone within hours of arriving, and that would result in a huge conversation about whether I'm okay or not and if I'm ready to be back on campus, which is not something I feel like having at the moment.

"I should probably just go get it. What street is she on?"

Jane gives me the street name and number. We say goodnight, and I head outside. I pause on the bottom step of the stoop, take a breath deep enough to taste the salt in the air, and then take off down the street.

3

Becca

I can taste the salt in the air. I let my head drop back and close my eyes, filling my lungs as far as they'll go. Even after a few years in Halifax, I haven't gotten used to being so close to the ocean. Everything changes here. The shoreline expands and contracts like the ocean is a pair of breathing lungs too, filling and emptying again and again, over and over, always taking something when it goes and bringing something new when it returns.

Sometimes I just sit down by the water and marvel at the movement of it all. Not much moves back home in the prairies, not unless you stop and watch the ripple of the wind in the fields. The waving stalks look a bit like water too sometimes, but they're always rooted in the earth, grounded in place.

Steady.

There's nothing steady about the ocean. It sweeps in whenever it wants and rolls and rages until it decides to leave. No matter how long I stare at the waves, I can never tell if I'm fascinated or terrified.

Sometimes I think I might be both.

The echo of footsteps in the empty street makes me lift my head and open my eyes. I'm sitting on the edge of the porch that runs the length of the big heritage home me and my roommates rent the top floor of. Down at the bottom of the street, I can see a girl making her way up the sidewalk.

Hope.

I recognize the army green sweats and white t-shirt she was wearing earlier. As she gets closer, her glasses glint in the glow from a streetlamp. She's got her hands in her pockets, and the bob in her step is the picture of the phrase 'out for an evening stroll.'

She's so fucking cute.

I shouldn't think it, but I do anyway. Hope Hastings is dangerously cute. She's so cute, in fact, that the first thing I thought when I saw the phone on the floor of the supply closet was, 'I hope it's hers.' I spent way too much of my summer trying and failing not to imagine what it would be like to see her again this semester. I pictured her smile, the sound of her voice, the way her glasses sit a little crooked sometimes and always make me want to reach over to straighten them. Once in a while, I'd even get so far I'd imagine trailing my fingers from her glasses to her cheek to her lips.

I grip the edge of the porch and squeeze so hard the wood digs into the heels of my palms. She's the last person on the entire campus I should be thinking about. She's my teammate. I'm her captain. We have rules for a reason.

Good reasons. Important reasons. Reasons I can't ignore.

I push myself to my feet and head down the sunken stone slabs that lead to the sidewalk. She pauses for a second like I've startled her, and then she grins and waves before picking up her pace to meet me.

She's gotten tanned over the summer, and the teal ends of her hair suit her so well. The last time I saw her—or rather, the time before I found her trying to steal an inflatable lobster earlier tonight—she had mascara running down her face, and her whole body looked slumped and broken, like an animal curling itself into a ball to hide its wounds. I'd never seen her like that. I'd never felt the need to *protect* her like I did then, the urge so strong it was more of an instinct than a thought. Other than when she was charging around the lacrosse field—and sometimes even then—I'd never seen her do anything other than smile and laugh.

She's good at making people laugh. At team parties, she's always the first one on the dance floor. She's led her fair share of karaoke parties in the locker room. She's always moving, just like the ocean, and maybe that's why I've been fighting not to sit and stare at her the way I stare at the shoreline since the day she showed up for tryouts two years ago.

"Hey, Becca."

She stops when we've reached the same square of sidewalk.

"Hey, Hope."

A beat of silence passes. She glances at the houses around us, hands still in her pockets. I try not to look at her lips. I try not to remember how it felt to hold her that night she fell apart. It was only a hug. It's what anyone would do for a heartbroken teammate, but I don't think just anyone would be itching to hold her again even now.

"Nice street."

A laugh bursts out of me before I can stop it, the tension in me searching for a way to escape. "I don't know if I can take credit for the street, but thanks."

She shuffles her feet and lets out an embarrassed

chuckle. "Yeah. Right. I just, uh, there are some nice trees on this one. Seems like a nice place to live."

The air between us is thick with something that really shouldn't be there. I can feel it pressing in on every side of me, like insulation that blocks out the rest of the world.

"I like it," I answer. "We only moved in at the beginning of last year."

"So you have roommates?"

"Yeah. I live with Rachelle and Bailey. I guess I'll have to move again when they graduate at the end of the year. I'm doing a fifth year to finish my degree."

She did not ask for all that information, but it comes out anyway.

"Right, yeah, I remember you saying a few times last year that you've got some courses to catch up on."

I nod. "Captain duties cut into my course load a little. Protecting Jim from kidnappers is a full time job."

We both chuckle at the lame joke, and Hope glances down at the pavement again.

"Yeah, about that. We got a bit...carried away? I'm sorry. I don't want you to think that I'm—that we're not serious about the team. Lacrosse first is the Babe Cave's code of honor."

I raise my eyebrows. "The...babe cave?"

She shuffles her feet again. She's extra cute when she's embarrassed.

"Uh, yeah. Ha. That's what we call our house."

I smile at her when she looks back up at me. "I like that."

"What?" She shrugs, and her voice gets playful. "Are you telling me you guys haven't named your house?"

"I can't say that we have."

"You should consider it. I'd highly recommend the experience."

I tilt my head. "Oh yeah? Got any suggestions?"

"Hmm." She squints and shifts her hips back and forth as she thinks. I try not to look down at them. "How about Cap's...shack?"

I make a sound between a laugh and a snort. Hope shakes her head.

"Okay, yeah, I'm terrible with rhymes. I'll workshop it."

"I don't know if Rachelle and Bailey would be down to name the house after me."

"I'd name a house after you."

The silence after she speaks seems to thicken the insulation around us. Her eyes go wide as soon as the words leave her mouth, and I can see her taking rapid breaths in through her nose.

"Right. Yeah. I am being suuuuper awkward tonight. Chatty McChatterson, as Jane would say. I should stop right now."

I want to reach out and grip her shoulder, but I keep my arms glued to my sides. "I don't think you're being awkward. I think you're..."

The only thing in this whole city that could make me consider jeopardizing everything that matters to me?

I force a chuckle. "Now I'm being awkward."

"We should make a club." She rocks back and forth on her feet as we grin at each other. "So, uh, thanks for grabbing my phone."

"Oh, shit. Right. Your phone. Let me get it. I left it on the porch."

Somehow, it took me all of two minutes to completely forget the reason she's here.

"I'll come with you. I need to see this shack."

We walk the few metres back to the house side by side. I can feel the heat of her arm just a few inches from mine. She stops for a second when I turn onto the pathway.

"Damn. You live *here*?"

The three story historic home with big bay windows, a chimney, and a giant oak tree in the yard *is* pretty impressive.

"Just on the top floor," I answer. "It's divided into a bunch of different units that all get rented out. I don't even know how many people live in the house in total."

"Is your room at the front?"

I stop to follow her gaze up to the roof of the house, where I can see my little window covered with the lace curtains that were already there when I moved in.

"Yeah, actually. It's that one." I point it out, and she nods.

"Cute."

I need to get this phone to her fast before I do something catastrophically stupid like ask her if she wants to see the room.

Staring at her in the shadows of the streetlight, just steps away from my front door, I can't help picturing what that would be like. I'd lead her up the creaky stairs, and we'd laugh as we tried to be quiet. I'd turn the little lamp on my dresser on to keep the lighting low. She'd tell me she likes the quilt on my bed. We'd walk over to look out the window. Our arms would touch.

I'd look at her.

She'd look at me.

We wouldn't need to say anything else.

"Here." I can't meet her eyes as I thrust the phone into her hands. I feel her fingers brush mine for a second, and it's pathetic, but even that seems like it could make me gasp if I let it.

I don't know what happened that night Ethan broke up

with her, but it woke something in me that I can't put back in the dark. I'd always *noticed* her before. Anyone would. She's hot and cool and funny, and the way she moves on the field is breathtaking. It's a combination of grace and aggression I've never seen in a player before. She's triumphant.

It's never a surprise to see her score an impossible goal; all anyone can ever think when they watch her play is *of course*. *Of course* the ball went in the net. *Of course* she made that pass. *Of course* she got around the defence. Her movement seems inevitable, free from dependence on anything around her.

Just like the sea.

I always noticed her, but I never let myself want her like this. I cut myself off. I kept distance between us. I barely even spoke to her outside of practice because I knew from the second I saw her just how dangerous the pull I felt could be. I fought it for so long I could convince myself it wasn't there, but now it tugs on my limbs even when she's not around, dragging me closer to her shoreline.

"Thanks. So, uh, I'll see you tomorrow morning, yeah?"

I nod and swallow down the lump in my throat. "We hit the field at eight."

"I'll be there. Sorry again about tonight."

"Hope, it—" I falter for a second when something shifts in her face at the sound of her name. "It's okay."

She nods.

"Have a good sleep." Her lips twitch. "In your shack."

I laugh for a little too long. I'm so tense my muscles are starting to ache.

"Goodnight. See you tomorrow."

She heads back the way she came, bobbing along with

her hands in her pockets just like she did on the way here. I shouldn't stand here watching her until she's out of sight. I should turn around and head inside to close the door on all of this as I pull it shut behind me.

But I don't.

I'm still standing there long after she's gone.

MY ALARM GOES off at a quarter to six. The soft chimes are supposed to gradually wake me up, but my eyes fly open long before they've reached their full volume. I fumble for my phone and shut the sound off so I can lay on my back in the quiet for a moment.

The grey light outside filters through my curtains, giving my room a dim glow. The space is small, just big enough for a twin bed, a desk, and two dressers sandwiched together, but it was close to campus and fit my nearly non-existent housing budget.

The house is silent as I lie there and watch the quilt my grandma made rise and fall where it's pulled up over my chest. With so many people packed into the units, this is about the only time of day there isn't some crashing and banging coming up from the lower floors.

I stay under the warmth of the blankets for another minute before I force myself out of bed. I pass the collection of art prints I got at a Halifax craft fair and the big mirror I have propped against one of the walls to make the room look bigger as I head for the bathroom.

I have my morning routine so down pat I'm pretty much on autopilot until I get out the door: brush teeth, drink smoothie, eat weird protein muffin thing, change into running clothes, tie shoes, grab keys, leave house.

It's an overcast morning, so there's no dramatic sunrise

to greet me, but the temperature is hovering right around perfect for a morning run. I smile to myself as I start stretching in the front yard. It's the first day of the first ever lacrosse summer training camp—the training camp Coach Jamal and I worked so hard to organize and get approval for.

When I got a scholarship from the Canadian Women in Sports Association after being accepted at UNS, I also won an annual donation to the team's funding. That's a big part of what took us from being barely more than a glorified intramurals team in my first year to where we are now: poised for a real shot at winning the ECULL Women's Championship this season. Just the thought has me tearing up the sidewalk at a speed way too fast to maintain for my whole run.

I know we're not playing in some huge, internationally regarded varsity league like I would have been if I'd accepted the invitation I got to go to school down in the States, but that's never stopped me from giving this team my all.

Every person on the UNS lacrosse team has their heart in the game. That means something. It shows in the way we play. It shows in the way we've performed and risen to the top. It's what gets me up before six in the morning and keeps me at the athletics centre late at night.

This team is something I can trust. It's something I can belong to and always have a place in. Sometimes it feels like the only thing I can count on, and I never want to come close to losing that again. After everything that happened in my freshman year, I've been regimenting my thoughts just like I regiment my morning routine: precise repetition with no room for mistakes.

I let my feet carry me through the sleepy streets. There are no sounds except the birds and the rumble of a few distant cars downtown. This is my favourite time of day to be outside. It feels like I'm watching the city shake off the last of its dreams, smiling down at it the way you do when you're waiting for someone you love to roll over in bed beside you and open their eyes.

The pavement under me starts to tilt into an incline as I make my way towards Citadel Hill. The city is notorious for the steep pitch of its streets, but I love the way my lungs burn as I trudge upwards. The hill makes up a park in the middle of the city that used to be an old military fort.

I wind my way along my usual route through the grass lawns, all the way to a lookout point where I can see Halifax stretched out on every side of me. To the east, it slopes down all the way to the sea. The harbour is already in action, white-sailed boats and huge cargo ships dotting the water.

A cool gust of air off the ocean lifts the ends of my ponytail. I breathe deep and smell the salt. Everything is at peace here. Everything has a place in a bigger picture that makes sense.

I'm a kinesiology major, but the courses for my minor in environmental science always make me feel like I'm standing right here on top of this hill, so high above a complicated world that it isn't complicated anymore. Studying nature in school never makes me fail to marvel at the patterns that tie us all together, the ones we move within each day without even being aware of the ways the world shapes us and we shape it.

Maybe I should switch my major.

I shake my head to push the pointless thought away, the one that still crops up from time to time. I'm too far into my degree to switch now, and my lacrosse schedule would make it too difficult to switch to a double major and still play on the team.

So kinesiology it is.

I don't want to lose the rhythm of my run, so I only pause for a few seconds before heading back down the hill. I run all the way to campus and slow to a walk outside the athletics centre. After a few laps of the lawn outside to cool down and a quick stretch, I swipe my card to get in and head for the lacrosse locker room. We share it with a few other sports teams, but it's better than having to use the ones for the student gym.

I've already claimed my usual locker for the year. I grab my backpack and gear and then head to the supply closet to grab a few things for practice. Coach will appreciate the head start. I load some pylons, jump ropes, and stretch bands into a milk crate and then shuffle my gear around so I can carry everything out to the field.

I glance up at the empty shelf that usually houses Jim the inflatable lobster, and I feel the corners of my mouth lift.

That's quickly followed by a spike in my heart rate and then a surge of guilt.

Now is not the time. It will never be the time.

I reach the field well before practice time and set the milk crate down on the close-cropped grass spray-painted with the markings of the game. Setting up the pylons is enough to distract me from Hope for a bit, and it only takes a few minutes before the same thrill of passion and purpose that sent me sprinting through the start of my run takes over again.

This is where I belong. It doesn't matter what happens anywhere else, because this field right here will always be my home.

4

Hope

"Mi amiga! Cómo estás?"

Iz comes pounding down the stairs and stops behind the couch in the Babe Cave's living room to give me an impromptu shoulder rub. I let my head drop back on the cushion and set the laptop I've been squinting at for the past three hours aside.

"Uh...Buen...o? Is that right?"

Paulina, Jane, and I are always begging Iz for Spanish lessons. I haven't managed to retain much from them.

Iz laughs and keeps working on my shoulders. I groan when they hit just the right spot. We had our fourth morning practice today, and my body is still getting re-acquainted with the intensity of university lacrosse training. The extra laps and sets of push-ups Coach Jamal punished us with after we showed up on the first day of training camp with a kidnapped lobster and raging hangovers may also be factoring in there.

Jim's triumphant appearance didn't inspire CJ's mercy like we hoped it would.

"Pretty much," Iz answers. "What are you working on? Your shoulders are like tense little rocks."

"I'll put that in my Tinder bio: shoulders like tense little rocks. Need massages."

They laugh again. "Could work, you know. Campus Tinder is dead at the moment, though. I would wait until the semester starts."

Now it's me who's laughing. "Of course you're on Tinder already."

Iz is the definition of the 'lover not a fighter' type. They're always pining after some girl and making big romantic gestures with flowers and curated playlists.

"You guys should be proud of me! You told me I had to stop asking out girls at Mario's."

Mario's is the campus sports bar, and it's always been Iz's go-to place for finding new objects of affection—meaning they've pretty much exclusively dated athletes and ended up with a pile of exes they run into around the department all the time. Iz can barely make it down the hall in the athletics centre without seeing some girl they've taken out for a three course pasta dinner or a homemade picnic in the park.

"You're right. I'm proud of you. Branching out is good."

They give me one last shoulder squeeze and then drop into one of the armchairs across from the couch, sitting sideways so their legs are slung over the side.

"I'm gonna end up like Becca if I'm not careful." They cross their arms and put on a fake scowl that's pretty close to one of Becca's unimpressed glares before adding a husky edge to their voice. "Do not try dating your teammates. Do not think about dating your teammates. Don't even say the word *dating* in front of your teammates. In fact, follow my example and take this rule to such an extreme that you will never date anybody who has stepped onto a sports field of any kind even once in their life."

Blood starts rushing in my ears. I do my best to make sure my laugh isn't too shrill, but I still sound a little demonic. Jane's suspicious looks and questions after 'The Jim Incident' have me on high alert.

It's not that I don't trust my friends enough to tell them I have a thing for Becca. I just know how things will go if I do, and I don't want to deal with it. I'd either have to tell them it's only physical attraction and then go along with all the jokes about being 'hot for captain,' or I'd need to tell them it's a full-on crush and endure the sympathy they'd give me about having it bad for someone things are never going to work out with.

Even I don't know which of those is more true. Sometimes I can reason with myself and believe I'd need to know Becca much better than I do to have more than a 'fuck, she's hot' infatuation with her, but the past few days have made that a lot harder than usual. Something is different between us, like we were circling each other in distant orbits and now we're moving on the same path.

It's not exactly a feeling I'm ready for. Not after Ethan, and especially not with the somebody who, as Iz has just pointed out, will do everything to fight feeling the same.

If she even feels the same.

There are too many *ifs* to say any of this out loud.

"Yo, earth to Hastings."

"Huh?"

I snap my gaze up from where I've been staring down at the coffee table and find Iz grinning at me.

"You need a nap or something?" They yawn like they could use one too. "*Mierda*. Practice was killer this morning. Becca worked us hard with those drills. I thought my legs were gonna give out."

I press my lips together and hold back a groan at the thought.

Becca standing on the field in tight leggings and a tank top.

Becca demonstrating a burpees and mountain climbers combo that put every muscle in her lower body on display.

Becca stalking around with her arms crossed, barking at us all in her growly, husky, 'I am the captain and you need to do this drill whether you want to or not' voice.

Becca stopping with the tips of her cleats just a few inches from my face to shout, "Is that all you've got, Hastings?"

Becca's eyes on mine when I jumped up into a burpee, neither of us glancing away for a second as she watched me pant and strain for her.

My legs almost gave out too, and it wasn't because of the burpees.

"Uh, yeah. I'm pretty wiped." I reach up to rub my temples. Even the Becca-induced panic hasn't been enough to make me forget I have a raging headache. "Maybe I should take a nap. Reading this shit is knocking me out."

They nod at my laptop. "What is it? You didn't tell me what you're working on."

"Oh." I glance at the screen. Even from here the letters look all wobbly. "One of my course textbooks only comes as an e-book, so I'm getting a head start working through it now, but I think I'm maxed out on reading."

Reading on paper has always been easier for me than reading on a screen. Just one of my many dyslexia quirks. I usually can't even resell my textbooks because I mark them up too much with ridiculous amounts of highlighter, underlines, and little hand drawn diagrams that clue me in to what the paragraph is about.

I always try to work through my textbooks and get a

grasp on what the different units and key concepts will be before the term starts. It's much easier not to zone out and miss the entire class if I've done that beforehand, but this stupid e-book is already making me feel completely lost after just the first few pages.

"Let me know if you need someone to record any of it," Iz offers. "You could take a study break and make us lunch in return."

A warmth covers my whole body, like somebody's just slipped a fluffy blanket over my shoulders and told me everything is going to be okay. Iz probably thinks they're only making a simple offer, but to me, it means the world.

All my housemates know about my dyslexia, and they're amazing about it. Whether it's offering to record themselves reading a textbook paragraph I just can't seem to absorb off the page, dealing with my very delayed replies in our group chat, or pulling an all-nighter with me so I can wrap up an assignment I still haven't finished after two deadline extensions, they always make me feel supported and valid, like I don't have to constantly prove dyslexia is an actual thing.

They're also great about respecting my independence. If they help me with something dyslexia-related, I usually do something for them in return. It's not like we keep a running tab of favors in our friendships; it's just that when it comes to dyslexia, I hate feeling like my friends are throwing me a constant pity party.

"That would actually be great." I give up on rubbing my headache away and stretch my arms above my head. "Are omelettes okay?"

"Fuck yeah. I think we have some ham for them."

"I'll see if Jane and Paulina want one." I flip over so I'm leaning over the back of the couch and take a deep breath in. "HEY HOES! YOU WANT AN OMELETTE?"

I hear the floor creak, and Paulina's door opens upstairs. Her shout booms through the house.

"YEAH, BITCH!"

We're not exactly a quiet household.

Jane's door on the ground floor stays shut, but I'm pretty sure I heard her cooking something while I was deep in the textbook vortex, so I don't bother interrupting her.

I get up off the couch and bring my laptop over to Iz. "I think if you just record these little info sections on the different chapters in the introduction, I should be good. Here, I'll open the recorder."

I get the microphone set up and also make sure to close the tab I've been ignoring all day: the one with my half-finished internship application. I'm getting closer and closer to the application deadline for a summer economics internship I've been dreaming about since first year, but something keeps holding me back. I've been blaming it on my pre-term workload even though I highly doubt that's the real reason I freak out every time I open the document.

It's easier than admitting my hesitation might have something to do with the things Ethan shouted at me months ago.

"Damn, I don't even know half these words," Iz says after scanning my textbook. "Such math. Much economics. Very money."

I laugh as I head for the kitchen. "As long as you can read them, we're good."

I hear them start recording something about microeconomic agents as I grab the egg carton, the ham, a couple green peppers, and some shredded cheese out of the fridge.

I first discovered economics after my high school

decided to offer an 'Intro to Econ' course when I was in the tenth grade. I'd always done well in the math and science side of school, but economics seemed like it might be too word-centric for me. My guidance counsellor urged me to take it anyway. I walked in on the first day expecting to switch out of the class by the end of the week, but we didn't even write anything for a while. We just talked. The teacher would move all around the classroom using everything from our pencil cases to the ceiling fans to illustrate economic principles. He made the whole thing feel like a conversation, like a game.

That's what it's always felt like to me. Economics is just like a sport. It's a quest for power. It's an exercise in anticipation. It's the ability to break a chaotic tumble of motion and sound down into a simple chain of cause and effect. When I learn about it, I feel like I'm playing lacrosse. My instincts take over. I get *in* it. I'm not stuck behind a piece of foggy glass, trying to wipe it clean just as fast as it gets fogged up again. That's how it felt to take classes like English and history, but when it comes to economics, I'm in there. I'm part of it.

I have the first omelette complete and the second one in the pan by the time Iz finishes recording. The smell of food lures Paulina down from her bedroom, and she helps me bring the plates out to the living room once I've loaded up all three.

"Mmm," she moans once we're all settled and she's taken her first bite. "Cheeeeese."

Iz points their fork at her. "Hey, weren't you gonna go vegan this year?"

She shakes her head. "I decided I'm too tall."

Iz and I glance at each other before we both double over laughing.

"You're too tall to be a vegan?" I demand.

She tilts her head and lifts her eyebrows like we're stupid. "It takes a lot to power six foot one of human. I don't have time to cook everything I would need to replace meat."

I'm pretty sure there are a lot of vegans who would have an answer to that, but I choose to use the opportunity to make fun of her gardening instead.

"I don't know. Maybe you could sprinkle everything with dead basil leaves like you did to our pizza the other day."

She glowers at me. "Do not speak ill of my basil. May she rest in peace."

With her long blonde hair, round face, and little dimples, Paulina is a bit too adorable to effectively glower.

"My apologies," I say anyway. "I would not wish to disrespect the fallen."

We turn back to our omelettes for a few moments before Iz asks what everyone's doing with the hour we have left before afternoon practice.

Paulina shoots me another Disney channel-worthy glare. "I am working in my garden."

"That sounds lovely. I'm supposed to have a video call with my brother," I answer.

Both their faces light up. Paulina squeals, and Iz bangs their fork on their plate in approval.

"Your brother is soooo cute," Paulina gushes.

"He's like a puppy!" Iz adds.

Despite being three years older than me and an adult human, that's a pretty accurate way to describe Zach. He is an adorable puppy. We have an older sister too, but Zach and I have always been the closest. I used to get into a lot of adventures—which other people called trouble—when I was a kid, and Zach followed me around like a patient golden retriever to make sure I didn't get stuck in a culvert

I was 'exploring' or decide to give homemade bungee jumping a try.

I did actually get that one set up before he found me and put a stop to it.

Iz and Paulina insist I say hi to him on their behalf, and after we finish our omelettes, I head up to my room to make the call. We've only got about half an hour to talk now, since I have to make it all the way back to the locker room and then the field for practice.

Half an hour until Becca time.

My brain has very unhelpfully decided to start referring to training as 'Becca time.' It's getting pathetic. I literally just threw the final photo of my ex into the trash a few days ago, and I'm already all over someone else.

Mentally speaking.

Besides interactions on the field and a few team-wide cuddle piles to celebrate our wins, Becca and I have never actually touched—until that one night when she held me after Ethan broke up with me in front of the whole team.

If you couldn't handle a serious relationship, you should have told me.

His voice fills my head, and once again, I start wondering if some of the things he said were true. If I was ready to be serious, would I even be thinking about Becca now? Am I just bouncing along from one distracting adventure to the next like I did when I was a kid, leaving it up to someone else to protect me and do all the hard stuff?

I flop onto my back on my bed and stare at the ceiling. There are a few unsettling cracks we all decided to ignore when we moved in. The macramé plant holder Jane got me for my birthday is screwed in over by the corner, swaying a little from the breeze drifting in my open window.

Catch and Cradle

"UGHHHHHHH!" I groan as I smack my hands on the blankets a few times.

I don't worry about freaking my housemates out. We're a very emotionally expressive household. Somebody's always making a weird noise somewhere in the building.

My phone lights up beside me a few seconds later, and I grab it and hold it above my face before accepting Zach's call. His smiling face fills the screen, his tousled blond hair making him look extra puppy-like.

"Hey, Dopey Hopey!"

"Don't call me that!" I wail.

His blue eyes—the exact same blue as mine—go wide. "Uhhh, okay. Is this a bad time?"

"UGHHHH!" I repeat my caveman groan and rock my head from side to side. "Sorry. I'm just in the middle of letting my feelings out."

He tries really hard not to grin. "By all means, continue. Seems cathartic."

"I think I did what I needed to do. How are you today, brother?"

"Can't complain. I—"

He gets cut off by a shout in the background. "Is that your sister? Let me say hi! *Allô, ma belle!*"

The phone gets ripped out of his hands, and his face is replaced by his girlfriend, DeeDee.

"Hope, how are you? How is your hair?"

Her French Canadian accent makes her miss the 'h' in my name. Her own hair is a bright bubblegum pink, and she's responsible for giving me the teal ombre of my dreams.

"It's great! It's barely faded at all." I grab the ends of a few pieces and hold them up for her to see.

"*Magnifique*! I'll give you a touch-up at Thanksgiving.

You are coming home, yes? Zachy Zach invited me. I've never done a big Thanksgiving!"

"I think so," I start to answer. "At least I—"

I pause when I hear Zach clear his throat from out of the frame.

DeeDee giggles. "I think Zach is upset I stole his phone. Here, we will do this."

After a few seconds of shuffling around and me getting a view of their ceiling, she straightens the phone so I can see her and Zach sitting on the couch in his apartment.

"Aww, you guys look so cute! And happy. And together."

Even I can hear the bitterness in my voice. Zach's face creases with concern, and DeeDee leans a little closer to the camera.

"You are better off without that asshole, *chérie*."

"Yeah," Zach adds, "and my offer to punch him still stands."

DeeDee and I cackle.

"Right. Yeah. You punching someone." I laugh for another moment and then turn serious. "But thank you. I appreciate the sentiment."

I may have drunkenly called Zach a couple nights after the breakup and ended up giving him and DeeDee a very slurred but detailed version of the whole story.

Minus the Becca part.

"Is that what your cathartic feelings release was about?" Zach asks.

"Kind of," I answer. "Like...the term hasn't even started, and I already feel overwhelmed. Feelings are hard. School is hard. If I didn't have the chance to chase a ball around and hit people with a stick every day, I'd have lost it already."

Zach chuckles. "You always tell me you're not

supposed to hit each other with the sticks, but then you say stuff like that."

"I mean, that's not what you're *supposed* to do..."

The two of them laugh, and after they give me some reassurance, we move onto talking about DeeDee's progress at haircutting school and Zach's work in ecommerce. I keep checking the clock to make sure I'm not late and try very hard not to mentally refer to it as the 'Becca countdown.'

That's difficult to do when I still have this morning's practice running on repeat in my head.

Is that all you've got, Hastings?

I wanted to show her exactly what I had. I wanted her to take it all from me. I wanted her to work me so hard I collapsed on the field, and then I wanted her to show me what I earned for being so good for her.

Not exactly the kind of thoughts I want to have while on the phone with my brother and his girlfriend, but I can't get them to stop.

"Hey, you guys," I blurt after I've announced I should probably start putting my contacts in. I hate wearing contacts so much I only put them on for the minimum amount of time required for practice and games. "How long do you consider the rebound zone to be? Like, how long after a relationship before any new person you're with isn't automatically a rebound? I'm just, uh, curious about what people's opinions are."

That did not come out as smooth as I hoped. They both give me knowing looks.

"Um, I guess it depends," Zach says. "Are we speaking hypothetically here?"

"Yes. Purely hypothetical."

DeeDee hunches forward to rest her elbows on her knees. "Well, I don't know what hypo...hypo whatever means, but people can be so judgey about rebounds. It's not even their business, you know? Nobody knows what you feel except you, and sometimes you feel things at times that don't seem right to other people." She turns to look at Zach. "But if it is what you feel, it is the right time to feel it."

I don't know if I want to gag or swoon at their adorable love.

DeeDee looks back at me. "Unless it's just, like, a sex rebound. Then you should *bang. It. Out.* What is it in English? Hit it and quit it?"

"Oh my god, DeeDee, don't talk about hitting and quitting in front of my little sister."

"Ah, *voyons*." She shields her mouth from him with her hand and whispers, "Bang. It. Out."

Zach shakes his head. "You know I can hear you, right?"

"You guys are too cute. I've really got to go now, but I'll call you again before the semester starts."

DeeDee blows me a kiss. "*Bisous!*"

"Love you, little sis." Zach slides his arm around her and waves at me.

"Love you guys!"

I end the call and drop my phone onto the mattress. I need to get up, but I just keep lying there for a minute.

'Bang it out' does not seem like the advice I needed, but I guess there's a difference between need and want.

5

Becca

I grab my phone from my bag on the side of the field and check for an update from Coach Jamal. Normally we get laps for going anywhere near our phones during practice, but Coach is late today, and I've been trying to track him down.

It's the last practice of summer training camp. I can feel the strands of hair that have slipped out of my ponytail sticking to my sweaty forehead. We've had a pretty mild week, but today is boiling with a humidex that's off the charts. Halifax doesn't usually get this hot. Everyone is gulping down water while they wait for me to locate our coach.

I let out a long exhale of relief when I see a text from him. I knew he was supposed to be spending a couple hours before practice looking after his daughter, and him going AWOL had me worried.

"He's on his way," I announce to the team. "He had a childcare emergency, so he's bringing the baby to practice."

Everyone starts jumping around and cheering. We only

met the baby once last year, when the team presented her with a 'Future Lax Rat' onesie and another one featuring the UNS Lobsters logo.

"Yes, I know, babies are exciting," I shout over the noise, "but he also gave me some drills to start with."

Most of the team starts booing, but even when they're overheated and pretending to be unamused, I can tell they're all caught up in the thrum of anticipation I can feel shifting in the field under my feet.

I have another year at UNS after this, and in all likelihood, I'll be captain again then too, but this year has an inescapable *do or die* feel to it. When I was a freshman, the team was only just getting whipped into shape and polished into something special. We nearly lost everything we gained after all my stupid mistakes turned the whole team into a war zone, but somehow we pulled it together in my second year and qualified to play for ECULL. Last year, we went all the way to the finals.

This year is going to be our year. I know it. I've given everything I can to take us to the top, to prove this team really does mean the world to me the way I always say it does.

To prove I belong.

"Okay team," I begin, "let's grab some sticks."

You'd think by now none of them would laugh at stick euphemisms anymore, but everyone still cackles and does whatever their version of provocatively grabbing their lacrosse stick is.

I try not to watch Hope, but it's like attempting to look away when you've noticed someone sexy undressing through their window at night. You know it's probably creepy, but you still keep staring.

She's laughing with her friend Jane as the two of them slide their hands up and down their sticks in long, slow, exaggerated strokes. I can see her bicep flex under the sleeve of her t-shirt, and she even makes her calf-length lacrosse socks look sexy.

It takes a lot to make lacrosse socks look sexy.

The two of them head for the middle of the field, and Hope glances over her shoulder at me before I can look away. Our eyes lock, and for a second, it's like we're back on the sidewalk that night she came to get her phone. There's an insulated box pressing in around just the two of us, one that blocks out every sound and traps the heat between us until it's hard to breathe or think or do anything except want each other.

Want each other?

I blink, and the moment slips away. Hope turns around, and I stand there asking myself what the hell I'm thinking. I don't know if she wants me. I could be making it all up. Anything that's happened between us could be interpreted as totally normal behaviour for two teammates.

And it should stay that way. It has to.

I grab my stick and the bag of lacrosse balls—affectionately known as the ball sack—and jog my way over to face the group.

"Okay! We're starting with some catch and cradle drills today. Split off into pairs. Your partner will pass you the ball, you'll catch it, run halfway up the field while cradling, run back, pass the ball off to them, and then they'll run up the field while cradling, etcetera, etcetera."

We'll add a few new players after tryouts this year, so for now, we're odd-numbered. I join my roommates Bailey and Rachelle as an extra partner after passing out the balls.

"Supple with the wrists while you're cradling," I remind everyone before we start. "You don't want to be floppy, but you don't want to be locked up like you're in a cast either. Keep the movement smooth. Tender, even. *Supple.*"

Once again, I really shouldn't look at Hope, but I do. She's staring at my hand as I demonstrate the wrist movement used to keep the ball in the stick's basket.

My mouth goes dry. If she was anyone else and if we were any*where* else, I'd be pulling her into the nearest dark corner to pin her wrists above her head. She chews on her bottom lip as I finish up demonstrating the drill, still not aware I'm watching her, and I grip my stick so hard my knuckles go white.

"All right!" My voice comes out hoarse. I clear my throat and try again. "Let's do this! Three, two, one, go!"

We make it through a couple of rounds. The team is in good shape, any rustiness after a summer off the field polished away by a solid week of double daily practices. I catch a perfect pass from Bailey, tipping my stick back a little to follow the arc of the ball and then bringing it forward to begin the rocking movement of cradling as I sprint up the field.

I let my muscles take over as my body settles into a rhythm it's known for most of my life. I started playing lacrosse when I was nine, and I went all the way to the national U19 team when I was in high school. That's when the American college scouts came looking, but with all the paperwork and flights and extra testing and costs involved, it made more sense to take the scholarship from the Canadian Women in Sports Association.

After a few more passes, I stop the drill and start getting set up for the next one. Coach shows up just before we're about to begin, and for the next ten minutes, it's pointless to even try getting anyone back on the field. They swarm around his daughter, Khadija, after he sets her carrier down on the sidelines. She's got chubby cheeks and huge brown eyes, and he even put her in her Lobsters onesie for the occasion. I walk over to stand beside him after I've finished obsessing over her with everyone else.

"Why don't I get this reaction when I show up to practice?" he jokes. "I have half the same DNA as her."

"I guess she gets the cuteness from her mom, then," I joke back.

He pretends to be scandalized. Coach has had that 'I totally used to be a frat boy but now I'm a dorky dad' vibe since before he even became a dad. He's always got a UNS baseball cap on over his curly black hair, and he has a fondness for aviator sunglasses.

He stood by me after everything that happened in freshman year, even after half the team left. I wouldn't have accepted the nomination to become captain without him sitting me down and telling me the team needed me to step up. I owe him. I owe everyone who decided to trust me, and I push myself to show it every day on the field.

He claps his hands together after a few more minutes of watching the team flock around the baby carrier like moths to a streetlamp. "Okay, ladies!"

I nudge his arm with my elbow.

"And people of all identities," he adds. "Please leave my baby alone and get on the field. We've got some lax to play."

By the time we wrap practice up, my whole body is drenched in sweat from the roots of my hair to my lacrosse socks. I'm panting for breath as my heart pounds in my ears and slows itself back to its resting rate while we make our way through some cool-down stretches.

"Beautiful work today, team!" Coach paces in front of us with Khadija clutched to his chest, and even my very gay ovaries have a reaction to the sight. "I have a few words prepared to bring this inaugural training camp to a close, but first I want to take a minute to acknowledge this beautiful field we play on and this campus we walk around every day as Mi'kma'ki territory. It's a privilege to be on this land, and it's a privilege to play this game that came from its native people. We all need to remember that."

I join the chorus of players thumping the ends of their sticks on the ground in answer. Before Jamal, I'd never had a coach dedicated to making sure the whole team remembers where lacrosse came from. It can be way too easy to forget we're playing a game that came from First Nations culture on the land that was stolen from those same people, but Coach never takes the easy way out when it comes to living with that truth.

"As for our playing" he continues, "if we can keep that up until November, we've got the season in the bag. You've given your all to this training camp, and it's paying off. We're prepared. We're ready. We're hungry."

I try to stay focused on the rest of his pump-up speech, but just the word *hungry* has me thinking about Hope's eyes on my hands during the drill. The rest of the team cheers, but I just breathe deep as I bend my head to my knee in a runner's stretch.

I can't do this. I can't let somebody throw me off course again. I have something good here, something stable and solid in my life that nobody is going to rip away unless I give them a reason to. My whole world here in Halifax is supposed to be the complete opposite of how things were back home.

I miss the rest of Coach's words and only tune back in when I hear him saying my name.

"Does our fearless captain Becca have any words for the team?"

I had an end of camp speech planned, but now I can't remember any of it. I step out of a lunge and face the group, doing my best to pull myself back into the moment as I scan their faces. There are only a few girls in my year left on the team—the ones who didn't accuse me of buying my way in with the donations I won and corrupting the entire athletics department.

I thought I was past all this, but my stomach is twisting itself in knots as I try to come up with some sort of inspiring message.

"This year," I begin, "is for us. Every practice, every game, every time we get up at six instead of putting our alarms on snooze, every sore muscle and bruise...It's for us. It's so there can be an *us*. We're not just a bunch of people running around with sticks doing their own thing. We're a team. We may not be the world's premier lacrosse program. We may not have a private locker room and funding for flights across the country, but that just means we've earned everything we *do* have. We've built it together. We're...a family."

A few people go, "Awww!" Coach lifts one of Khadija's hands up to make her look like she's doing a fist pump.

"That's what's going to take us to the top this year," I continue, the words flowing now. "That's what's bringing the trophy home. We didn't tattoo lobsters on our ankles for nothing, right?"

"RIGHT!" the team shouts back.

"Right," I agree, "so let's spend this season showing everyone what UNS has got. Claws *out*!"

Everyone starts screaming and stomping around, doing the weird lobster-inspired dance we made up on one of our road trips. Coach covers Khadija's ears to protect her from the noise, but he's laughing as I join the group and lift my arms up to make them into claws.

They weren't just pretty words; this is my family. This is the family I'll always fight to keep.

THE LOCKER ROOM is empty when I head in to take a shower. We've had it pretty much to ourselves all week, but it'll be packed on a regular basis now that the semester is starting up. Coach and I stayed out on the field strategizing long after the team left. They've all headed home to get ready for our team dinner at the campus sports bar by the time I make it to my locker.

The clang of the metal echoes through the empty room when I swing my locker door shut and head for the showers. My clothes are still damp and stuck to my body. It's hot enough outside that I'll probably have to rinse off again after I walk the few blocks home, but I can't go another minute without washing the practice sweat off.

I strip out of my clothes and gear before setting the spray of water as cold as it will go. My muscles tense from the shock but relax after a few seconds. I sigh as I tip my head back and start massaging my scalp.

There's nothing like a cold shower after a long, sweaty practice.

I stay in for longer than I normally do. By the time I'm patting myself dry with a towel, my hands have gone a little pruney. I throw my stuff over my shoulder and leave the stall with my towel wrapped around me like a dress.

Back at my locker, I pull on some fresh underwear and a pair of old grey sweatpants I cut into shorts. I have my head shoved in my locker as I dig around for the extra sports bra I know I have in here somewhere when I hear footsteps behind me.

"Oh hey, I didn't—oh."

The greeting starts out loud and confident before ending with a soft, almost breathless *oh* as the footsteps come to a halt.

My own breath catches, and my whole chest blooms with heat. I'm hyperaware of every bare inch of my skin as I turn my head to look over my shoulder.

Hope is standing there in a baggy t-shirt and tight running shorts. Her hair is piled in a messy bun on the top of her head, the ends of it beaded with water like she just had a shower too. She's staring at my back, her eyes wide behind her glasses. Even under her oversized shirt, I can see the rapid rise and fall of her chest.

My whole body is tingling, and I can't move. I can't speak. I can't do anything except stand there half-naked as she raises her gaze to look at my face.

Her neck is starting to flush a deep pink.

"You, uh—you have a tattoo," she stammers, her voice so much softer than when she's out joking around on the field.

For a second, I don't even register the meaning of the words.

"Huh?"

"Your, uh, yeah. Tattoo. I didn't know you—you had that."

I force myself to swallow so I can speak. "Oh. Yeah."

It would help if I actually had words to say. I can't stop thinking about what would happen if she stepped closer, if I turned around.

My hands have started digging through my locker again of their own accord, like they need something to keep themselves busy. I feel my fingers catch on the fabric I was looking for.

I swivel my head back around and pull my bra all the way out of the locker. My hands shake a little as I lift them up to pull the bra over my head, tugging it down past the two lines of text inked onto my upper back. My arms don't even feel like they're attached to my body. I hear Hope clear her throat behind me.

"I didn't know anyone was in here. I, uh, forgot something in my locker."

I hear her take a few steps, and then the clicking and whirring sound of a combination lock fills the silence. I risk turning to take another look at her. I can see the tension in her shoulders. There are a few drops of water sliding from her hair and down the back of her neck.

I want to lick them off her skin.

"That tattoo," she says after she gets her locker open. I look down and start digging for a shirt in my backpack before she can catch me staring.

"Yeah?" I ask after a few moments pass.

I look back up, and this time she's watching me. Her eyes are on my bare stomach, and her lips are parted just a bit.

There's no way I'm imagining this. I can't be. That is not how you look at someone you haven't thought about touching.

"Is it..." She drags her attention back up to my face like her eyes don't want to obey.

I don't want them to either. I want her to keep looking at me like that. I want her to keep looking at me for so long one of us has to do something about it.

Fuck. Fuck. Fuck.

Part of my brain is blaring a warning siren, but it's not loud enough for my body to listen.

"Is it from a poem?" she finishes.

Once again, it takes me a few seconds to get any meaning from the words.

"Oh. No. It's a song, actually." I find a white t-shirt in one of my bag's pockets and knead the fabric in my hands as I keep talking. It's easier to fight the urge to move towards her if I'm talking. "By Ben Howard. You probably know it. Keep Your Head Up? It's like his biggest hit, which makes it kind of basic that it's my favourite by him, but it is."

"I don't think I know it," she says, a trace of embarrassment in her voice. "I've heard of Ben Howard, but I don't think I actually know any of his songs."

She chuckles, and I pause long enough to look down and realize I've been coiling my t-shirt into a rope.

"Sorry. I sounded kind of douchey there, didn't I?" I laugh too, and it gets a little easier to breathe.

"We all have our douche moments. Is that your only tattoo?" she asks. "Besides the lobster, of course."

"Never forget the lobster." I shake my t-shirt rope out, and she leans against the row of lockers behind her. "But yeah, that's my only other one."

"I figured. There's not much else of you left to see."

I freeze.

She freezes.

Her eyes look like they're about to bulge out of her head, and her whole neck and the skin above her t-shirt collar are now a burning red.

"Uh, wow. I just said that, didn't I? I just meant, uh...umm..."

I let out a laugh that's borderline frantic. "Ha. It was funny."

I busy myself with getting my shirt on. I'm so distracted I almost try to shove my head through one of the sleeves.

"The one on your arm," I say after getting all my limbs through the correct holes of the shirt. "It's really nice."

"Oh, thanks." She strokes the ink on her left bicep. "Chickadees are my mom's favourite, and I guess somewhere along the line, they became my favourite too. I got it just before I left home. We have a lot of chickadees where I'm from."

"Ontario, right?"

I don't know where I pull that information from, but it seems like a safer subject than asking about the location of any other tattoos she might have.

"Yeah." She grins. "A little no-name small town no one has ever heard of. We're basically a village."

"That sounds really nice."

I mean it. Growing up on the outskirts of Calgary didn't have much of a community feel to it.

Then again, my own family didn't have much of a community feel to it.

"It is." Hope nods. "I make fun of it a lot, but only because I love it so much."

"Do you miss it?"

"Hmm." She drums her fingers on a locker. "Less now than I did when I first moved away. Halifax feels like home now too, in a way. I do always love going back, though. It feels weird when it's been more than a few months. In second year, I went to Ethan's for Christmas, and—"

She cuts herself off, a twinge of pain crossing her features. The sight makes me think of that night I bumped into her running out of the end of year party. If this week has shown me anything, it's that that night changed far more between us than I thought.

I want to wipe all her hurt away. That same burning need to protect her roars to life somewhere deep in my chest.

"Actually, never mind," she says after a moment. Her voice has gone flat and dull.

"Hope," I say, my voice quiet too. I like the way her name feels on my lips, soft and sweet. "I know that I, um, wasn't in the room when it happened, but I've heard...I mean, those things he said..."

Hope's hands curl into fists. "Yeah, that's what happens when you break up with your girlfriend in front of her entire lacrosse team and like thirty other random people. They talk about it."

"I'm sorry I mentioned it," I rush to add. "I promise nobody on the team is talking behind your back, unless it's to call him an asshole, and if they even try gossiping or whatever, I'll put a stop to it."

She lets out a long, heavy breath. "I'm not mad that people are talking. I'm not mad at you for mentioning it. I'm just...I'm so fucking mad that...*Fuck.*"

She brings her fists to collide with the locker door behind her. The rattling sound echoes through the room.

"Sorry," she says when the noise fades. "It just sucks to have somebody get in your head like that, you know?"

I know better than she realizes. I can still remember everything they said about me in freshman year.

"For what it's worth, anyone who could say even half those things about you clearly doesn't know you at all."

I have my hands clasped tight in front of me. I wish I could walk over and hug her, squeeze her shoulder, even just give her a playful little punch on the arm—any one of the things I'd normally do to cheer a teammate up. I at least have enough sense left to realize this moment is far from normal, so I stay where I am.

"You're one of the most passionate players I've ever seen. You're dedicated, responsible, creative, smart, tough. You...I can only imagine that anybody you're with would be lucky to date you."

Fuck. Shit. Fuck. Shit.

I just blew past the road sign for 'Friendly, Casual Support' at full speed.

"Thank you, Becca."

The way my name sounds coming out of her mouth has me digging my nails into the back of my hand. Even that's barely enough to keep me from pinning her to the lockers and finding out if her lips taste as good as they look when she says it.

She smooths her hands down her thighs and then takes a step forward. "I should probably get going."

"Yeah. You should."

I flinch at how harsh I sound, and her eyebrows crease with confusion. I just need her out of this locker room. Now. Before something we'll both regret ends up happening.

"I mean, I should too," I add in a more even tone. "We still have to get ready for the dinner."

"Right. Yeah. The dinner. Okay, I'll see you tonight."

She heads out with whatever piece of clothing she came to get from her locker, bobbing along with that bounce in her step that always makes her look like she's got some thrilling news to share with the world. I know it's weird I don't offer to go with her, seeing as we now know we only live a couple streets apart, but even a ten minute walk in broad daylight in the middle of the student neighbourhood seems like too much to handle with her right now.

And possibly ever.

The season hasn't even officially started yet, and I already don't know how I'm going to get through it.

6

Hope

"You guys, the sparkles are digging into my vagina!"

Paulina comes waddling down the stairs to join me and Jane in our living room as she tugs on the hem of the high-waisted, sequined red booty shorts she has on. She's topped them with a UNS t-shirt that has her last name and lacrosse number printed on the back.

Jane and I are wearing matching outfits. It's the team's official 'celebration ensemble.' The end-of-training-camp dinner is the first time we're busting them out this year.

"Seriously, guys, these are not made for people who are six foot one," she moans as she settles herself on one of the arm chairs. "I have the camel toe of the century. I'm going to lose circulation to my clit."

Jane and I burst out laughing. Paulina rolls her eyes and adjusts one of the floor fans we have going to keep the living room from turning into a sauna while the two of us sit on the couch clutching our stomachs.

"That'd be quite the medical feat," Jane says once we've calmed down and earned ourselves a few glares from

Paulina. "I think you look great. Here, have a beer. It will help."

She passes her one of the bottles of red ale from a Nova Scotia brewer. Normally we stick to beer that's more suited to a student budget, but red ale seemed perfect for celebrating our UNS spirit.

I've also been using the beer to placate my panic over whatever the fuck happened with Becca in the locker room today. If tonight's going to be our one exception to the team-wide alcohol ban we all swear ourselves to until November, I'm sure as hell taking advantage of the chance to drink my worries away.

"Maybe it will help restore some feeling to my labia," Paulina grumbles before taking a sip.

I nearly spit out my own sip. I fight to swallow it down and end up caught in something between a laugh attack and a choking fit. Jane gives me the side-eye.

"Perhaps you should slow down there, eh? That's your second already, right?"

She is right. The last time I drank in this household, it ended with me nearly falling to my death during a botched robbery interrupted by Becca herself. If today's Locker Room Incident has proved anything, it's that I can't be trusted not to embarrass myself around her drunk *or* sober.

There's not much else of you left to see.

I said that to her. I literally said that to her.

Iz comes thundering down the stairs just as I'm making a silent pledge to be more responsible tonight. They've already got their bright red high top Jordans on, and they've somehow managed to make sparkly booty shorts look delightfully butch.

"*HOLA, CHICAS!* ARE Y'ALL READY TO PARTAYYYY?"

The rest of us cheer as they do a somewhat successful

attempt at moonwalking across the living room before kicking back in the chair next to Paulina.

"You want an ale?" Jane asks. "We should head out soon, but you have time to drink one."

"Fuck yeah!" They lean forward and take the offered bottle. "No ragrets, right?"

I groan. "Maybe we should...direct the no ragrets energy in a different way tonight?"

Iz and Paulina gasp.

"Who are you? Jane?"

Then Jane gasps.

"I am offended." She turns to me. "You did say you wanted to make this a year to remember."

She raises her bottle, and I suck it up and join in the toast. I did want to make this a year to remember. I probably should have specified whether I wanted to remember it as triumphant or disastrous.

We all finish our beers in time to head for the sports bar. Even with the sun slipping down in the sky, it hasn't cooled off much outside. I can already feel sweat gathering at the waistband of my shorts. In Paulina's defence, they aren't very comfortable.

"How you doing, Hopey?" Jane asks me. She grabs my arm and links it through hers while Paulina and Iz continue their own conversation a few feet ahead of us.

"Currently, I'm asking myself why the team decided to go with sequins."

She shimmies her hips as she walks. "Because sparkles are fun."

I laugh and bump her hip with mine.

"But seriously," she urges, "you okay? Training camp has been so intense that I feel like our bestie rhythm is a wee bit out of sync."

I grin. "You know I love it when you say things like 'wee bit.' You're the cutest."

"No you." She rests her head on my shoulder for a few seconds.

Our shadows stretch out in front of us in the fading orange sunlight. I sigh.

"I thought I was more over the Ethan thing than I am." I shake my head when I realize that's not exactly true. "I mean, I'm over him. I'm definitely not pining away for him or anything, but it's just...I opened up to him, you know? I told him about how hard things are for me sometimes, how dyslexia can make university a living hell, how juggling sports and assignments that take me twice as long as anyone else made me think I might not be ready for a relationship at all. I just...I thought he *got* it. I thought he knew what he was getting into. I thought we were going to handle it together. Maybe I didn't prepare him enough. I mean, maybe he's right that I didn't try hard enough."

"Hey!" Jane tugs on my arm. "That is *not* true. You did lots for that guy. You were a great girlfriend, and you were always honest with him, and you know what? Sure, he was always allowed to decide that wasn't enough for him, but he did *not* have the right to do it like that."

I nod and squeeze her hand as we turn a corner. "Thank you. This is why you're my best friend."

"Anytime, my dear. I hate seeing him get even a minute more of your time. This is *your* year. This is your night to be with your team and have fun, and I don't want to let any of his stupid yammering get in the way of that, yeah?"

Only Jane would use the phrase 'stupid yammering.'

"Yeah," I agree. "You're right."

We're only a few minutes away from the bar now. We spend the time talking about Jane's boyfriend and how things are going for them—perfect, as usual. They've been dating since shortly after frosh week in first year, and I wouldn't be surprised if they end up married someday.

"Oh my god, it's JIM!"

Iz's shout interrupts our conversation. We've just turned onto the bar's street, and sure enough, there's a crowd of girls wearing sequinned booty shorts outside, holding a giant inflatable lobster over their heads.

I will never get tired of UNS life.

"JIM!" I shout. "Our beloved Jim!"

The four of us sprint to the bar. The red neon letters over the door spell out *Mario's* in looping cursive letters. A few of the bulbs have been burnt out for years, making it look like the sign says *Mari's*, but anyone who mentions it risks getting barred for life. For a giant, beefy Italian guy obsessed with sports, Mario is pretty sensitive when it comes to his bar.

That's also probably why he's blocking the doorway, refusing to let Jim inside.

"I have TVs in here!" he's in the middle of saying when we catch up to the group. "You know I live for the Lobsters, ladies, but he's going to have to stay outside."

I glance around the crowd again to be sure, but I already noticed Becca and her housemates aren't here yet. She always shows up for team events, but she's known for heading out early. Becca takes the dedicated athlete lifestyle to the next level.

Hence her devotion to the 'no dating teammates' rule —which really doesn't give me any reason to have a mix of hopeful and terrified butterflies dancing around in my stomach.

I don't even know what I'm hoping for, or what exactly I'm afraid of. She's my captain. I'm her teammate. It's been that way for two years already, and there's no reason to think it's changing now.

Except for the way she looked at me in the locker room today. When I walked in and saw the smooth, pale skin of her back with her bright red hair pushed forward over her shoulders, I almost dropped to my knees. She's that beautiful. She's more gorgeous than I've ever even imagined, and I've imagined a lot. The freckles on her face match the ones dusted along the tops of her shoulders, and that tattoo was so delicate, so poetic, like a hidden piece of her I've only ever glimpsed and finally got the chance to see spelt out across her skin.

"*Che cavolo!*" Mario's exasperated voice pulls me back into the present. He lets out a stream of Italian words and strokes his thick moustache before throwing his hands in the air. "Fine, fine! You can bring him in, but he stays by the door. No dancing with the lobster on the bar."

"So are you saying we can dance on the bar?" someone asks.

He shakes his head and mutters something in Italian again. "Always the crazy ones, this lacrosse team."

We all cheer and stomp when he finally clears the doorway so we can head inside. We cheer and stomp a lot when the whole team hangs out. We also like yelling, singing, clapping, and banging random objects together. There are a lot of words you could use to describe the UNS lacrosse team, but quiet isn't one of them.

Jim gets propped against an empty coat rack while the rest of us help Mario push a few tables together. Normally this place is packed to the rafters every night, but people are busy moving back to campus this weekend, so it's a rare occasion when there's room for the whole team to sit together.

I take a deep breath of that signature Mario's smell: the tang of cheap beer with sticky overtones of sweet cider, lingering notes of melted cheese and tomato sauce from the pizzas the bar serves all day and night, and a trace of musk that fits right in with the sagging leather armchairs and scratched-up barstools dotted around the brick-walled room. Almost every available surface is covered in Italian flags and Lobsters memorabilia.

There's something about stepping into Mario's that feels like taking a load off your shoulders—or an inflatable lobster, depending on the day.

This is the first bar I ever got drunk in. Even when we're not drinking, this bar is where our team celebrates every win and mourns every loss. This is where we go to unwind from a long training session or rev up for an important game. It's where we share our fears and our hopes, where we laugh until we cry or cry until we laugh. This is where *moments* happen. Just a few feet from where I'm standing is the spot where I kissed a girl for the very first time in my life, under the glow of a hockey match playing on one of the TVs.

That was frosh week, a couple months before I met Ethan.

"Corona buckets all around?"

Now that we're seated, Iz has taken over the role of conveying our order to Mario, probably so they can have an excuse to chat up a group of soccer girls by the bar. It seems like their habit of pursuing people who will inevitably turn into exes they awkwardly see around the athletics centre all the time is still going strong.

But it makes them happy, and maybe that's what this year of 'no ragrets' is all about.

"Buckets all around!" I shout. The team cheers in agreement.

Maybe I could just be happy tonight. Maybe I could leave it all behind: Ethan, the breakup, my dyslexia-induced worries about the semester, and even the pressure to have a memorable year itself.

Maybe I could just drink beers with my teammates and have a good time.

"Ooooh, Cap's looking good tonight!"

One of the girls sitting closest to the door draws all our attention with her shout. Becca and her two roommates are walking into the bar, unintentionally arranged like some sort of glamorous all-female pop star trio in their sparkly shorts.

Becca.

In sparkly booty shorts.

In *red* sparkly booty shorts.

Her legs go on for miles, all toned muscle and creamy skin. Her hair is down and a little wavier than normal, and somehow the black eyeliner that looks like it was smeared on her against her will by one of her roommates before they left the house has an effortlessly gorgeous effect.

Everything about her is a flashing danger sign.

"Hope?"

I rip my eyes away from Becca and turn to look at Jane beside me. Her head is tilted to the side as she squints at me.

"You good?"

I bob my head a few times.

Words. Use words. Convey that everything is fine.

It *is* fine. This is a fun night out with friends. I can handle a fun night out with friends.

"Fo sho, Jane of the jungle! Let's get this party started!"

THE PARTY SHOULD REALLY BE ENDING. It's sometime past midnight, and we got kicked out of Mario's a while ago. A good chunk of the team went home after that, but the rest of us all stumbled our way back to the Babe Cave to keep things going here.

"Play some Lorde!" somebody shouts as the last notes of the Rihanna song blasting in the living room fade away. "Play Team!"

I join in the cheering that's probably driving our neighbours nuts. If both properties on either side of us weren't student houses too, I'm sure we would have been evicted a long time ago.

Paulina's phone is hooked up to the speakers, and she shouts a few slurred commands for Siri to play the Lorde song that's one of our team anthems before giving up and doing things manually. The dreamy, layered vocals of the intro fill the room. I lift my arms up and start to sway along with everyone else.

I'm at that point when the bright-eyed boldness of drinking a few too many beers has mellowed to a soft, warm glow. Everyone around me looks so beautiful as they start shifting their hips and shaking their heads when the beat drops. Someone is holding CJ Junior up in the air, thong and all, and my laugh gets drowned out by the music.

Even Becca looks free and happy as she grooves along beside Bailey and Rachelle across the room. Normally she doesn't stay out this late at team parties, but tonight she's shaking her hips with the best of them, and for the first time, the fact that she's so stunning doesn't fill me with panic or dread.

I just appreciate her for what she is: a gorgeous woman giving herself a chance to let go and be free, if only for the length of this song. It really hits me then—how tightly wound she is all the time, coiled up like a spring shoved inside a locked box. Immovable. Solid and still.

Everyone on the team seems to think that's just who she is, but I see how much work she puts into tucking herself away. I see the change in her when that spring shifts and threatens to break loose.

I see it sometimes when she looks at *me*.

By the time the song ends, my throat is dry from singing along. I know I filled my water bottle at some point, but I'm pretty sure I left it sitting on my desk when I went up to my room to charge my phone.

I leave the crowd in the living room and head up the creaky stairs as another song starts blasting. My steps are a bit sluggish, but by now most of the alcohol has worn off. There's a light on under the bathroom door, but the rest of the second floor is dark. I head into my room and turn my desk lamp on. The sounds of the party are a little muffled now. I pick up my water bottle and chug down a few swigs.

My muscles remember just how tired they are as I lean against my desk. We had double practice today, and I worked through some more of my textbooks and course overviews during our afternoon break. My eyelids start drooping, and I wipe my mouth off with the back of my hand before flopping down on my bed with my legs hanging off the end. The party will be winding down soon, and I need a little break from being on my feet before I head back for the grand finale.

The bathroom door opens and closes a few times as I lay there, and I hear people passing up and down the hall while shouts and laughter from downstairs follow them. I'm really fighting to keep my eyes open now, and I've almost started slipping into a dream when someone's voice at my door makes me turn my head.

"Hope?"

Becca is standing in the gap left by my half-open door, one of her hands hovering over the handle like she's not sure if she should open it all the way or pull it shut and leave me here on my own.

I'm not sure what she should do either.

"Oh, hey," I answer.

Smooth.

I push myself up into a seat, and she takes a step inside.

"You okay? I hope I didn't wake you up."

"I think I passed out for a second there," I admit as I adjust my glasses. "You may have just saved me a couple hundred dollars. I snapped the arm off a brand new pair of glasses by falling asleep on them once."

Here I am, rambling about glasses. My mom always says if there's silence, I'll find a way to fill it. She's usually right.

"They're nice," Becca says as she takes another step forward. "Your glasses. You had different ones last year."

I blink at her for a second as I let that settle in. She noticed.

"Uh, yeah. Thanks." I take them off and start polishing one of the lenses with my shirt even though they're perfectly clean. "You don't think they're too hipster? My brother keeps making fun of them."

Becca laughs, and the low, husky sound makes my breath hitch.

"I think they're great. They fit with your whole, like, tattoo and blue hair thing."

I slide them back on and laugh. "So you do think they're uber hipster. I see how it is."

"No, really, they're—"

"I'm kidding, Becca."

She's shuffling around like she's nervous.

"Do you, uh, want to sit down?" I offer.

My heart is already pounding, and it only gets louder

when she hesitates for a second and then sits down next to me on the edge of my bed. Our bare thighs are just a few inches apart. I can smell her shampoo, something light and flowery mixed with warm vanilla. My fingers dig into the bedspread.

"Is that him?" she asks.

"Huh?"

I come back to reality and find her pointing at a framed photo of me, Zach, and our older sister Emily on my wall. We're all wearing dorky Christmas sweaters.

"Oh, yeah, that's Zach and my big sister Emily."

"They look like you. Except for the blondeness, of course."

I flip the ends of my hair over my shoulder. "Alas, I was not blessed with the Hastings clan's luscious golden locks."

She chuckles and glances down at her clasped hands in her lap. "Well, blonde is overrated anyway."

"Maybe I should give being a redhead a go."

She laughs and reaches up to run a hand through her own hair. "Trust me, you do not want to deal with this. Men are so creepy about it."

"And the ladies aren't?"

Shit. Too flirty. Much too flirty.

It's hard to keep the conversation platonic when all I can think about is straddling her lap and burying my own hands in that glorious auburn wonder of nature.

Clearly I've just answered my own question about the ladies being creepy.

Becca shrugs. "When it comes to the ladies, it does have its perks."

Okay, that was flirty. Are we flirting?

"Damn." I chuckle in a failed attempt to diffuse the tension. "Becca Moore, player extraordinaire."

She snorts. It's way too cute.

"The only thing I have time to play is lacrosse."

"Spoken like a true player."

We're both laughing now. She swivels her head to scan my room, taking in all my decor. I watch her face, waiting for a reaction, but she keeps her expression fixed in the same slight smile as she looks around.

"This is nice," she says after a moment. "Your whole house is so...homey."

"That's what the Babe Cave is all about. You should come back sometime when Jane has one of her scented candles lit. The one that smells like fresh bread really gets the homeyness going, and it's much easier than actually baking bread."

I'm rambling again, but Becca doesn't seem to mind. She braces her hands behind her and leans back a little, relaxing her posture as she continues surveying my room. I try not to let my eyes drop to her tits.

Why does she have to have such amazing tits?

"It must be nice to be so close. Bailey and Rachelle are great to live with, but we don't have the whole, like, bond of sisterhood thing going on, you know?"

I nod. "Do you have any sisters or brothers back home?"

She shakes her head. "It's just me."

"I'm sure that has its perks too. No fighting over the TV or who gets the shower and stuff like that."

"Honestly, that would have been kind of nice." She shrugs. "My aunt's house was so quiet growing up."

"Your aunt?"

I feel her tense up beside me. "Oh, uh, yeah."

She chews on her lip for a second, like she's debating how much more to say.

"My mom was kind of in and out, and my dad has a

two weeks on, one week off schedule on the oil fields, so I mostly lived with my aunt."

She's trying to hide it, but I can hear the pain and loneliness in her voice, and it makes my chest ache. I lean back so we're level with each other.

"That must have been tough."

She dips her chin in a nod. "Sometimes. Sports helped. I played soccer when I was really young, and then I switched to lacrosse. I've always had a team, so it kind of feels like I didn't totally miss out on having siblings. It brought me and my dad closer too. He was big into hockey growing up, so sports have always been a bonding thing for us."

Her arm is so close I can feel the heat of it on mine. When I turn to look at her, the dim light from my desk lamp catches in her brown eyes and makes them spark.

"I'm glad you had that." My voice has dropped to a whisper.

"Me too."

She's whispering too, and the only thing I can see now is her eyes. She's so close. She's closer than she's ever been before, and when she's looking at me like this, I can believe I haven't been making it all up. I can believe she wants me too. I can believe that moment when I raked my eyes down her bare back in the locker room has been on her mind all day just like it's been playing on repeat in mine.

"Becca—"

"God, I'm tired." Without any warning, she lets out a big yawn and flops onto her back beside me. "Training camp was amazing, but I think a break from double practice will do everyone good. We need to rest up a little and then buckle down once we get tryouts sorted."

Right. Lacrosse. Our lacrosse team. Our lacrosse team

of which she is captain and I am a player forbidden from thinking such thoughts about her.

At the moment, that's just making them seem all the more appealing. She's rubbing her eyes, and it gives me a chance to look at her stretched out on the bed.

My bed.

Becca Moore is lying on my bed in tight little shorts with her shirt riding up high enough for me to see a few inches of her stomach.

"Yeah. Tryouts will be fun. They always are."

I follow her lead and collapse onto my back too. If I stay sitting up, I'm not going to be able to resist the temptation to keep staring at her even after she notices. It doesn't give me any relief to be lying down beside her, but at least I can force myself to keep my eyes glued to the cracks in the ceiling.

"Coach wants you to help run them."

"Huh?"

"We need a couple experienced players to help with tryouts, and Coach said you'd be perfect for it." She shifts on the mattress. "I think you would too. We just need a couple reliable people who are passionate about the team —and really great on the field, of course."

'Reliable' is not a word that's always been associated with me. 'Passionate,' sure, but I don't think the first thing people describe me as is 'reliable.' There's been times I've daydreamed about doing more for the team, like when I get called on to lead a warm-up or give everyone a pump up speech that ends with a standing ovation. Something about those moments feels *right* and exciting in a way I can't explain, but I've never taken the thoughts seriously. We already have an excellent captain, and besides, I'm still the dyslexic girl who has to work her ass off just to balance sports and school.

"Does CJ remember I recently tried to kidnap Jim after too many shots of Jane's crazy whiskey?"

I feel Becca's laugh vibrate through the mattress. "That was actually really cute, you know. Your face when I walked in...It was so cute."

I stop breathing. She just called me cute. She thinks that I, specifically, am cute.

"Oh yeah?" I ask after a moment. It's a stupid response, but I don't know what else to say.

My voice has gone quiet again. I'm hyperaware of every inch of space between us and how easy it would be to obliterate them all. I want to pull her into me. I want to forget about all the reasons we shouldn't and let ourselves explore every justification for why we should.

"Yeah. I..." She trails off, and I hear her swallow. "Yeah."

Don't look at her. Don't look at her. Don't look at her.

But of course I do. I turn my head just enough to see her face at the exact same time she does the same thing. She looks so soft in the glow from the lamplight. Her lips are shining like she just licked them. I want to lick them too.

I want to lick her, touch her, *take* her.

I want to feel what it's like when she takes me. I've never wanted someone so bad for so long. Even before things shifted between us, I still *wanted* her.

Back then it was a fantasy, but now it's real and here and so close all I have to do is reach for it. Even the anticipation is better than anything I imagined, sweeter and sharper than any thoughts I've ever let myself have.

I can hear her breathing. I can feel my own chest rise and fall. I inch my head just a fraction closer to hers, and she doesn't pull back.

Becca. Becca. Becca.

My brain is chanting her name, using it as a metronome to pound out the rhythm of my pulse. In this moment, she's everything. I need her. It's more than just want.

I move even closer. She gasps mid-inhale and stops breathing altogether. Her chin lifts, bringing her lips in line with mine, and then our mouths are pressed together.

My eyes close. For a moment, we stay completely still. I feel numb, like I'm floating outside my body, but then her lips shift. She breathes in, and all my senses roar back to life. My hand reaches to cup her cheek, and now we're kissing—really kissing. Her mouth is hungry on mine, and when she grips my hip and pulls me closer, I let out a moan that makes her growl.

I shiver. I need more of her. She feels amazing. She *tastes* amazing. I sweep my tongue along her bottom lip without breaking our kiss. Her hand slides up my waist. I want to feel her touch under my shirt. I want to be under *her*.

The sound of the front door opening reaches my room, and we both go still. I hear everyone calling out their good-byes as a few people leave the party.

Becca pulls back to look at me, and her eyes go from hooded and hungry to round and terrified in a matter of seconds.

"Oh fuck. Oh no. Oh my god, I'm so sorry."

"Becca—"

Before I can ask her what the hell she's sorry for, or even really process what's going on, she's pushing off the bed and jumping to her feet.

"Fucking hell, how did I let that happen? Oh my god."

"Becca, wait."

She covers her face with her hands and starts breathing so hard I'm scared she's hyperventilating.

"Becca." Half my brain is still lost in the kiss, but I force myself to stand up too. "Becca, it's okay."

"No, no, no." She drops her hands and looks at me while shaking her head. "It's not okay. I'm so sorry. I shouldn't have done that."

"You didn't *do* anything." I keep my voice soft. "*We* kissed."

She winces, and it hits me like a punch to the stomach.

"That was a mistake. Just...I can't...I have to go. I have to go now."

She gives me one last frantic, haunted look and then leaves the room before I can get another word in.

I don't chase after her. My feet won't move. All I can do is stand there and let that word sink in.

Mistake.

I can feel the blunt weight of it slamming into me over and over again. Whatever that kiss was, it was not a mistake. I will never be able to call something so incredible a mistake.

Even if she can.

7

Becca

I've made the biggest mistake of my life. Last night was worse than anything I did in freshman year—not because it was anywhere near as catastrophic, but because I knew just how catastrophic it *could* be, and I did it anyway.

I did it again.

I kissed somebody I shouldn't have kissed. I laid the only thing that's ever really felt like a family to me on the line just so I could make out with a hot girl.

I roll over on my side in bed and pull my pillow out from under my head. I squish it down over my face to block out all the protesting thoughts, but it doesn't work.

Last night wasn't just about making out with a hot girl. It wasn't like that with Lisa, and it wasn't like that with Hope, either. This wouldn't have happened in the first place if that was all it was about.

I press the pillow hard enough over my face to groan into the fabric without the entire house hearing. I let everything out in a long burst of frustration and rage. Then I do that again. And again.

By the third venting session, I feel better enough to sit up.

It's late, judging by how much light is streaming in through my curtains. I can't remember the last time I woke up later than the sunrise. I spent the summer in Halifax, working at one of the school's labs and doing some part time hours at a kayak expedition booking office downtown. I only started work at nine, but I still kept up my usual sleep schedule.

I check the clock on my bedside table and see it's just past nine now. I'm not sure when I fell asleep. It feels like I spent the whole night lying flat on my back, paralyzed by the constant replay of just how badly I fucked up with Hope.

I drag myself out of bed before I can get pulled into the loop again. When I catch a glimpse of myself in the mirror, I have to stop and laugh. If this whole situation were a joke, the way I look would be the punch line. My hair is a wild, autumnal forest that could easily be concealing several birds and an entire family of squirrels. I forgot my roommates Bailey and Rachelle coerced me into wearing eyeliner last night, and it's now smeared across the tops of my cheeks and all the way up to my eyebrows. I'm still wearing my shirt from last night over a raggedy pair of plaid pajama shorts.

I let out another snort after doing a full scan of the disaster zone that is my body and then stop to check my phone on the way to the bathroom. There are a couple text alerts, and my stomach lurches when I realize why I feel a flutter of excitement about that.

Even with all the millions of reasons not to staring me straight in the face, I'm still wishing the texts will be from Hope.

I lean against my bedroom's doorframe and let out a

breath of what should be relief—though it feels dangerously close to disappointment—when I see they're from my best friend Kala. She's asking if I'm still down to get brunch today.

"Shit," I mutter. I forgot to text her when her flight got in yesterday. She knew I was at lacrosse practice and couldn't come to the airport, but I still feel like a shitty friend.

I send her a stream of 'welcome back to Halifax' texts filled with an uncharacteristic amount of emojis and let her know brunch is on me. Keeping up a friendship with someone not on the lacrosse team—and thus not bound by its intense schedule—has been difficult since Kala left the team after first year, but she's my only friend from Calgary at UNS. She's been one of the most important people in my life since we met on our very first lacrosse team, so we make it work despite all the difficulties of her not being on the UNS team.

And all the reasons she left it.

By the time I get myself cleaned up, put on something presentable, and manage to pile my damp hair up in a bun that looks intentionally messy and not like an actual mess, it's time to head downtown. I could wait for a bus, but I'd rather spend thirty minutes outside.

Campus is much busier than it has been all week. With the semester starting tomorrow, the streets are filled with moving vans and parents' cars stuffed with boxes and bins. People are lugging home textbooks fresh from the bookstore and setting up picnics on their lawns so they can sit around greeting their neighbours. The walk calms me down a little, and the closer I get to the waterfront restaurant, the more the smell and sound of the sea work their spell on me.

Still, that's not enough to fool Kala. After we've spotted

each other on the sidewalk and made the typical we-spent-a-whole-summer-apart squealing sounds while hugging, she pulls back and raises an eyebrow.

"Seems like we've got something to talk about over brunch."

I don't bother trying to deny it. When it comes to Kala, I have no secrets, and she'll get it out of me whether I try to hold back or not. I spend a lot of time with the team, but I don't have the same heart to hearts with even Rachelle and Bailey that I do with Kala.

I tell her it can wait until we at least get our order in. The hostess leads us out to a table on the ocean-facing patio. A big yellow umbrella blocks out some of the heat that's building from the morning sun. We've been here enough that neither of us needs to look at the menu. This place is cheap and has a great view, which makes it popular with students, locals, and tourists. The patio is almost completely full already, and it's not even noon.

Our waitress heads off with our order, and Kala leans across the table to stare at me, her dark curtains of chin-length hair falling into her face.

"Becca Moore, are you hungover?"

I *am* squinting at the light reflecting off the water, and my head is killing me.

"Uh, maybe?"

She sits back. "Yeah, girl! Letting loose for senior year."

"It's not really senior year for me," I remind her. "I still have so many courses if I want to complete my minor, and I have to do a full extra year *and* stay on the lacrosse team for them to extend my scholarship."

She huffs. "Like you would ever leave the lacrosse team."

She laughs like she expects me to join in, but I can't even force the sound. Just trying makes heat prick the corners of my eyes. I glance away and roll my shoulders back to keep them from slumping, but she's already noticed something's wrong.

"Becca? You've got to tell me what's up with you. You're clearly upset about something."

I can't believe I'm about to fucking cry. I have no right to cry about this.

"I...I just..." I stammer as I fight to get myself under control.

"Ah, ah, ah, none of that hiding your feelings bullshit. That doesn't work on me. I know you too well."

She knows me better than anyone. I let a few moments of silence pass, filled by the din of clanking plates and chatting diners. Seagulls caw far above our heads.

"I fucked up." My voice comes out thick and monotone as I stare down at the worn wooden table. "I...I really fucked up. *Again*."

"Becca." She reaches across the table and squeezes my arm for a second. "You've got to stop being so hard on yourself about all that."

I shake my head since the lump in my throat won't let me answer. It's been a long time since we've really talked about any of this.

"Hey, come on. It's okay."

She tugs on my arm until I give in and let her drag my hand on top of the table. She clasps it with hers and lifts my limp arm up to lead us in a two-person version of doing the wave.

It was the first step of our secret handshake in the seventh grade. The whole thing was an elaborate, full-body routine that required at least two metres of empty space around us.

I've always felt so safe with her—safe enough to do dumb stuff like this no matter how old we get. I think that's what led us to turn towards each other in high school, back when we were figuring out who we were and who we liked. We found a safe place in each other to face this scary, amazing thing we were both discovering about ourselves.

I see now that we never really had chemistry as anything more than friends. Kala and I figured that out pretty quickly after we tried to date, but I can also see how things might look to anyone watching us laughing and holding hands at this table. That's always been the worst part about how things turned out with Lisa: I could see the problem so clearly, but I still couldn't make it right.

Kala lets go of my hand after a moment and settles back in her chair. "So, are you going to tell me what happened?"

I take a deep breath in and hold it like I'm bracing for a punch to the face.

"I kissed someone." I wince. "On the team."

She doesn't say anything for a while. Her immaculate black eyebrows rise a fraction of an inch, and she starts tracing the edge of the table with one of her fingers.

"Okay," she finally says. "Why?"

"Huh?"

Whatever I was expecting her to say, it wasn't that.

She taps on the table a few times and then points at me. "You once told me that the first time you kissed Lisa, it wasn't even really because of *her*. It was because you had just failed an assignment for the first time in your life. You didn't know if you could handle being on the team, being away from home, and living up to the expectation that you'd be this, like, lacrosse goddess bringing all this new funding in and revitalizing the team. Half the team was pissed you were even there at all. Then Lisa showed up like this perfect escape."

I have to chuckle at that. Associating the word 'perfect' with any part of the Lisa situation is humor at its darkest.

"You're one of the most determined people I know," Kala continues. "Most people would call it stubborn as hell. It takes a lot to knock you off course, and you've basically made your whole 'no dating teammates' rule into a religion. So what made you set that aside? Was it this girl? Was it something in your life right now?"

"I—I mean, we're not, like, *dating*," I stammer as my pulse kicks up. "We kissed. Once. Last night. I was kind of drunk. I haven't, you know, *set anything aside*."

She lifts her eyebrows again. "Do you want to?"

"That's not even part of the equation. Teammates don't date teammates. It's a rule, and everything falls apart when it doesn't get followed. I shouldn't have kissed her, and now I don't know how to fix it."

She reaches up to tuck her hair behind her ear and stares out at the ocean for a moment.

"You know, Becca, it's not an official rule of lacrosse, or even the athletics department. It's just a team culture thing that you—"

"Kala."

I feel a twinge in my chest. Of all people, I thought she'd understand why this is so important to me. She knows what the team means to me. She's the one who sat with me in my dorm room while I spent half my freshman year freaking the fuck out on a daily basis.

She turns back to me. "I'm sorry. I get it. I do. As your best friend, I just feel the urge to sometimes remind you that you are, in fact, a human being. You're not *just* the lacrosse captain, which brings me back to my question. Why do you think the kiss happened?"

I'm about to say 'I don't know,' but I clamp my mouth shut and force myself to think about it, really think about it. Kala might be onto something here. If I can figure out why it happened, I can stop myself from letting it happen again.

Of course, asking myself why I kissed Hope just makes me think about kissing Hope. Her blue eyes wide, her face leaning closer and closer to mine. The warmth of her breath on my lips before she met them with her own. The way she sighed and moaned against me. The curve of her hip under my hand.

I wanted to touch so much more of her, but it wasn't just about the touching. I wanted to be close to her, in any way I could. Sitting with her in her room felt like stepping into another world. *Her* world. I wanted to learn about everything: the pictures on the walls, the clothes in her closet, the lines inked onto her skin. I wanted to know her. I wanted to explore her step by step like a new city. I wanted to memorize every street and neighbourhood, learn how they looked in the morning and how they sounded at night.

I didn't just want to kiss her. I wanted to *be* with her.

"Oh, I see how it is." Kala's face has lit up as she sits there watching me pick through my memories. "You liiiike her."

I don't know if I shake my head for her benefit or mine. There has to be more to this. There has to be another reason why I let things go so far.

"She's really cool," I say. "I've always thought she was really cool, and she went through a horrible breakup last year. We kind of hung out for a bit after, and I just...I don't know. It felt like we could be friends. Maybe all I really want is to hang out with her more, and the stress of fourth year and captaining again and knowing I have a whole other year left just got to me and messed all my feelings up.

Oh, and the Corona buckets. We can't forget there were Corona buckets involved."

She grins. "The Mario's special."

"Ugh, remind me never to drink again. You were right about the hangover. This sunlight is killing me."

She reaches over and pats my shoulder.

"Okay, so let's go with your, um, theory," she says in a voice that makes it clear she's even less convinced than I am. "What happens next?"

"Well..." I roll my shoulders back a few times. "I guess I'll tell her I'm sorry it happened, that it was a mistake, and that we'll just be teammates like we've always been from now on."

Kala winces. "Ouch."

"She'll be fine," I insist. "I really don't think she's going to have any trouble finding someone else to kiss."

"I meant ouch for *you*, Becca. She clearly means something to you, and you're just going to cut it all off? I mean, what if you could have a really nice friendship? You and I have *actually* dated, and that hasn't stopped us from staying friends."

"Thank god for that." Now it's me patting her arm. "I don't need to be messing around with complicated friendships. I already have the best friendship I could ever ask for."

She fluffs up her hair. "Well, when you put it like that..."

"Speaking of, I've been a shitty friend. We haven't talked at all about your summer. How was the family?"

She groans just as our server approaches with two plates of eggs Benedict balanced on a tray with a couple giant glasses of freshly squeezed orange juice. We spend the rest of the meal talking about her summer job working for her dad's investment firm. Her family is pretty right wing, and she's still deciding whether or not she's ever going to tell them she's bi.

She wasn't even sure she wanted to come out on campus at all, but that got decided for her when Lisa took it upon herself to out Kala to the whole team. Freshman year wasn't exactly a picnic for either of us, and that's part of what made it so hellish: knowing I'd roped my best friend into my own mess when she already had more than enough to handle.

By the time we've paid and headed out of the restaurant, I'm more convinced than ever I need to pull the plug on anything besides a cordial acquaintanceship with Hope.

No matter how gorgeous her eyes are.

Or how fucking amazing she is at kissing.

Or how she makes me laugh with all her dorky moments.

Or how being alone with her feels like putting the whole world on pause and just *being* for a while.

I think that's what's hardest to turn my back on—even harder than the kissing. I've only really gotten a taste of what spending time with her is like, but I haven't clicked with someone like that in a long time. I haven't really *let* that happen. My role as captain comes first. It has to. It's who I am.

"Study date this week?" Kala asks once we're back out on the sidewalk.

She's a business major and has an even more intense study schedule than I do. I wouldn't be surprised if she's already prepping for assignments.

"Of course! I'll text you my practice schedule, and we can figure something out."

We hug goodbye, and she heads off to finish getting settled back into her apartment. I consider going home to look over my new textbooks, but I know I'll probably just end up pacing around my room, so I head for the athletics centre to burn off some energy.

I have a few sets of workout clothes stashed in my lacrosse locker. I change out of my t-shirt and denim shorts, trying and failing to shut down the mental replay of that day Hope walked in here while I was half-naked.

"No, no, no," I chant to myself as I slam my locker closed. "None of that. It's done now. It's done."

The student gym is all but empty. I power through a few stretches and then switch one of the ellipticals on. I know I should go slow to warm up, but I'm craving a sweat. I need a fast enough rhythm to lose myself in the strain and power of my body for a while.

Twenty minutes later, my legs feel wobbly and my flyaway hairs are sticking to the sides of my face. I can feel the sweat pooling in the band of my sports bra, and my lungs are heaving. I feel lighter, though. Clearer. It's like a layer of haze has been wiped away.

I do a couple dumbbell sessions after that and then head back to the elliptical to finish off the workout. When I finally power the machine down, I feel like I've stepped back into my body after being stuck floating around outside.

This is me. Becca Moore: lacrosse captain, straight A student, model scholarship recipient. Focused. Determined. As Kala would say, stubborn as hell.

This is who I want to be.

I'm still panting after I've finished my stretches. I grab my water bottle and chug half of it down as I head for the gym doors. I wipe my mouth off with the back of my hand and then screw the bottle lid on before looking up to reach for the door handle.

Only I don't reach for it.

I don't do anything except stand there and stare at Hope where she's frozen on the other side of the glass.

She has her hair up in a ponytail and headband, and she's wearing skin-tight leggings and a tank top. My heart is going haywire, but suddenly my desperate lungs don't even know how to take another breath.

Neither of us moves. She watches me from behind her glasses. I tighten my grip on my water bottle to keep it from sliding out of my hand.

The moment only breaks when some sound on the other side of the door makes her turn her head. I use the distraction to summon up a surge of adrenaline that lets me grab the handle and take a few steps past her.

"Becca!"

I'm frozen again by the sound of her voice. I have my back to her now, and I don't turn around.

"Becca, you..."

My arms are clamped to my sides, and I can feel my hands starting to shake. I don't know how I want her so much so soon, but I do.

"I..."

I try to say 'I can't,' but I only manage the first word before I need to start moving again. I need to get out of here. When I'm with her, I forget every reason I shouldn't be.

The empty halls are a blur in my peripheral view as I speed my way to the locker room and yank the door open. I'm panting again, and I've only just walked over to rest my forehead against the cool metal of the nearest locker when the door swings open again behind me.

"Becca, what the hell? Did you literally just *run away* from me?"

Hope's whole body is tensed like she's ready for a fight. She stalks over and stops when she's only a couple feet away, tilting her head to let me know she expects an answer.

"I..."

"I'm not a ghost," she says when it's clear I can't come up with anything else. "I'm not floating around haunting you. You don't have to run in the other direction when you see me."

"I'm sorry." I have my back up against the lockers now. "That was...dumb of me. And weird. I'm sorry."

My face heats as I say it. I really did just run away from her, like a panicking little child.

"You also don't have to keep saying sorry. I know you...I know you regret last night. I know you wish we didn't...I just feel stupid, okay? I feel stupid when you say sorry for it."

She still has her shoulders set in a tight line, but her face crumples a little, just for a second.

"Hope." I pause to take a breath after I say her name. Just the sound of it seems to shrink the distance between us. "You don't have anything to feel stupid about. It's not that I didn't want to...to do that."

It's like we're shy, inexperienced teenagers all of a sudden. I can't even say the word *kiss*.

"So why did you leave like that after?"

Her voice is so soft now. Dangerously soft.

"Because..."

There are a million *becauses*. I can feel them buzzing around my head like annoying flies, but I can't catch a single one.

"We were drinking," I finally say. I know that really doesn't have much to do with what happened, but it's the easiest reason to verbalize.

It was also clearly the wrong one to pick. She flinches like I've slapped her.

"I'm so stupid." Her chin trembles. "God, I feel dumb."

She takes a step back, and I take one forward. I can't hurt her. It *hurts* to hurt her.

"Hope, don't say that. I didn't mean it like that. I meant that...I've thought about you a lot, okay? I wonder about you. I worry about you. I...admire you. I feel this need to know more about you, and then last night, when everything felt so free and easy at the party, I just...I had to be close to you." I close my eyes for a second, just to remember what it felt like, just to hold on for a little longer. "That wasn't fair to you, and that's what I'm sorry for."

When I open my eyes again, we're almost chest to chest. I can hear her breathing. Her knuckles brush mine. I should pull my hand away, but I don't. I stand there shaking as she trails her touch up my arm and then strokes my skin just above the collar of my t-shirt.

She's so close now. I could dip my head an inch and kiss her again. I can taste it already, but at the last second, I twist my face to the side. Her lips land on my neck instead, and that's almost worse. Need flares in my body, hot and demanding, and it's too much. It's all too much.

"Becca?"

She stops just as the first tears seep out of the corners of my eyes. I try to hold my sob back, but the sound rips its way out of me.

"Becca, it's okay. Hey, it's okay. I'll stop."

She goes to back away, but I reach out on instinct and grab her hand. I'm really crying now, letting out huge, embarrassing sobs that echo in the locker room, but I still don't want her to leave.

I can't lie about it or explain it away: I don't want Hope to leave.

8

Hope

I don't know what I expected when I followed Becca into the locker room, but it did not include ending up on one of the benches with my arm around her shoulders while she cries.

Yet here we are.

I've never seen her fall apart like this. I've never seen her lose control whatsoever, except maybe last night. Even during the few totally hopeless lacrosse matches the team has faced, she's always been the person we look to to keep us from breaking down.

I pull her in closer as she takes a few struggling breaths. We've only been sitting here about a minute, and she already seems to be calming down. As I stare around the empty locker room, I can't help thinking this is an exact role reversal of the night Ethan dumped me.

Except Becca doesn't have a recent ex-boyfriend, and I have no idea why she's crying.

"Aw, come on." I try for a joke, since everything else I've said just seems to have made her cry harder. "I can't be this bad at kissing. Did I have beer breath or something? Oh my god, did I burp in your mouth?"

She lets out a watery laugh, and I feel a little thrill of success. She swipes at her eyes and sighs before sitting up straight. I slide my arm off her, but we're still sitting so close our thighs and shoulders are pressed together.

The crying has kind of dampened the sexual tension, but being close to her still makes me feel all warm in a way that isn't even sexual at all. It's just *nice*. Whatever the hell else is going on, this part is nice.

"I'm sor—"

"Stop it, Becca!" I bump her shoulder with mine. "No more apologizing about last night, okay? It happened. We both liked it. We've established that."

I sound much calmer than I am. In my head, I'm still trying to process the fact that I just had my mouth on her neck.

So much for dampening the sexual tension.

"What do you want to happen now?" I ask.

Personally, what I want is to get back to the neck kissing, but that doesn't seem to be the world's greatest idea.

"It's not really about what I want." She still sounds a little shaky. "We're both on the team. I'm the captain. There are rules to follow, and we both owe it to everyone to follow them."

"I mean, technically, it's not, like, an official rule..."

She shakes her head. "It means just as much as one."

The conviction in her words is so strong it startles me.

"I get that. I really do," I say after a moment. "This team means so much to me, and it makes total sense that everybody wants to avoid drama. We need to if we want to be the best players we can be, but I mean, we aren't *just* lacrosse players. We're people too."

Again, she shakes her head. "It's not just lacrosse to me. It's not just a team. I..."

She trails off and sighs like she doesn't want to get into things, but I just sit there waiting until she's ready to talk again. I can tell this is something she needs to get out.

"Look, it's just...when I realized going to school in the States and playing for a big league wasn't going to work out, I was devastated," she begins. "Totally devastated. I just felt *empty*. Even my plan to major in kinesiology was inspired by lacrosse. This sport made me feel like I had something to count on when even my own family couldn't give me that. It's always been more than just a fun hobby, or even a career goal. After playing for the U nineteen team, I was banking on a full ride from an American school, but all I got offered was partial funding. It wasn't enough, and I realized I'd pinned literally every hope for my entire life on this one thing."

I never had to worry about scholarships. My parents aren't millionaires or anything, but there was never any question of whether they'd be able to fund undergrads for me and my siblings. If I'd really wanted to, I know they would have even been okay paying for me to go to school abroad.

They always told me they were happy to help with any dream I believed in. That's what got me through some of my hardest dyslexia days: knowing if I worked hard enough, I had a family who could help me get anywhere I wanted to go.

I think back on all the late nights and extra tutoring I put in so I could graduate with flying colours and be accepted at every university I applied to. Then I imagine that even after all that, it still wasn't enough for me to actually *go*. My chest aches for Becca.

"Then the Canadian scholarship came through," she

continues, "and I ended up here, and it was better than I could have imagined. The funding I won for the lacrosse program along with my scholarship made so much possible. It felt like we were all building something. I mean yeah, some people thought I bought my way onto the team with the funding and weren't exactly quiet about it, but for the most part, it was like I just...fit. Like I belonged. Like I was home."

I nod. "I know that feeling. UNS is special like that."

"It's the *only* place that's been special for me like that."

The crying is starting to make more sense now.

"You're not just scared to break the rules. You're scared to lose that."

"Yeah," she whispers. "I am."

I want to wrap my arm around her again, but I force myself to stay still. "I would never try to take that away from you or jeopardize it. I'm sorry if it seemed like that's what I was doing."

She shakes her head, and the corner of her mouth lifts. "Now I want *you* to stop saying sorry. That's not what I thought you were doing, and I played a part in it too."

"Yeah, maybe it's you who had the beer breath."

It's a bad joke, but we still laugh together.

"When did this whole no fraternizing with teammates rule start, anyway?" I ask. "Everyone always says there was drama a long time ago, but nobody has any details. It's like an urban legend or something."

I wait for her to laugh along with me, but she tenses up again.

"Right?" I prod when she stays silent. "Or do you have some sort of secret knowledge passed down from captain to captain?"

She shrugs and then rolls her shoulders a couple times.

"It's just like...breakups are messy, you know? I think

people always have the best intentions for how they're going to handle stuff like that, but when shit hits the fan..."

I force a chuckle that comes out sounding strangled. "Yeah, when you put it like that, it kind of makes sense that everyone's so intense about it. Shit does have a tendency to hit the fan during breakups. I would know."

She leans forward so she can get a better look at my face. "That really fucked you up, didn't it? I'm so—"

She catches herself before she says sorry again, and we both grin.

"I've been feeling way better about it lately," I admit, "and I am *so* done with him. I think I'm just freaked that he's gonna be back on campus. We haven't talked since that night, and we run in the same circles. One of the girls on the team is dating his best friend. We're bound to bump into each other at some point."

"Do you want to talk to him?"

"Hmm." I tap my heels on the floor tiles while I think. "Maybe there's some sort of closure I should go for, but honestly, I think he said everything he wanted to say, and maybe it's a waste of energy trying to say anything back."

"Well, I can tell you with complete certainty that he doesn't deserve a minute more of your time."

She says it with almost as much conviction as when she talked about what lacrosse means to her. It's stupid of me, but a lump forms in my throat when I hear her standing up for me like that.

"It's true."

"Thanks."

We go silent again, but it still feels like we're speaking, like there's a constant exchange between us even when we can't find the words to say. One kiss shouldn't make me feel so connected to her, but there's nothing else to describe it as except a connection.

"So, um, I know we haven't exactly come up with a game plan here, but this bench is making my ass go numb." I shift around on the metal slats to illustrate my point while I work up the courage to say what I want to say next. "What if we went and got a coffee or something?"

"Hope..."

"Just to talk," I clarify. "Just to figure this out. I..."

I just want to keep being near you.

"I could use the caffeine boost," I finish.

She fiddles with the edge of her shorts. I have to look away from her thighs and remind myself we really are just going to talk.

"Okay." She pushes herself to her feet in one swift motion and turns to face me. "If you're okay with giving up on your workout, that is."

"Huh?"

She nods at my outfit. "You were going to work out, right?"

"Oh. Yeah, right." The entire day thus far was completely wiped from my memory as soon as I saw her walking out of the gym. "No problem. I wanted to do something to wake me up, so coffee works too."

She laughs then—a real laugh, not a nervous chuckle or quiet huff of air. The full, throaty sound feels like the sun on my face, warm and bold and unafraid of anything.

She only remembers she needs to change once we've already left the locker room. I wait outside while she goes back in to throw some fresh clothes on. I was planning on walking home in my gym outfit, so I just take my headband off and smooth down my hair while I stand there.

She comes back out in some jean shorts and a loose, dark green t-shirt. The colour makes her hair look extra fiery.

Just talking. Just talking and coffee. That's all.

"Where do you want to go?" I ask as we head down the hall, our shoes making the polished floor squeak.

"I don't get coffee on campus very often," she answers. "Do you have any favourite places?"

"Oh, I'm the queen of the all-night study session." We reach the lobby, and I pull one of the front doors open and hold it for her. "I think all the campus baristas know me by name."

"That doesn't surprise me," she says after thanking me for holding the door.

I don't know who I'm kidding here; even holding the door for this girl makes my stomach flip.

"Which part?" I ask, doing my best to ignore the gymnastics class happening inside my digestive system. "My last minute cramming, or my caffeine dependency?"

She laughs and shakes her head. "No, I meant the fact that they all know you. You're very...easy to want to know."

"Oh." I walk along the path beside her as I try to work out how I should take that, or how much I should let it mean. "Or maybe I just tip really well."

She laughs again, and I can't get enough of the sound. It's like I'm drinking it up drop by drop, always thirsty for more.

The campus is much busier than it's been all week. A few groups are spread out on picnic blankets on the lawns, and most of the benches and tables we pass are filled with students. A guy darts in front of us to grab a Frisbee flying through the air and then runs back to join the other guys playing the game. The air smells like grass and flowers and the last of summer's long days.

"I can't believe the term starts tomorrow," I say. "The summer felt like it was taking soooo long, but now it seems like I've barely had a break since exams last year."

"Yeah," Becca answers. "It seems like they go by faster and faster."

I nod and then burst out laughing a second later. "Wow, we sound like such grandmas, talking about the years flying by. I really need this coffee to restore my youth and vitality."

"I'm curious to see where you get coffee that restores your youth. You're setting some high expectations here, Hastings."

I like when she calls me by my last name. I always have.

"Well, Captain Moore, you're about to find out. That's it right over there."

We've reached the edge of a lawn that faces a street lined with student-oriented businesses. There are a few grab-and-go restaurants, a print shop, a massage therapy office that seems a little out of place, and right on the corner is my favourite cafe in all of Halifax.

"The Lobster Trap," Becca reads off the wooden sign jutting out above the door. "Clever."

"They've trapped this lobster, that's for sure."

The mini patio in front of the floor-to-ceiling windows has just enough room for a bench and two little round tables with chairs. Inside, you can see the wooden counter running along the edge of the room with barstools dotted along it. The floor space is taken up by a few clusters of armchairs and lobster-red sofas. I hold the door for Becca again, and the soft tinkle of a bell rings out.

The sweet scent of sugar and frothy, warm milk hits us first, followed by the rich and bitter undertone of coffee beans. A folk band that sounds kind of like The Lumineers mixed with some Nova Scotian flair is playing above the sound of clanking mugs and chatting students. The place's signature light fixture—made of a couple antique, wooden lobster traps—dangles from the ceiling in the middle of the room.

"This is really cool," Becca says from beside me. "I can't believe I've never been here before."

"Wait until you try the coffee."

I lead the way to the counter, where a couple people are lined up, contemplating the menu.

"Are you a secret coffee connoisseur, Hastings? I didn't know that about you."

"Ha. I wouldn't go that far. I really don't know what makes coffee good, other than whether I like it or not."

She laughs. "Does anything else really matter?"

"Hmm." I tap my finger on my chin. "I guess not."

By the time we make it up to the cashier sporting horn-rimmed glasses and a huge collection of bracelets on both his arms, I'm ready to order my usual iced mocha, but Becca is still squinting at the letter boards tacked to the wall.

"Um…" She glances between me, the boards, and the waiting cashier. "Maybe just like…a cup of…coffee?"

I don't think she has any idea how cute she is. She's always marching around as this fearless team leader, but the second she lets her captain facade down, she gets all sweet and hilarious.

"Oh, come on, Becca," I joke. "You've been staring at that menu for like ten minutes and all you came up with was a cup of coffee? Live a little! Have a specialty latte!"

"A latte is coffee, right?"

Now even the cashier is trying not to laugh.

"Yeah," I answer. "Mostly. Unless it's made with tea."

"This is confusing."

"You're right. It's like learning a new language."

If I want to try something other than a mocha, I always ask the cashiers what's new instead of trying to decipher the signs. It's a good thing I don't mind chatting with strangers, or dyslexia would be a lot harder to handle in daily life.

"Um, okay..." She scans the signs one last time. "I'll do the iced lavender specialty latte. That sounds...lavendery."

I chuckle as the cashier punches the order in, and Becca shoots a dramatic scowl at me.

"Remind me to never let you be my coffee journey guide again. I feel so shamed."

"It's your coffee hazing. Everyone has to go through it."

The cashier clears his throat. He's giving off some strong queer vibes, and he looks like he's caught between staring fondly at Becca and I's it-shouldn't-be-flirting-but-it's-totally-flirting routine and just wishing we would hurry up so he can help the next people in line.

"Will you be paying separately or together?"

"I'll get it," I answer before Becca can say anything. "As repayment for your hazing."

The only empty seats I can spot are singles, so once we have our drinks in hand, Becca and I head for the bench outside. It's padded with red cushions and gives us a view of the tree-dotted lawn across the street.

For the first few sips, we don't say anything, but there's no awkwardness to the silence. It feels like we're letting the moment settle over us. Part of me is still trying to catch up with how *normal* this feels, how right, like Becca and I have been getting coffee together for years. It shouldn't be possible to be so calm after what happened in the locker room just twenty minutes ago, but that's exactly what I feel: calm.

She makes the world stop for a while, like everything beyond this bench can wait.

"How's the lavendery lavender?" I ask once I'm halfway through my mocha.

"I thought my hazing was done, or are you still making fun of me?"

"This isn't hazing anymore. This is just regular making fun of you."

"Oh, I see how it is." She lifts her chin up. "I'm going to sit here and enjoy my lavender latte whether you make fun of me or not."

"I admire your perseverance."

We're both struggling not to laugh. I take another few sips as I grin around the edge of my cup.

"Are you looking forward to your courses this semester?" I ask as a girl passes by on the sidewalk, staggering under the weight of an armload of textbooks.

"Mostly," Becca answers. "I don't have many courses for my minor this term, and those are usually my favourite, but the kinesiology ones still seem like they'll be good."

"Remind me what your minor is again."

"Environmental science."

"Right, yeah." I nod. "If it's your favourite, how come it's your minor?"

Her forehead creases, and I hurry to backtrack. "That was kind of nosy. You don't have to answer that."

"No, no." She shakes her head. "It's a good question. I...I've actually asked myself that. Kinesiology has always been the plan, and I do like it. I just didn't know how much I would like environmental science too. I've thought about switching to a double major a few times, but I'm always so busy with captain stuff, and it's a little late to make the switch now anyway. "

It's the first time I've heard her sound anything besides obsessed and elated about being captain. There's almost a hint of regret in her voice.

"Mhmm." I nod, watching her. "What do you like about environmental science?"

"I—" She cuts herself off and drums her fingers on the side of her cup, staring over at the lawn for a few seconds before she turns to me. "You really want to know about this?"

"Of course." I slide my glasses up my nose and smile at her. "If you want to tell me."

"I do."

We stare at each other for a moment, and I can feel my smile fading as something starts to flicker and heat up between us again. I want to hear more—about her, about what she likes, what she doesn't, how she sees things, what she feels. It's like I'm taking an Intro to Becca course and it's the most fascinating thing I've ever studied.

"Um, well..." She takes a sip of her drink and goes back to staring at the lawn. "My environmental science classes sort of feel like...like learning to see, you know? It's like becoming aware of all the puzzles wrapped in puzzles wrapped in more puzzles that make up everything around us. Or maybe puzzle is the wrong word. Maybe it's more like paintings. It's like those art historians who do all those intense scans and investigations of famous paintings to uncover all the layers and techniques and all the ways the painting changed as the artist was making it, only the painting is...the world, and we're figuring out how it was made so we know how best to preserve it."

Her whole face has lit up with passion and a breathtaking confidence. When she's on the lacrosse field, she always looks like she could set everything around her on fire through sheer force of will, but in this moment, she looks like she *is* the fire.

I know I'm staring, but I can't help sitting there blinking at her until the silence really does get awkward.

Becca lets out an embarrassed chuckle. "That was kind of a weird explanation. I know—"

"No!" I interrupt. "No, not at all. That was...inspiring. It made me want to sign up for environmental science courses."

She chuckles again and stares down at her cup in her lap.

"That's actually kind of similar to how I feel about economics," I tell her, "except for me, it really is like a puzzle within a puzzle within a puzzle. It's a way of taking it all apart and putting it back together again. There are so many parts that work together in all these unexpected ways. I'm not, um...I've never been super into reading and writing."

I don't know why I can't make myself say, 'I'm dyslexic.' I've said that exact sentence to dozens of people without breaking a sweat or even thinking much about it. It took a few years after my diagnosis to stop seeing dyslexia as a badge of shame, but eventually I realized it doesn't define me any more than people are defined by a food allergy or being left-handed. It's just a thing my body does, and sometimes it makes my life harder, but other times it makes my life really cool too.

The years before the diagnosis were much harder. That's when teachers would call me unfocused and lacking in initiative on all my report cards. That's when I'd find myself in detention for acting up and not understand what I'd done wrong. That's when kids would look over and see my completely blank test at the end of an hour. They'd whisper things about me.

Ethan said some of those same things loud and clear when he broke up with me.

"The thing about economics," I continue, forcing myself to abandon that train of thought, "is that it's actually really...active. You have to learn all the terms and stuff, of course, but once you do, it's way more about looking at the way things move and interact in this big picture in your head. It's like a sport. When I have to write an essay, I pretend I'm being a sports commentator."

Now it's me looking down at my cup while my cheeks get hot.

"Wow, I can't believe I just told you that. I am a dork."

"You're not a dork!" Becca gives me a light jab with her elbow. "I mean, you are, but not about that. That's really cool."

My ribcage is tingling from the touch. She actually makes me *tingle*.

"Thanks."

I take another sip of my drink and realize I've gotten to the bottom of the cup. Becca's about finished too. I should have gone slower. I could sit here with her for hours. The building's awning keeps us out of the sun's glare, and the early afternoon heat is just strong enough to make the iced drinks worth it.

Not that I need an excuse to drink an iced coffee. Even winter can't keep me away from ice-cold caffeine.

"Damn, I'm finished already. They make such good mochas. You should get one next time."

I feel her tense up beside me, and I freeze too when I realize what I've just said.

What it could mean.

Next time.

"I guess we should probably talk about what we're supposed to do now."

I might be imagining it because it's what I'm hoping for, but I hear the hesitation in her voice, like she doesn't want to spoil this moment with reality any more than I do.

"Probably," I echo.

"This was...really nice. Getting coffee. I don't really talk with people like this a lot. I mean, I hang out with the team, but..."

I know what she means. When she shows up for team parties, there's this aura around her, like she's presiding rather than participating. I guess it makes sense for a captain, but I see now what I've always suspected: she's lonely. Even with the team she thinks of as a family, she feels alone.

"Becca, I know you don't want to mess things up with the team, and I respect that. I agree it's not a risk we can take." I pause for a second and go on when she doesn't reply. "I just think that going to practices and games while pretending we don't know each other any better than we did a couple weeks ago is not going to be...convincing. I don't want things to get weird because we're trying so hard to *not* make them weird, you know? So maybe we, uh, don't have to try that hard. We could stop all the rest of it and just, like, get coffee together sometimes? Hang out? This sounds really cliché, but I do want to be your friend."

I expect her to call me out on my bullshit plan, because to be honest, it *is* kind of a bullshit plan. The static sparking between us every time our arms accidentally brush is proof of that.

It's true, though. I want to be her friend. I want more conversations like this, even if that's all we have, and it'll be much easier to keep things from getting weird with the team if we're acting like two people developing a friendship, not two people who made out at a party and then swore to never speak again.

"I do want to try those other specialty lattes..."

My head jerks up in surprise. I was sure she was going to shoot me down.

"You do?"

"I think you're right. We can't just decide to avoid each other for the whole year. It will impact the team, and that's the whole point of not getting involved with teammates in the first place."

I fight to keep my shoulders from drooping. Of course she's only thinking of the team. I shouldn't have expected more.

"And..." She taps on her cup again, her eyes trained to her lap. "I want to be your friend too. I really do."

My heart jumps into my throat. I have the urge to jump up and do a 'becoming friends with Becca' dance, but some part of my brain has the decency to remind me to be cool.

"Right. Cool. Yes. Let's do it."

She lifts her head and holds her cup up. I clink the side of it with mine, and we make a silent toast to whatever the hell we just agreed to get ourselves into.

9

Becca

"Okay, first question. How many of you have played lacrosse before?"

We're halfway through the second week of the semester, and today is the first of our two lacrosse tryout sessions. There are a dozen girls standing on the field in front of me while Hope and Bailey flank me on either side. Coach Jamal is yet again dealing with a baby care emergency, so for now, it's on me to lead the tryouts.

About half the girls raise their hands. Most of them are freshmen, but there are a couple upper years looking to give lacrosse a go too.

"Don't worry about experience." Hope takes a step forward, smiling at the girls who've never played before. "Lacrosse is a pretty straightforward game to learn, and you never know who's going to be a natural with a stick."

She says the last part in an exaggerated seductive voice, and everyone laughs. I force a chuckle too and try to ignore the way that voice makes heat bloom somewhere low in my stomach.

I start leading the group through a quick warm-up, and

Hope keeps cracking jokes that wipe all the nerves off the prospective players' faces and have them chatting and making jokes of their own. She just *sparkles* when she's doing stuff like this. I knew she was the perfect person to help out with tryouts. She's a natural at lacrosse, but over the years she's been on the team, I've seen her step up as a natural leader too. She doesn't look for the chance to lead, but when Coach happens to give it to her, she excels.

"Let's go over some really basic game rules," I announce once the warm-up is done, "and then we'll work through some simple drills to get us going."

I review the objective and general rules for lacrosse, along with a quick description of the different positions. Hope, Bailey, and I make up three quarters of the team's attackers—or offence—and the team also includes four defenders, three midfielders, and the goalie.

"We'll partner up and start with some basic throwing and catching, and the more experienced people can add in some cradling too." I pick up my stick and take a few steps back. "Cradling is the technique we use to keep the ball in the stick's basket while we're moving it up the field. We'll go over all the important points for stick handling, but first, Hope, do you want to demo with me?"

She raises one hand in a salute. "Aye, aye, Captain."

I shake my head and grin. She's such a dork. As I watch her run over to grab her stick and then jog back to meet me, I realize it didn't really matter whether we decided to do this whole 'being friends' thing or not. I never could have ignored her, not really. I'm tuned into her now, like a radio signal that lets me adjust the volume but never fully turn things off.

Deciding to be friends with her last week has been a lot more effective than I thought it would. Talking to her feels so natural, even when it's still laced with the memory of

Catch and Cradle

how she tasted. We haven't had our proposed second run of specialty lattes yet, but we've hung around talking after practice and texted a bit during the week.

I never realized how little I actually socialize. Kala and I keep up with each other's lives, but scheduling hangouts around lacrosse is hard. Scheduling *anything* around lacrosse is hard. I barely even have time to get phone calls in with my dad. I've taken on so many projects as captain that with the exception of schoolwork, I'm basically doing or thinking about something lacrosse-related from the minute I get up to the minute I go to bed.

Even though she's on the team, hanging out with Hope makes me feel like I can let that all go. It makes me feel like I can just be *me*—which is confusing, because for most of my life, lacrosse has *been* me.

Hope sets up with the ball a few metres away. I get my stick in position and wait for her pass. She sends the ball in a perfect arc through the air, and I tip my basket back to feel it land with a light thud. I jog a few feet up the field, flicking my wrists in the cradling motion, and she sprints ahead of me to accept my throw.

We move like two parts of the same machine as we complete the pattern a few more times. We've drilled this enough that we're moving on pure muscle memory, caught up in a dance that's as effortless as breathing.

Catch and cradle. Catch and cradle.
Breathe in, breathe out. Breathe in, breathe out.

By the time I accept the final pass and rest my stick on my shoulder, the whole field has gone silent.

"Okay, okay, stop showing off," Bailey jokes while the tryout candidates gawk at us. "You're going to make them think it's as easy as it looks."

Hope jogs up to stand beside me. I glance at her, and she flashes me a grin. My pulse has kicked up from the exercise, and I smile back as the rush of endorphins washes over me. Nothing feels as good as being on the field. I can tell the same thrill of energy is moving through her too.

"Let's do this!" I call out. "Partner up!"

The rest of tryouts take the better part of an hour to get through. There are a few standout experienced players, and one of the girls who's never even held a stick before shows a lot of promise.

Coach showed up about halfway through. He comes over with the clipboard he's been taking notes on when it's only Bailey, Hope, and me left on the field.

"Good work today, girls. Sorry again for being late. We have a new nanny starting next week, so I won't be running into any more problems."

Hope leans on her stick and pretends to pout. "No more Khadija at practice?"

"The wife will still bring her on game days. We'll make a Lobster of her yet." He taps his clipboard. "Speaking of, let's talk about possible new recruits. Hastings, who are your picks?"

Hope blinks and looks over her shoulders like he might be talking to someone else.

"M-my picks? I thought I was just here to demo."

"You're one of our best players. You know what we're looking for as well as Becca and I do," Coach insists. "You must have seen some standouts today."

"Um, I mean..."

She glances at me, and I nod for her to go on. She was a pro out there with the girls today. I know she must have an answer.

She takes a deep breath and continues. "Okay, so seeing as we're currently lacking in our midfield section since Tasia and Alexa both graduated last year, I'm gonna go with a bit of a hot take on this one. Hear me out."

Catch and Cradle

I thought I knew from within the first few drills who the girls to watch were, but as Hope goes on with her explanation, I realize just how much I missed. She can remember every girl's name and what their strengths and weaknesses were, and she's already matched them to what we're lacking in our current team. I glance at Coach and see his eyebrows have risen over the top of his aviators. Bailey is staring at Hope with her mouth hanging wide open, and I feel like I'm close to doing the same.

She'd make a great captain.

The thought crosses my mind for the first time ever, with a loud, piercing clarity I can't ignore. Hope would be excellent at leading this team. If I were passing on the torch, she'd be my first and only pick. I know Coach would agree.

But of course, I'm not passing on the torch. Not yet. Being captain of the UNS lacrosse team is who I am. I've fought through so much to be here. I almost lost Kala's friendship just to stay on the team. I *did* lose a lot of people when I stayed. Getting the captain nomination made it all worth it. It felt like I belonged and always would. For so long, I just wanted somewhere to belong, and I found it here.

I don't know who I'd be if I lost that. I don't know who I am without lacrosse.

But what if I could find out?

"And that's why I think we should pick her," Hope concludes, cutting off my train of thought before it gets too crazy. I zoned out and missed her last few sentences, but I still join in Coach and Bailey's applause.

"What?" Hope looks between the three of us. "Why are we clapping?"

"We're clapping because you just did my job for me, Hastings." Coach tucks his clipboard under his arm.

"Have you ever considered running the national team's draft for them? Maybe I could hook you up."

"So you're saying you agree with me?"

Coach chuckles. "Yes, Hope. That was a fantastic assessment."

"Oh." She taps the end of her stick on the ground a few times. "Thanks, C—I mean, thank you, Coach Jamal."

I bite back a laugh. He still doesn't know half the team calls him CJ, or that Hope's household apparently has a garden gnome named after him.

"Thank you. You three better head home now. Early practice tomorrow morning."

Bailey laughs. "It's, like, not even seven, Coach."

He claps his hands together in a *chop chop* motion. "Then you will have no excuse for being tired tomorrow. I, on the other hand, have a very uncooperative infant to attend to."

We say our goodbyes, and the three of us carry all the tryout gear back to the supply closet before heading for the locker room.

"Do you guys want to grab dinner?" Hope asks after we've all changed—with me exerting every ounce of effort not to look over my shoulder at her the whole time. "I'm starving."

"I'm meeting up with my boyfriend," Bailey answers, "but we should do a team breakfast run tomorrow. We haven't done that yet this season."

"Oooh, good idea!" Hope pulls out her phone. "I'll send a message to the group chat."

She types something out and then looks up at me before I have time to glance away and pretend I wasn't already staring at her.

The 'being friends' plan isn't entirely flawless.

"You down for dinner, Becca?"

"I—yeah." I swallow. "I'm down."

The slam of Bailey's locker door makes me jump. "I'm out, hoes. Have a nice dinner."

I don't know if it's paranoia, but I swear there's something suspicious in her eyes when she looks back over her shoulder and waves before leaving the room. She's one of the few players who've been on the team as long as I have, which means she's one of the few people who were there for The Lisa Experience.

I know she lost friends because of it too. Anyone who stayed on the team did. A whole social circle got ripped in half when everyone was forced to choose between me and Lisa.

"I was thinking Pita Pit." Hope steps up beside me, one strap of her backpack slung over her shoulder. "I've had a Pita Pit craving all day."

I edge away from her on the pretense of closing my locker. If we're going to keep hanging out, I need to be more careful.

"Pita Pit sounds good."

"And then maybe we could eat in the park?"

I agree before I can stop myself.

Just a casual summer evening spent having an impromptu picnic in the park with a girl who's kissed my neck.

Nothing non-platonic about that.

I ROLL down the top of my pita wrapper and take my first bite. Hope and I are sitting on a bench at Citadel Hill with a very platonic two feet of space between us, marked by the backpack I dropped onto the bench as soon as I sat down.

"Mmmm!"

Hope is already three bites into her pita and clearly satisfying her craving.

"'At's 'ood!" she says around a mouthful of food.

I laugh and turn away from my view of the harbor to face her. "You seem happy."

"Mmmm!" she repeats. She closes her eyes and does a contented little wiggle with her shoulders.

"You deserve a celebratory pita. You were great today."

She swallows and tilts her head to the side. "You sure? I thought maybe Coach was just trying to be nice and, like, supportive of my nonsense rambling."

"He's nice, but he's not *that* nice. You were amazing with your results and with the girls. You brought the best out of them. That's hard to do in a practice, never mind a tryout."

She shrugs. "I just wanted them to have fun. It's hard to tell what someone's strengths are if they aren't feeling comfortable. I guess some people work well under pressure, but I think you can do more when you feel safe."

She's gotten quieter now, showing that contemplative, almost reserved side of her that doesn't appear during practice or when she's hanging out with the team.

"That makes sense."

It sounds like she's speaking from experience, like there's heartache hidden in the way she helps other people, but I don't know how to ask about it.

We spend the next few minutes eating and watching people in the park. The sun is making its way down to the edge of the water, streaking the waves with gold that filters up through the city streets. We sit above it all, looking down the green lawn in front of us that's dotted with picnic blankets and beach towels like a patchwork quilt.

I'm the first to break the silence. "Can I ask you something?"

"Go for it."

"It seems really hard for you to believe you did a good job today. Is that true?"

She's done with her pita now, and she curls the wrapper up into a ball with her fist before sighing.

"Yeah, I guess that's probably true."

I wait to see if she'll add more. I'm about to tell her we can drop it when she starts talking again.

"I think I might be going through some kind of weird doubting myself phase at the moment. I've been trying to ignore it, but it must be bad if other people are noticing it too."

"I'm sorry. I didn't mean to make you feel bad by bringing it up. I just thought maybe there was something different I could do for the next tryouts, like maybe I said something hurtful, or Coach did, or something."

She shakes her head. "No, no. That's not it at all. You guys are awesome. I'm just..."

She gets up instead of finishing her sentence and walks over to the nearest garbage can so she can pitch her wrapper inside. When she comes back, she sits down and stares straight ahead as she starts speaking so fast I do a double-take and struggle to keep up.

"I have dyslexia. I'm dyslexic. It's, like, not even a big deal. I got diagnosed pretty late and it took me a while to feel okay about it, but then I had lots of great people help me learn to deal with it. Now it's just a normal part of my life I feel totally okay about, except..."

She pauses and takes a few quick breaths, still staring out at the ocean.

"Except it still *does* make things difficult. University is *so* hard. Everything takes me forever, and it's way harder to get academic support when you're in a class with a hundred people than a small high school, you know? When

I first started at UNS, I wasn't even sure I would try out for lacrosse. It felt like I was pushing my luck, like I should just be happy I even got into university in the first place. I *need* lacrosse, though. I need that outlet, so I make it work. It takes a lot of scheduling and a lot of prioritizing and a lot of discipline, but I make it work."

Her hands are balled into fists in her lap, her forehead creased with all the determination I can hear in her voice. She looks fierce, like she's ready to re-shape the world around her through sheer force of will.

The more time I spend with her, the more layers I see pulled back, always revealing something new underneath. She's way more than just happy-go-lucky Hope Hastings. She's more than the girl who makes everyone laugh in the locker room. She's more than the girl who shines on the field. She's more than all the struggles she's describing. She's a whole universe slowly unfolding itself in front of me, and there's something humbling and precious about that.

"I didn't think I could fit a relationship into all that," she continues. "I told Ethan that. I opened up and told him everything I was scared of, every weakness I thought I had, and he said it would be okay. He said we would take it on together, but in the end...he just threw all my deepest fears in my face. In front of everyone."

I can't help it. I reach over and wrap my hand around her clenched fist. Heat flares low in my stomach at the contact, but I ignore it. There are more important things going on.

"Hope, you have to know all anyone got out of that situation was realizing he was a complete jackass. Nobody thought it reflected at all on you."

She looks up from staring down at our hands and locks

her eyes on mine. The glow of the sunset picks out the flecks of hazel in the bright, clear blue.

She has eyes like a river.

"I know what he did was bad and wrong and totally unacceptable," she tells me, "but what if there was some reason in what he said? Maybe I didn't try hard enough. Maybe I don't have what it takes to try hard enough. He said he started keeping things from me because he didn't think I could handle them. I just...I can't stop thinking about it." Her hand twitches under mine. "I haven't felt like this in years. I thought I was over feeling bad about dyslexia, but I guess not."

She sighs, and some of the moment's intensity breaks. I pull my hand away, and she goes back to looking out at the city and the sea.

"It's really stupid. Nothing has actually changed, but I'm questioning everything. I'm almost past the deadline to apply for this summer economics internship. I have it all finished, but every time I go to hit send, I just...can't. I start wondering if it's going to be too much for me."

"Hope." I nudge her foot with mine to make sure I have her full attention. "Nothing about you is stupid. Nothing at all. I mean, just today I was thinking about what an amazing lacrosse captain you would make. I would trust you with the whole team, and I can't even think of a single other player I would say that about."

She lets out a shocked laugh. "Captain? I mean, maybe tryout manager, but *captain*?"

"Absolutely, and I'm not just saying that to be nice. You know I don't hand out lacrosse-related compliments just to be nice."

She laughs again. "That's true. I remember in first year, you once told me that if I wanted to be a cross-checking troll, I should get off the field and go live under a bridge."

I clap my hand over my mouth and double over with laughter. "Oh my god, did I really say that?"

"Yeah, it was quite the criticism."

"I can't believe I called you a troll. Oh my god." I clutch my stomach as I fight off another laugh attack. "I mean, in my defence, you did used to get kind of aggressive with the cross-checking."

"But a *troll*, Becca?" She throws her hands in the air and shakes her head, but I can see her biting back a grin. "Where did you even come up with that?"

"I have no idea. I guess I just wanted to make sure I kept our star player from racking up penalties."

She scoffs. "First I'm a troll. Now I'm a star player."

"You've always been a star player."

"Oh really? In first year, I didn't even think you knew my name."

"I always knew your name."

My voice is low, and my words spark some new heat—a heat even the backpack and two feet of bench between us aren't enough to ward off. If anything, the distance just makes me burn with an even stronger need to be close to her.

"You did?"

"Of course."

I've always noticed her. I've always felt her like a change in seasons, like a shift of scents and colours, of sounds in the air and wind on my skin. Sometimes she's the first crackle of dried leaves in the fall and sometimes she's the mud and melting of spring, but she's always a change. She's always a collection of warning signs there to remind me I spend every day of my life pulled around the sun by a force I can't feel or see.

Maybe it's dramatic, but it's true. I feel Hope like a force, and until now, she's always been a force as vague and distant as the centrifugal motion of the solar system. The pull I feel toward her was never something I had a role in. It was never an action I took or tried to take. She was just *there*, and now, somehow, she very much feels like she's *here*.

"Becca..."

"We should head back." I jump up off the bench and stand facing away from her as I pull my backpack on. "Coach was right. Early morning practice tomorrow."

"Right. Yeah."

I turn around and find her slipping her own backpack on. The top of her chest has the slightest tinge of a pink flush to it, and for a second, all I want to do is lick her collarbones and see how deep I can make her blush.

Which is exactly why I need to leave. Now.

"Thanks for getting dinner with me." She shifts her weight from side to side. "And for what you said. About Ethan. About...me."

"I meant it." I press my lips together, but my next words slip out anyway. "You're amazing, Hope. You really are."

10

Hope

Jane sets a salad bowl down in front of me and then passes two more out to Iz and Paulina. We all gasp and clap in appreciation of the beautifully presented strawberry, balsamic, and feta creation served on a bed of mixed greens.

"My end of summer speciality," Jane says as she takes a bow.

We're crammed in around the round table we have tucked in a corner of the Babe Cave's narrow kitchen. We usually have our family dinners in the living room, but momentous occasions call for an actual table. Supper on the eve of our first lacrosse match of the season definitely counts as a momentous occasion. We're almost halfway through September already, and we lucked out with scoring a home game to kick things off.

"It's so pretty I don't even want to eat it." Paulina gazes down at her bowl like she's staring at a painting.

I've been studying all day and can't remember if I ate lunch or not, so I don't hesitate to spear a huge forkful of greens and dig in. I groan out my approval as I chew, and Jane sets her own bowl down with a satisfied smile.

"Chef Jane has done it again," she says, bringing one hand to her mouth and kissing the tips of her fingers.

Now that the craziness of the semester has set in, it's rare that all four of us get time to sit down for a meal together. We try to have semi-regular family dinners, but mostly our group dining experiences consist of eating on the fly as we head to practice or devouring takeout during quick study breaks.

"How is everyone doing?" I ask between bites of salad. "Like, *really* doing? Let's have a Babe Cave catch up session."

It's been almost a week since Becca and I's Pita Pit Experience—as I've started calling it in my head—and I know I've been so busy with school, lacrosse, and lying on my bed replaying the feeling of her hand on mine that I haven't exactly been the most attentive roommate or friend.

"Oh, I didn't tell you guys! My sister got her first ultrasound." Paulina sets her fork down and beams at us. "The baby is healthy and such a cute little blob! I can't believe I'm going to be an auntie."

Jane claps her on the shoulder. "You're going to be a great auntie."

"What's aunt in Polish?" I ask. "Is that what the baby will call you?"

"Oooh, I hadn't even thought of that!" her eyes light up. "How does *Ciocia* Lina sound?"

"Like a thing I cannot pronounce, but very cute," I answer.

"What about you, Iz?" Jane asks after we've all finished another few bites of salad. "What's your Babe Cave update?"

"No babies to report, but uh..." They run a hand over their freshly shaved head. "I'm going on a second date with that girl I met at Mario's. The volleyball player. I know you guys are going to make fun of me, but I like her. A lot."

To no one's surprise, our pizza dinner to celebrate the end of training camp resulted in Iz taking yet another UNS athlete out on a romantic date.

"We can stop teasing you if it really bothers you," Paulina tells them. "We really do support whoever you want to date. You're just following your heart, you know? There's nothing wrong with that."

My own heart twinges at her words. That's exactly what I'm craving to hear from someone—*anyone*—but even if I did come clean and somehow gained their approval, there isn't all that much to approve.

Becca doesn't want more. Becca *can't* want more, and I need to stop daydreaming about alternate realities where we're some kind of happy couple the whole team is thrilled for.

"Aww, thanks Auntie Lina." Iz shifts in their chair and opens and closes their mouth a few times like they're working out what they want to say next. "Speaking of acceptance, I'm kind of, um, worried about the season. This is the first time I'll be spending a whole season out as non-binary, and it just really sucks to think of all the misgendering that's going to happen. Having our team renamed to Women's Plus around campus was amazing, but the league itself hasn't done anything like that, and maybe I'm just being difficult—"

"Iz," I cut them off, "you are not being difficult. You have every right to play a sport in a way that acknowledges who you are. Sports really need to catch up in the gender department. We're really lucky to have you, and I know the whole team feels the same."

Jane starts clapping. "Hear ye, hear ye!"

"Fuck yeah!" Paulina shouts. "Claws out to tear up the gender binary!"

The three of us start doing a modified version of the lobster claw dance in our seats and don't stop until Iz has gone from worried to laughing and dancing along.

"Okay, Jane." I make a claw-snapping motion at her as the dance comes to an end. "What about you?"

"Well..." She nibbles a strawberry on the end of her fork and makes a show of coyly twirling the fingers of her other hand in her hair. "My life hasn't been much more exciting than endless study sessions and dragging my ass to practice, exceeeept for last night at the boyfriend's when we may or may not have used a cock ring for the first time."

Everyone's jaws drop. Jane usually describes herself as vanilla, but every once in a while she'll come out with some crazy declaration and then refuse to give us any actual details about it.

"I won't confirm or deny details, but I'll say one thing." She drops her voice to a whisper. "*Game. Changer.*"

"Oh my god, Jane! You can't just leave us hanging," Iz whines. "This is like that story about the butt plug."

"You mean the story about that time the smoke detector went off and we all had to run out of the house in the middle of the night because Jane and her boyfriend set her curtains on fire, and Jane wouldn't give us any details besides blaming it on a butt plug?" I deadpan.

"I blamed it on a butt plug *and* my Cherry Nights scented candle."

Jane glares while the three of us scream with laughter. I forgot about the candle part.

"I c-can't believe you have a-a-a candle called c-*cherry*

nights," Iz stammers. They're laughing so hard they're wiping tears off their face.

"It sounds like a-a-like a..." I clutch my stomach and fight to get the words out. "Like a weird v-virginity candle or something."

"For your virgin butt!" Paulina shouts.

We all totally lose it—except for Jane, who sits there shovelling salad into her mouth and pretending to ignore us.

"Do you have a special candle for using the cock ring?" I ask when I can talk again.

Iz splutters and almost spits out the sip of the water they just took.

"I am *not* talking about my candles with any of you," Jane answers. "I will not take any more of this friggin' mockery."

Friggin' is one of my favourite Nova Scotia-isms of hers.

"Okay, okay, we'll stop mocking," I assure her.

She shakes her head. "Too late. I'm done. Let's move on to what's up with you, Hope."

What's up with me?

Just the question is enough to sober me up from the memory of Jane's candle story. I'm not even sure what *is* up with me. After talking with Becca on Citadel Hill and hearing her go so far as to say I'd make a great captain, I started thinking about how I *really* want my life to look this year—not just with her, but with everything.

How I want to feel.

Who I want to be.

What I want to do.

Despite our vow of *no ragrets* and my promise to make this a year to remember, I've really just spent almost the whole first month of school being afraid and uncertain.

"Soap of Hope." Iz reaches over to pat my hand. "What's up? You just got all sad."

I set my fork down and stare into the remains of my salad. "Can I ask you guys something? And can you be completely honest?"

I glance up and find them all nodding, their faces pinched with concern.

"Do you think I'm responsible?"

"Hope!" Jane springs to her feet and comes to stand behind me. She bends down and wraps her arms around my neck. "Of course you're responsible. You're one of the most responsible people we know, right guys?"

Iz and Paulina nod.

"Yeah, sometimes I even wonder if we even have a fourth roommate because you're studying so much," Iz answers.

"And the best thing about you is that you're responsible *and* fun!" Paulina adds. "You can have a good time and just dive into things and go with the flow, but you're also great at keeping your shit together. It's impressive."

"You're a miracle!" Jane loosens her suffocating neck hug a little and rests her chin on top of my head. "And we love you very much."

My chest swells, and I can feel my eyes start to sting.

"You guys don't, like, hide stuff from me because you think I can't handle it, right? You don't think I have too much on my plate?"

"Oh my god, Hope, we would never decide that for you." Jane lets me go and crouches down beside me instead. "The only time I'm going to tell you how much you can have on your plate is when it's food I made. You're getting an extra large helping of my spaghetti tonight whether you like it or not."

I chuckle and swipe at my eyes. "Thanks, guys. It's just

been a rough start to the year. I'm about to miss my summer internship application deadline, and I'm just like, maybe I shouldn't even bother, you know?"

"*What?*" Jane grabs both my hands. "Nonsense! You've been talking about that internship since freshman year. When is the deadline?"

"Uh, tonight."

"How much do you have left to write?"

"I mean, I'm done all the writing. I just have to submit it."

Jane stands up and assumes her fisherman's wife stance. "Hope Elizabeth Hastings! Go and get your laptop."

I can feel myself starting to smile. "But dinner—"

"Spaghetti can wait! Get your friggin' laptop and bring it here!"

Five minutes later, our salad bowls have been cleared and my friends are all gathered behind me as I sit with my laptop open on the table. I've filled in the application form, uploaded all my documents, and have my cursor hovering over the 'submit' button.

The internship is a six week summer position with the government in Ottawa. It's a mix of summit-like seminars and group sessions combined with practical experience, and they only accept twenty people a year. From what I can tell, hundreds if not thousands apply.

"Go Hope! Go Hope! Go Hope!" Iz, Paulina, and Jane chant as they watch me raise my finger to click.

I freeze just before I do it. The internship includes a lot of discussions and talk-based learning, but there's still going to be plenty of reading and writing involved. It's an intense position even for people who don't have dyslexia. Their website says they want 'the next generation of innovative, quick-thinking economists ready to excel.'

Is that really me? The girl who can't even spell innovative *correctly or read it without seeing the letters get all squiggly on the page?*

"Go Hope! Go Hope! Go Hope!"

The chant continues to ring out behind me as Paulina shouts, "You can do it! Use that little lobster claw and click!"

"I'm a lobster!" I yell, my finger still hovering above the keyboard.

"You're a lobster!" they all echo.

"And you can do anything!" Jane adds.

Maybe it's okay that I don't totally believe it. Maybe I don't have to. Maybe that's what being a Lobster means—what being a friend means: believing in the people you love so much that they always find their way back to believing in themselves.

I click the button. My friends cheer.

I can do anything.

11

Hope

"I CAN DO ANYTHING!" I shout around my mouth guard as I hoist my stick in the air.

The words come out sounding more like '*Ar 'an 'oo anyfink,*' but that doesn't stop my teammates from understanding me. We're all fluent in mouth guard-speak at this point.

Bailey taps her stick to mine as we set up for the game to resume. I just scored a where-did-that-even-come-from goal that brings us up to a four point lead. The crowd gathered on the bleachers is going nuts. We're down to the last five minutes of the game, which means we've basically already declared victory.

I glance at the sidelines and see CJ signalling for everyone to keep their focus on the game. It's not time to party just yet; stranger things have happened than a miraculous end-of-the-game turnaround.

Although I have to admit, my goal was pretty damn miraculous itself.

I catch sight of Becca, her red hair hanging in a thick braid down her back. It thumps against her jersey as she jogs into position. The two of us have been unstoppable today. Her pass is what set me up for my nearly impossible goal. It's like I can sense where she's going to be before she even gets there. We've always worked well as attackers together, but today we're on fire.

Maybe we've got this all wrong. Maybe the whole team should be making out if it results in us playing this well.

The face-off grabs my attention and turns me into a single-minded machine. I watch the thrashing mass of sticks and limbs in the centre of the field like a lion waiting for its shot at the prey. My mind slows the movement down, tracking the ball amidst all the chaos, searching for the first sign of where it's going to end up.

Now.

I sense it more than I see it. I haven't even fully confirmed the ball is in our possession before I'm sprinting to where I need to be. Becca catches a pass from one of our midfielders and instantly gets swarmed by defenders. She lobs the ball out of the mess and over to Bailey. I tear up the field towards the opposing team's goal, making sure I stay far enough ahead of her that she can see me.

The field is a red and blue-streaked blur of activity. They don't call it 'the fastest game on two feet' for nothing. There is no standing around in lacrosse.

The ball pitches up and down the field a few times, getting snatched by the opposition and then reclaimed by us in a pattern that continues on and on for the next few minutes. The air smells like turf and sweat. My heart pounds in my ears, blocking every other sound. My whole body is flooded with adrenaline that brings the world around me into sharp definition.

I feel strong.

I feel capable.

I feel *hungry*.

I want the win so bad it's like a gnawing in my stomach that fuels every breath I take. Ever since I submitted my internship application, I've been riding on a high that pushes me harder and takes me further in every part of my life. I'm tired of being scared and unsure. I'm tired of letting someone else's words knock me on my ass.

Hope Hastings doesn't sit around on her ass. Hope Hastings gets up and fights.

I grind my teeth against my mouth guard and take off sprinting up the field again, riding out the last few minutes of play. Our team doesn't get another point in, but by the time the end of the game is signalled, we've kept the other team from scoring any more.

A six to two win for our first game in the season against one of the biggest schools in Canada.

As soon as it's officially announced, the rest of the world rushes back into focus. The screaming of the crowd and my teammates is piercing, wild, and so joyful it makes my heart feel like it's about to burst into Lobster-shaped confetti. I run as fast as I can to throw myself into the group hug collecting in the middle of the field.

I can do anything.

I blink back the tears as I whoop and pound my teammates on their backs.

I don't know why I ever let myself believe otherwise. This moment right here is proof of everything I need to know: there's nothing I can't accomplish.

"HOLY SHIT, THAT GOAL!"

Jane hauls me out of the pile-up so she can give me a hug of her own. She's already ditched her mouth guard. She backs up so we can do a chest bump. I oblige, and we slam our bodies together. It leaves us winded and rubbing our boobs—the same result as every time we do a chest bump, but we keep doing them after winning games anyway.

It seems like everyone on the team has something to say about the goal. By the time we've gotten through all the post-game formalities, I've gotten compliments from almost every single player.

"Hastings, get over here!"

Most of the team is still milling around, slinging back water and talking with friends who came out to watch the game. I turn from where I've been talking with Iz and find Coach Jamal waving me down. He's holding Khadija and standing with Becca a few meters away.

I haven't had a chance to get a word in with Becca since the end of the game. I'm still buzzing with the high of the win. I can't even stand in place without bouncing up and down on my toes. It's all I can do not to sprint over and grab her face to pull her into a triumphant kiss.

This feels like the moment for a triumphant kiss. I've been beaming at everyone for so long my cheeks are starting to hurt. I feel so light, like a giant weight dropped off my shoulders in the middle of the game and left me flying.

"What up, Coach?"

I jog over and tickle one of Khadija's feet to distract me from how close I am to Becca. A few strands of red hair have slipped out of her braid, and they're now curling around her flushed, freckled face. The whole team is glowing, but Becca is shining. Even Khadija's cute baby laugh isn't enough to keep me from stealing glances at her.

"Becca and I were just talking about that goal. What a shot. I think I've seen somebody score from a position like that maybe…four times? And that's since I started playing lacrosse myself."

"Oh wow, so we're going back to ancient history," I joke.

Becca giggles. I don't think I've ever heard her *giggle* before.

"Hey now." Coach puts on a stern face. "Just because you're the star of the game doesn't mean I can't order you to do push-ups if you keep talking like that."

"How many do you want?" I ask as I rock back and forth on the balls of my feet. "I could do laps too. I feel like I could go all day."

He shakes his head and laughs. "Let's save some of that energy. We've got a long journey to get to our next game."

Our next game isn't for two weeks, but it's all the way in Montreal. We're in for a twelve hour drive since we have to ration out funding for flights.

The cons of being the only coastal team in the league.

"My wife is giving me some kind of signal about bottles," Coach announces, "so I better get this baby back to her. Good job again, Hastings. You too, Moore. You're quite the pair."

I glance at Becca and see she's gone stock-still just like me. My pulse has picked up like I'm back in the game, and my throat is so dry all I can do is make a weird squeaking sound in answer. Thankfully, CJ is already walking away and doesn't hear it. I stare at the back of his red coach t-shirt and then force myself to swallow and turn back to face Becca.

"So, uh, seems like we're quite the pair."

I cringe as soon as I say it. I expect her to shoot daggers at me and silently warn me to knock it off, but my jaw drops when all she does is smile—partially because I'm shocked, and partially because she's just so goddamn beautiful.

Catch and Cradle

"Yeah, we did good out there today. *You* did good out there. Coach is right. That goal was spectacular."

"I wouldn't have made it without that pass from you."

She laughs. "I wasn't expecting you to score from there. I was just as shocked as everyone else. You were like the ball whisperer today."

I gawk at her. She stares at me blankly for a second and then claps her hands over her mouth as I start laughing so hard I lose my breath.

"Did you really just use the phrase *ball whisperer?*" I choke out after a moment. "Really, Becca?"

"*Lacrosse* balls!" she insists as she doubles over with laughter too.

"I've been called a stick master before. Now I'm the ball whisperer. I'm just working all the equipment."

"I mean..." She pauses to suck in a breath. "I could have said you were really great at penetrating the crease."

I snort and clutch my stomach, but as cringey as it is, it still turns me on to hear her joke about the crease—AKA the half moon-shaped line that marks the no-go zone around the goalpost. I can see her cheeks getting a bit red, and she avoids my eyes as our laughter dies down.

Turns out the word penetrate *can* be sexy if you're desperate enough.

"Becca..." I push my luck and take a step closer. I still feel invincible, and if there was ever a moment to ask her if she wants to hang out again—on purpose and for a long time, not just as a quick post-practice hang out or coffee run—this would be it. "Do you—"

"Hey, look! It's the stars of the show."

I freeze as the bottom of my stomach drops and a shard of icy dread shoots up my spine. The reaction is instant. I've been braced for this moment all semester, and

141

it's finally here. I don't even need to turn around to be sure it's him.

I should have expected this. His best friend is dating one of my teammates. He hangs out around the jock crowd just like me and all my friends. I thought he'd have the decency to stay away from my games this season, but I guess I gave him too much credit.

"Hope! Hey. Was hoping I'd catch you."

I can't move, but it turns out I don't need to. Ethan strolls up from behind and comes to stand in front of me and Becca. From the corner of my eye, I see her cross her arms over her chest and plant her feet in a wide stance a couple inches ahead of me. I'd probably feel grateful, if I could feel anything at all.

Instead, I just stand there with my mouth hanging open like a gaping fish in the harbour as I take the sight of him in. He hasn't changed. I don't know why I thought a single summer would make a difference, but I realize now that part of my brain was expecting him to be taller and broader and just *more* after everything that happened. In my memories of the last time I stood face to face with him, it felt like he was looming over me, like I was this tiny little mouse crouched under his shadow.

As I look at him now, the opposite seems true. He looks small. Unexceptional. Desperate even, as he stands there shifting his weight from foot to foot and running his hand through his sandy blond hair in an effort to look casual. It's pathetic, really, that he thinks I'd want to talk to him at all.

I find my voice.

"What do you want, Ethan?"

"Uh..." He drops his hand to his side. "Just to, like, say hi."

I cross my arms over my chest and take a step past Becca until Ethan and I are only a few inches apart.

"Hi," I say, the word sharp and short.

The adrenaline of the game is still pumping through my veins. I'm not going to shrink. I'm not going to let anyone make me shrink ever again. I spent the whole summer in a spiral over one conversation with this guy. I'm not going to let him take my year. I'm not going to let dyslexia take my year. It's *my* year, and I'm going to live it.

No ragrets.

"Are we done here?" I ask when he just stands there blinking at me instead of coming up with a reply.

"I—I mean, I just thought maybe we could...um...we..."

"There is no *we*, Ethan." I move even closer. "We aren't going to get a drink or have a talk or whatever it is you came over here to ask. Your window for apology closed a long time ago. I texted you three times this summer to ask if we could talk, and you only even replied to one of them. I didn't owe you that, and I don't owe you anything now. You disrespected me in front of everyone I care about at this school. You broke my trust and made a very private conversation an extremely public one. It wasn't me who didn't take our relationship seriously. It was *you*. You bit off more than you could chew and then made *me* the problem, but I am not going to make myself less for you or anybody. Ever."

My heart is pounding so loud in my ears it's hard to hear the chatting and laughing of all the people milling around on the field, but my voice is clear and even. The post-match celebration continues around us, everyone but Becca oblivious to the showdown.

I glance back at her out of the corner of my eye and see her looking between Ethan and I with a barely contained grin on her face.

She looks proud, and something in my chest roars to

life at the sight. I want to spin around and throw my arms around her neck. I want to tackle her to the ground and kiss her right here on the field. Everything in me is burning—burning with a fire that sparked and flared into an inferno as soon as I scored that goal. I followed it through the air with my eyes and felt everything else get singed away.

There's nothing left but power. I feel unstoppable, like I could have anything I want.

What I want is Becca.

I don't know what's going to happen today. My whole body is thrumming with the certainty that *something* will, but first I need to deal with this dude in front of me.

"I think we're done here," I say.

Ethan stands there opening and closing his mouth a few times.

"Hope, I came over here to ask if we could talk," he finally gets out. "I want a chance to say I'm sorry. I really fucked up, and I—"

"Like I said," I interrupt, "window of apology is closed. We're done here, Ethan."

His eyebrows furrow into a glare, and his shoulders tense.

"Fine, whatever. This is why we broke up in the first place."

He turns and heads back for the bleachers. I wait for the sting of his words to hit, but instead, they just bounce right off me. I barely even hear them. I turn around to face Becca after he's taken a couple steps, and the two of us start beaming as soon as we lock eyes.

"Holy shit, Hastings!" she shouts. "You're a boss."

I shrug. "I have my moments."

"You obliterated him! That was iconic."

I'm smiling so wide my cheeks are starting to hurt. "It helped to have you here."

Something flickers in her eyes, so fast I only just manage to catch it. "Oh, don't even. That was all you. You're amazing."

The fire in me climbs even higher, and before I can decide if it's a good idea or not, I throw my arms around her neck just like I've been aching to do since the game ended. I know to anyone else, we'll just look like excited teammates hugging, but as soon as I'm holding her, all my senses go into overdrive.

I can smell something flowery in her hair mixed with the salty tang of sweat on her neck. Her body is warm against me, her curves pressed to my chest, rising and falling in time with mine as our breathing gets faster and faster. For a few seconds, that's the only part of her that moves. She's gone completely still, and I'm about to pull away thinking she doesn't want the hug when her arms wrap around my waist.

I really am burning for her. Everything is heat and hunger and the bright red of her hair.

I can't pretend we're friends anymore. I can't pretend I don't want this. She has to know. She has to want it too, and right now, I can't see any reason to stop. I played one of the best matches of my life today, and these feelings for her just made me work harder, run faster, be better. I'm *better* with her. What about this could possibly be wrong?

I'm about to pull back enough to look at her face, to see if she's standing on the same ledge I feel myself edging closer and closer to, when the sound of someone calling my name makes me whip my head around.

Becca's arms drop to her sides. I let mine fall from around her neck.

"Hope Elizabeth Hastings!" Jane is sprinting toward us,

Iz and Paulina trotting along behind her. "Please tell me I just saw you serve it to Ethan like the rotten leftovers he deserves."

The laugh that bursts out of me is slightly manic. I'm still trying to process the hug.

"What does that even mean?" I ask.

"It means you're a hero!"

She slams into me at full speed and crushes me in a hug of her own. I grin at Becca from over her shoulder, still a little dazed, and feel a few sparks crackle in my stomach when she smiles back.

Something is happening, something I couldn't stop if I tried.

I don't want to stop it, and I don't want to slow it down anymore.

"Party toniiiiiight!" Iz shouts as they crash into me and Jane and worm their way into the hug. "It's celebration shorts time."

12

Hope

Dry season never stops the lacrosse team from having a good time. Even fueled by nothing but the free Italian sodas Mario gives us to celebrate our win, we still manage to be the loudest group in his bar. He makes fun of us for eating more than the football boys as the staff keeps bringing us pizza after pizza.

I reach for what's got to be at least my fourth slice as I strain to hear the story Paulina is telling about one of her herbs. All the thumping music, clinking glasses, and rowdy conversations make it hard to hear anything quieter than a shout. The place is packed to the rafters tonight, and the team is spread out over a few different tables.

Becca and her roommates are sitting with me and mine. She's directly across from me, and we keep locking eyes, smiling and looking away, then locking eyes again.

It's very gay.

So gay, in fact, that I should be worried about our friends noticing, but I'm not. I don't have room to worry. I'm full of lemon-flavoured Italian soda and an unshakeable belief that tonight is *my* night.

I hold Becca's gaze the next time she looks at me, trying to squeeze all the words I can't say into a few seconds of eye contact. She stares like she hears me, like she wants to answer, and this time neither of us have any Corona buckets to blame it on. This is real.

This is happening.

"I just don't understand why it died," Paulina wails. "Rosemary is supposed to be easy! Am I being sabotaged? Is that what's going on? Should we get a security camera?"

"Oh, *Ciocia* Lina." I pat her on the shoulder, using the nickname we've all adopted after a few lessons in Polish pronunciation. "Is that what we should get you for your birthday? A security camera?"

Her face lights up. "Would you?"

"Guys, seriously?" Jane asks. "A security camera? For *herbs*? Are we running a grow-op?"

"Good idea!" Iz chimes in. "The Babe Cave could use a little extra income."

"You mean our gnome brothel isn't pulling its weight?" I ask.

The four of us burst out laughing while Becca and her roommates look between themselves like they're trying to figure out what the hell is going on.

"We lead a colourful life in our house," I explain.

Becca joins in the laughter. The conversation returns to Paulina's struggles with rosemary as we all finish our pizza. I've just wiped the cheese off my fingers when a new song comes on the speakers and makes the whole team screech and jump to their feet.

"RIRI!" I shout as we form a makeshift dance floor between our tables.

We like Rihanna a lot.

"We the best music!" Iz screams out, doing their best DJ Khaled impersonation. "DJ KHALED!"

Turns out dancing to 'Wild Thoughts' while staring at the subject of your own wild thoughts through a crowd as she shakes her sparkly-shorts-covered ass is a pretty transcendent experience.

Becca is just so gorgeous—always, but especially in moments like this when she lets herself go and shrugs off the weight of responsibilities she always seems to carry with her.

I want her to let go with me. I want to know what that feels like.

We all dance our way through another few songs until somebody knocks over a pitcher on one of the neighbouring tables and Mario flies over to yell at us for disturbing the peace. I like to think we ensure he gets his exercise, but it's more likely the lacrosse team is responsible for the grey hairs streaking the sides of his head.

It's almost ten by the time we settle down and stop dancing. More and more people are filtering into the bar. Most of the team decides to head out and either call it a night or find a more low-key place to celebrate. Game days always hit hard, and even I can feel the exhaustion starting to sink in.

"Anybody coming to the Babe Cave?" Paulina asks once a big group of us have gathered in a red-sequinned herd outside the door.

"We're off to this guy's place," Bailey says from under the arm of her boyfriend, who showed up during the dance party. She jerks her thumb at a few other guys and Rachelle.

A lot of the crowd went straight from the game to Mario's, but Ethan didn't show his face at all. I end up grinning every time I think about that.

"Becca, you calling it a night?" Rachelle asks.

Becca's standing a few feet to my left. She shifts her

weight from side to side, looking around the group. I hold my breath as I wait for her answer. She could come to our place. I didn't even have to make the invitation myself. I don't know what I'm hoping will happen, or what even *can* happen, but the night doesn't feel done.

I don't feel done with her.

"Um yeah, I think I am. I'm wiped out. I'm just gonna head back to the house."

I let my breath out and feel my chest sink.

"Okay, be safe!" Bailey answers. "Text us when you get there."

"We can walk together. You're only a few streets away, right?" Jane asks Becca as people start to disperse.

"Yeah, that's right."

"Great! We will convey our captain home."

Jane leads the Babe Cave crew plus Becca up the sidewalk towards home. I fall into step beside Becca, and it's like I can feel the heat of her arm brushing mine even though we're at least a foot apart. There has to be something I can say, some magic word I can speak to seize all the possibilities hanging like a thick, intoxicating fog in the air, but instead we just stay silent.

I can feel that fog clearing inch by inch the closer we get to her house, but I can't find a way to step back into it. We're losing our chance. I don't know how I know it, but I do. Something about this night is different, and I don't know when or if another one like it will come.

"This is my street. I'll just say goodbye here."

I turn to face her as makes her announcement to the whole group. Everyone spends a few minutes talking about how great the game was and saying goodbye, but I barely speak at all.

And then she's leaving, passing in and out of the glow of the streetlights as she gets farther and farther away from me. Part of me has enough sense left to realize how weird I look standing here staring after her, so I pull it together enough to follow my housemates as they head for our street.

"You all right, Hope?" Jane asks when we're in sight of the Babe Cave. Paulina and Iz are up ahead, singing the chorus of 'Wild Thoughts' and doing weird vocal impersonations of the guitar solo.

"Oh, yeah, just tired."

She gives me a shrewd look. "You sure about that?"

"And maybe I ate too much pizza?"

She chuckles. "How are you feeling about Ethan?"

I shrug. "Honestly? I'm pretty done feeling anything about Ethan. I've been doing better and better about it all ever since I sent in the internship application, and winning the game helped too. I didn't realize how much I needed to say what I said to him today, but now it's over. He's just a guy who said some shitty things to me. I don't have to let that define me anymore."

She slings her arm over my shoulder. "That makes me very, very happy to hear."

We catch up with Iz and Paulina at the house, and everyone declares they're ready for bed as soon as we've kicked our shoes off. I trudge up the creaky staircase and into my room. My bed squeaks when I flop down on the mattress and shimmy out of my shorts.

I can still see Becca walking away from me up the dark street every time I close my eyes.

I toss my glasses onto the bedspread and rub my temples. I only have my desk lamp on, and the dim glow reminds me of the night we kissed. She was lying right here on this bed with me. I can feel the ghost of her fingers gripping my hip.

A shiver runs through me. I can feel her everywhere. I

lay there for so long the sounds of my roommates trudging in and out of the bathroom fade into the silence of sleep. I can't stop thinking about Becca's hands.

I let out a shaky breath as I skate my own hands up the sides of my body. I hook my thumbs under the hem of my lacrosse crewneck and pull it up over my bra. Heat builds between my legs as I imagine her standing over me. Watching me. Wanting me.

I slide my hands under the cups of my bra and flick my thumbs over my nipples. Goose bumps break out all over my skin as I gasp.

I have to have her. I don't want to lie here imagining like I have for years, not when the real thing is just a couple streets away.

Not when she might want me just as bad.

I sit up and slide my glasses back on before hunting around for some joggers and a hoodie. Once I'm dressed, I open my door a crack and see both Paulina and Iz's bedroom doors are shut with no sign of lights on behind them. I hold my breath the whole way down the staircase, keeping to the edge to minimize the creaking. I can smell the lingering traces of some flowery candle in the living room, but Jane's door is closed with the lights off too.

I slip my Keds on, trying to brainstorm some excuse to use if Jane happens to catch me, but I'm too filled with adrenaline to think straight. I step out into the chilly night and pull the front door closed as softly as I can behind me. I hover on the front step for a minute afterwards, straining to hear any sounds of movement in the house, but it stays quiet.

My breathing gets faster and faster as I speed-walk up the street. I don't even know what my plan is. I just have to get to her.

By the time the big tree in her yard comes into view,

Catch and Cradle

I'm wishing I wore a heavier sweater. The days are still warm, but autumn is definitely here at night. I run my hands up and down my arms as I step onto the path that leads to the house's old-fashioned glass panel front door.

When I glance up, I see the light in her room is still on. I remember which window she pointed out last time I was here. The lacy curtains are a softer, frillier choice than I would have expected for her.

Something in me calms at the sight. My breath slows. My head clears.

I just want to be near her. Everything feels better when I'm near her.

I pause when I reach the doorstep. I have no idea which of the several doorbells is for her unit, and I don't want to be the person who wakes the whole house up at midnight.

I walk back into the middle of the yard and take my phone out of my hoodie's pocket. I pull Becca's number up in my contacts and bring the phone to my ear as it starts to ring.

"Hope?"

"Becca."

I hear her sharp inhale. A few moments of silence pass as the two of us just breathe.

"I was about to joke and ask if you forgot your phone again," she says in a quiet voice, "and then I realized you're calling me on your phone."

Her breathy laugh zings through my body, lighting me up.

"Knowing me, I really would think I lost my phone while calling somebody on it."

She laughs again. "So to what do I owe this midnight call?"

"Um, well..." I look down at my feet and kick a little

rock on the path back and forth between them while I try to work out what to say.

The longer the call stretches on, the more I realize this was possibly a shitty idea. It's not exactly a chill move to show up outside someone's window unannounced in the dead of night.

"So, I have a hypothetical situation for you," I tell her.

"Intriguing."

"Ha. Right. Yeah." I kick the rock off into the grass and look back at her window. "Are you in your room?"

Her breath catches, and I feel the heat flare between my legs again. "Yes."

"Like on your bed?"

"Y-yeah."

I close my eyes. I can picture her there, her phone pressed to her ear, her long, milky white legs stretched out on the blankets.

"Okay, stay right there and answer this question." I pause for a second. There's no going back after this. "If I was hypothetically standing in your front yard right now, would you come down and let me inside? Or would you be really freaked out and want me to leave? Both are acceptable answers."

The line goes so silent I start to think she's hung up. Panic squeezes my chest.

Shit shit shit. Fuck. Bad decision.

I'm about to ask if she's still there when the sound of her voice prompts me to start breathing again.

"If we're talking hypothetically..." She trails off, and I can picture her chewing on her lip as she hesitates. "If you were outside right now, I'd come down and...fuck, Hope, I'd kiss you again. I can't stop thinking about kissing you again."

Now it's me going deathly silent.

"Hope? I'm sorry. I—"

"Becca." I'm gripping my phone so hard I'm scared I'm going to crack the case. "Come to your window."

I hear her breathe out, and then there are some shuffling noises before a shadow appears behind the lacy curtains. One of them gets pulled aside, and I see Becca's face framed by her hair hanging loose and wavy over her bare shoulders. She's wearing a white tank top with thin little straps. I can't see her freckles from here, but I can imagine them sprinkled along the tops of her shoulders and down her back.

I haven't been able to stop imagining them since that day in the locker room.

"Y-you're here," she stammers. I watch her lips move high above me.

"Will you let me in?"

I brace for her to say no. She has every reason to say no.

"This is...probably a bad idea."

"Yeah," I agree, "it might be."

Neither of us moves.

I watch the rise and fall of her shoulders as she breathes. I'm covered in goose bumps again, but it's not from the cold.

"Stay right there, okay?"

The call clicks off before I can answer. She turns away from the window, leaving the curtains swaying. I'm still standing there staring up at them when the sound of the front door creaking open echoes in the quiet street.

Becca steps out onto the porch, and I know if she asked me to drop to my knees right then and there, I'd do it. I'd crawl to her. She's practically glowing in the dim light from the streetlamp. Her feet are bare, and she's wearing grey sleep shorts under her tank top with a pale pink knitted cardigan thrown on top.

I've never seen her wear pink before.

"Hope, we shouldn't do this."

I wince like she's just slammed the door in my face. She didn't have to come all the way downstairs to tell me that. It wouldn't hurt so much to hear it with a sheet of glass between us.

"Right," I say through gritted teeth. The pain and embarrassment have me clenching my jaw to keep from breaking down right here. "Of course."

"But I...I still want to."

She takes a step farther onto the porch. I don't move. I don't know which way this is going.

"When I'm with you, everything feels right. Everything feels simple, which is crazy because it's not simple and it hasn't even been that long since we've...gotten close, but I hate feeling like my head's going one way, and my heart..."

A lump rises in my throat when she looks at me with more longing than I've ever seen in her eyes before. I've never felt so wanted in so many ways. None of my crushes during my wild kiss-all-the-girls days back in first year made me feel this way. Not even Ethan made me feel this way in the whole time we dated.

This is something rare. This is not something you're supposed to pass up.

"Just forget about the rest," I rasp. My throat feels raw. I take a few steps toward her. "For tonight, let's just forget everything else. I can't keep ignoring it, Becca, and I don't want to lose you because of that."

She shakes her head. "I don't want to lose you either."

I'm at the edge of the porch now. I wait for her to stop this, to tell me to go, but when she doesn't, I climb the short set of steps to stand in front of her. The shadows of the leaves in the tree shift and twist in a swaying choreography across her skin.

"Do you still want to kiss me?" I whisper.

She nods. Her bottom lip has dropped open, and her gaze is pinned to my mouth.

"So kiss me, Becca."

For a second, I think she's going to pull back, but then she lunges for me. One of her hands fists in my hair and the other grips my waist. Her mouth crashes into mine, desperate and demanding.

I'm just as hungry for her. I moan against her as I cup my hands behind her neck, pulling her closer. I always need her closer.

She parts my lips with hers and sweeps her tongue inside my mouth. She tastes sweet and heady with a hint of spice, like some warm autumn drink spiked with a dizzying shot of dark liquor that works its way through my veins as soon as it hits my tongue. Her hand slips under the bottom of my hoodie, and my back arches, pressing my chest into hers.

I realize she doesn't have a bra on, and I groan. She tightens her grip on my hair and tugs enough to make my scalp sting as she flicks the back of my teeth with her tongue.

No one's ever done that to me. The shock of the sensation makes me gasp into her mouth. I haven't even decided whether I like it or not before I'm already desperate for more. She does it again, and I feel my knees start to get wobbly.

I'm the one who walked up here and ordered her to kiss me, but I'm just putty in her hands. I'm completely, totally hers.

"You like that, huh?" she pants when we break apart to

catch our breath. Her forehead is pressed to mine, the tips of our noses touching.

"Yeah, that—that felt so good."

"I can't get over how good it feels to kiss you."

I tilt my chin up and bring my lips to hers again. This kiss is softer, slower, but just as overpowering. There's an ache between my legs that won't let up. The need flares through my whole body every time I feel the soft curves of her chest brush mine.

I rest one of my hands on her hip, squeezing as we start to pick up the pace again. There are so many places I want to touch her. I hook one of my fingers under the band of her shorts, and she lets out a muffled cry against my lips.

"Fuck," she hisses. "You have no idea what you do to me."

"I think," I pant, "I do, if it's anything like what you do to me."

"I just *can't* stop kissing you."

She pulls me into her again, and this time our kiss is bordering on furious. I need her so bad. Her mouth isn't enough. I want all of her.

"Becca, you're going to have to decide if we're going upstairs or if I'm pushing you up against the wall of this house." I feel my neck flush as I say it. I can't believe I'm being this bold. "If you want me to stay, that is."

Her eyes are hooded and hazy. She still has one of her hands tangled in my hair.

"You want to come inside?"

"Yeah." I swallow. "I do, if that's what you want."

"I want that." She nods like she's confirming it with herself. "I want you, Hope."

We break apart, and she reaches for my hand before

pulling the front door open. I follow her into the dark entryway, her fingers intertwined with mine.

13

Becca

Hope is in my room. I stand in the doorway, frozen as I watch her walk over to the window just like I imagined that night she first came to meet me outside.

"That's a beautiful quilt," she says, glancing over at my bed while she toys with the edge of the curtains.

"Oh. Thanks. My grandma made it."

I don't know why I'm talking about my grandma. I don't know why I'm talking at all. I should be kissing her. I just want to keep kissing her. Kissing her is the only thing stopping me from having a complete emotional crisis about what we're doing.

Kissing her blocks everything else out. I've never felt that kind of freedom. I've never really, truly understood the words 'live in the moment' until I first had my lips on hers.

"It's, um, funny you said that," I stammer as I step into the room.

I pull the door shut behind me even though Bailey and Rachelle are still out and probably will be all night. The wood muffles the buzzing sound of the outdated fridge in our kitchen.

"Oh yeah?" she glances over her shoulder at me. "What's funny?"

I trail my fingers along the edge of my dresser as I take a few steps closer.

"I've...I've thought about bringing you up here. I guess this is kind of creepy, but I've thought about what you might say, what you'd think of my room..." I glance down at the floor as an embarrassed chuckle climbs up my throat. "I thought about you complimenting that quilt."

She chuckles too. "It is a great quilt. I love all the colours."

The fabric scraps are all mix-matched shades of blue, green, and yellow. I cross over to my bed and bend down to smooth a few wrinkles out.

"Me too."

My breath catches when I feel Hope approach behind me. I straighten up when her footsteps stop. She's so close I can feel her breath on the back of my neck.

I shiver at the brush of her fingertips on my neck when she sweeps my hair to the side. She tugs on the neck of my unbuttoned cardigan, guiding it down over one of my shoulders. Her lips land there next, moving over the strap of my tank top and up my neck.

My eyes close. I lean my head to the side to give her better access. I can feel her kisses everywhere. When she lets her teeth scrape the skin just below my jaw, I can't hold back my moan.

"You like that, huh?" she murmurs, teasing me with my own words from earlier.

"I do," I whisper. My eyes are still closed. Her voice feels like it's surrounding me. "So much."

I like everything about her. When we hugged on the field today, I almost kissed her right then and there. There's something about her I can't ignore, no matter how many reasons I have to do the complete opposite.

She's special. *We're* special. The more moments I have with her, the more I realize we're building an *us*. Somewhere along the line, we started forging a connection link by link, like a necklace wrapped around us both. We're still only just beginning, but those shimmering links feel heavy and inevitable.

What she said outside the house is true; this night is different. Everything is urgent and immediate, from the thump of my heart to the heat of her lips. It's been a long time since I trusted anything just because it felt right. I'm always analyzing, always checking the risks, always playing it safe. Even on the lacrosse field, I'm cautious. I never would have gone for that shot she made today, but she took a safe pass from me and turned it into something spectacular.

Maybe tonight, I can be spectacular too.

She sets her hands on my hips, and I arch my back, grinding into her as her grip tightens. She licks the soft skin below my ear and pulls me closer until my back and ass are flush with her chest and hips. One of her hands snakes around my body and under my tank top. I gasp as her fingers skate up my stomach.

"I almost lost it when I realized you weren't wearing a bra," she says in a low, purring voice that's one of the sexiest things I've ever heard.

"I'm about to lose it right n—"

My words get cut off by another gasp when she cups one of my breasts and squeezes. We both moan as she slides her other hand around and starts doing the same on the other side. She has me so turned on it almost hurts when her thumbs brush my nipples.

"I want to see you," she says after a moment. "Please."

I almost grab her hands and pull them back on me when she starts to slide away, but I want her to see me just as bad. She steps back enough for me to turn around, and I let my already lopsided cardigan slip off and drop to the floor.

Her mouth is hanging open, and her eyes are on my chest. I grab the bottom of my tank top and peel it over my head.

"Oh my god." When I look back at her, she has one hand pressed over her mouth as she stares and stares like I'm a painting she flew halfway around the world just to see. "Becca, you are so gorgeous."

I'm aching for her. I need her touching me again.

As if I've said it out loud, she steps forward and pulls me to her. She strokes my chest with both her hands, pinching my nipples this time and making me bite my lip to keep from crying out.

"Maybe this is a weird thing to say, but I've thought about these, uh, a lot."

I let out a breathless laugh and see her cheeks go red.

"That's very flattering."

It's more than flattering; it almost makes me feel tender, like this is a moment we've been headed towards without knowing it since the very first time we met. Another link in the chain forms and snaps into place.

"I want to see you too, Hope."

She looks up at my face, and her eyes widen. I reach for her hoodie's zipper without hesitating and start inching it down.

"Oh fuck," I mutter when I've got the zipper all the way to her stomach. I thought she'd have a shirt underneath, but she's wearing nothing but a bright teal bra.

I yank the zipper the rest of the way down and strip her out of the hoodie. She's got a gorgeous body, from the smooth plains of her stomach to the delicate skin stretched over her collarbones. Her sweatpants sit low on her hips, emphasizing the slight dip and flair of her waist.

"I've been thinking about you too." I hook a finger under one of her bra straps, still drinking the sight of her in. "This matches your hair. It's cute. Did you do that on purpose?"

"I mean..." She takes on the same teasing tone as me. "I had to look good. I did think there was maybe a chance you would see my bra tonight."

"I appreciate the effort." I reach for the clasp. "But I do really need to get this off you."

As soon as she's standing half-naked in front of me, we both lose all control. She's just too gorgeous for me to go slow anymore, and she seems to feel the same. We're a desperate tangle of limbs and mouths and fingers when we tip over and land on my bed. I shift us around until she's under me, my hands braced on either side of her body as I trail my mouth over her tits, kissing, licking, and nipping while she shudders and buries her hands in my hair.

Every part of her tastes sweet. I could spend all night getting to know her body.

When I lift my head enough to look at her, her eyes are dazed and unfocused behind her glasses, which are sitting crooked on the end of her nose. I grin as something tightens in my chest, and I reach up to straighten them just like I've imagined doing so many times.

"You okay?"

She bobs her chin in a few frantic little nods. "Very okay."

I chuckle. "Good."

I set myself up so I can start kissing my way down her stomach. She still has her sweatpants on, and I need to see more of her. I need to see all of her. I'm already soaked from just the thought of touching her between her legs, teasing her, stroking her, *tasting* her.

"Becca."

I go still and lift my head at the urgency in her voice. It's a different kind of urgency than before.

"Everything all right?"

She looks at the end of the bed behind me instead of meeting my eyes. "Uh, yeah. I just have to tell you something."

"Of course."

I roll off her and move so I can lie beside her instead. It's a tight fit in the single bed, and I'm pretty much pinned to the wall, but there is literally nowhere on earth I would rather be in this moment.

"What's up?"

She fiddles with the edge of my pillowcase and keeps staring at the end of the bed. "Okay, so, I thought I would be all cool and not bring this up, but I don't want to...do something embarrassing, so maybe it's better to mention it."

I wait for her to go on, brushing my hand up and down her arm so she knows it's okay to take her time.

"All right, soooo...I actually only came out and started doing things with girls when I got to UNS. Then I got in a relationship with a dude a few months later that lasted until the end of last term, so...This is embarrassing, but I didn't feel ready to, like, go all the way when I was hooking up, so I've never actually gone down on a girl. One girl has gone down on me, but I've never, uh, done it myself."

A rush of tenderness fills my chest until it feels like it's about to burst open. She's clearly having a hard time saying this out loud, but she trusted me enough to tell me anyway.

I lay my hand on her shoulder. "Hope."

She still won't look at me. "I know that's not exactly sexy—"

"Hope, there is nothing wrong with that, and it has nothing to do with how sexy you are. Also, we don't have to do anything you're not ready for. I'm *very* happy to just go down on you, or we don't have to do anything else at all. I'm perfectly happy to just lay here and talk to you if that's what you want."

She shifts onto her side and finally meets my gaze. Her eyes flash with hunger.

"Trust me, I want to do way more than talk. I'd really like to...taste you."

I have to fight not to groan.

"I just thought you should know," she continues, "in case you didn't, you know, want to do that to me if I'd never—"

"Hope." I sit up and lean over her. "I really do not care about your experience level either way. All I care about is what would make you feel good right here right now, whether that's giving or getting or all or none of the above. It's all good."

"Right. Yeah. *Ugh.*" She twists her head to the side and buries her face in the pillow for a second, letting out a muffled groan. "Why am I making this so awkward? UGH!"

"Hey." I hook a finger under her chin and turn her head back to face me. "Right here, right now. That's all that matters."

I'm saying it for both of us. If I focus on anything else, the rest of the world is going to come crashing into the room to steal this moment away.

This moment is too perfect to lose.

She nods, and I take that as my cue to bend down and kiss her again. We start off soft and slow, but it doesn't take me long to remember how much I want her. She reaches to squeeze my ass hard, and I know she feels the same.

"I want these off you," I mumble against her lips as I tug on the band of her sweatpants. She doesn't break the kiss, but she does lift her hips enough for me to start tugging the pants down. I give up when she slips her tongue in my mouth and let the distraction take me over for a while. She flicks my teeth with her tongue just like I did to her, and the sensation gets me so wet I can feel it every time I move.

"Off. Now," I pant when I finally pull away. I wait as she strips the pants the rest of the way off to reveal a plain pair of dark blue underwear. I can see how wet she is, and it's all I can do not to rip them off and bury my face between her legs.

I want to take a little more time, though, so instead, I straddle her and slip one of my thighs between both of hers. She gasps when I grab her hips and pull her onto me. I lean forward, increasing the pressure until she cries out and starts bucking against my leg.

We find a rhythm, and she rides my thigh until we're both panting and slick with sweat. I shift so I'm kneeling between her legs and spread them wider. She smells so good it's making me dizzy. I keep my eyes on her face as I trail a finger up the soaked fabric of her underwear. She gasps and then bites her lip when I flip my hand around so I can cup her whole pussy, the heel of my palm pressing over her clit.

The thin layer of fabric between us is making things even hotter, but I need her skin too bad to keep waiting. I need to touch her—*really* touch her, like I've been craving since I looked out my window and saw her in the yard.

She lifts her hips so I can strip her. I don't look away from her pussy even as I toss her underwear across my room. She's absolutely mesmerizing, her perfect pink folds slick and dripping with how bad she wants this.

"Oh my god, Hope." For a few moments, that's all I can say. I just sit there kneeling with her spread in front of me, a million possibilities shifting through my mind.

A million ways to touch her, taste her, make her mine.

I start stroking my thumbs along her inner thighs, getting just close enough to make her twitch.

"This is sexy," I say, taking a moment to trail my finger over the strip of hair she's left above her pussy.

"O-oh yeah?" she stammers.

I grin. "Yeah, it actually doesn't surprise me that you're the landing strip type. It suits you, and it's *so* hot."

She starts to say something but has to stop and suck in a breath when I lower my head without warning and kiss the thin patch of hair. I keep going, teasing her with kisses and licks along her inner thighs and outer lips.

"O-oh." Her hands fist in my hair again. "That...*Oh*."

I hover over her clit, watching the way my hot breath makes her tremble, and then I trail my tongue in one long, slow lick up and down the length of her. She sighs my name, and it urges me on. I keep my tongue focused on her clit as I thrust two fingers inside her. She's so wet I could have fit three. I can hear her panting and squealing as she pulls on my hair, but I'm so lost in the taste of her I almost forget this is supposed to be for her benefit, not mine.

I can't tell which one of us is enjoying it more. She tastes so good I pull my fingers out for a moment just so I can thrust my tongue inside her. I growl as I go back to licking her clit, and this time I really do slide three fingers into her. Her back arches, and she lets out a long, low moan before she starts thrusting onto my hand.

I fuck her hard, furiously, as I keep going on her clit. I

tune into the subtle signals of her body, learning just which spots make her go wild. She starts tightening around my fingers, and I know she's getting close.

"I want you to come for me," I say against her skin. "Come for me, Hope."

She bucks against me, once, twice, and then her whole body goes rigid before her spine curves in a violent arch and her desperate shrieks fill the room. I don't let up until she's totally spent, lying limp on the bed and gasping for breath.

I sit up and lock eyes with her as I drag the back of my hand across my mouth. She twitches.

"*Fuck.*" My voice comes out low and hoarse. "Fuck, Hope."

She closes her eyes and bursts out laughing. "Yes, yes you did fuck me."

I start laughing too. "You're delirious."

"Yeah, I think I am." She starts rolling her head from side to side, still laughing in a breathless, euphoric kind of way. "How did that feel sooooo good?"

"I take it you enjoyed yourself?"

"Fuck, I don't think I've ever come that hard with someone."

A rush of satisfaction fills me as I lay down beside her. She rolls over and clings to me, the two of us coming down together as she catches her breath.

"I want to do that to you," she says with her mouth just under my ear.

My thighs squeeze together, but I do my best to stay calm.

"You know you don't have to. I promise you, that was more than enough for me."

"I want to." She pulls back to look at me. "Can I?"

I need her so bad I'm twitching, and the same need is

written all over her face. Her eyes are wide as they stare into mine, waiting for me to let us both fall off this ledge together.

"Yes." I pull her back to kiss me and mumble it again against her lips. "Yes."

She kneels between my legs like I did to her, and I strip out of my shorts and underwear at the same time. I'm burning with how much I want this, and the awe and wonder in her face when she looks down at me makes me ache even more.

"You're so wet," she says in a hushed voice. "Oh my god, Becca, you're perfect."

She strokes along my outer lips, and I moan. Every inch of me is straining for her, desperate to feel her touch. She slides a finger up the very centre of my pussy, and I can hear how wet I am. My hips start to rock, and she doesn't wait to slip her finger inside me.

"Fuck. Fuck, that feels so good."

"Do you want more?"

I nod and clutch at the blankets as she slides another finger in and starts thrusting in time with the motion of my hips. The thumb of her other hand finds my clit.

"Fuck, you could make me come just like that."

She slows her pace. "I want to give you more."

I gasp when she pulls out and spreads my legs wider with both her hands. She lowers herself to her stomach and props her weight on her elbows before looking up at me. I can see the hesitation gathering in her expression.

"Will you, um..." She chews on her lip for a moment. "Will you tell me what to do?"

She wants me to tell her how to eat my pussy.

Just that question makes me feel like I could come.

"I know it's not very sexy to, like, ask for instructions." She flushes, misreading my silence. I'm too turned on to even answer her right away. "I just thought that to start, we could—"

"It is *very* sexy," I interrupt. My chest has started heaving with my strained breaths, and that's all I can get out.

"Oh." She seems to catch on to what she's doing to me as she takes the sight of me in.

"Yeah. That...I would like that."

"Okay," she murmurs, glancing down again. "How should I start?"

I've never given someone directions before, not like this. There's something so intensely intimate about it, and it's layered with an eroticism that hangs in the air and fills my lungs with every panting breath. I'm almost suffocating from it, and we haven't even started yet.

"I'd like it if you kissed my thighs," I murmur, "and up over my hips too."

I figure that's a safe place to start, but as soon as she begins, I realize it's anything but. Her hot breath and soft lips sear me everywhere she touches. She grazes her teeth along one of my hip bones just hard enough to sting, and I lose it.

"Fuck, Hope. I need you to lick me. I need you to lick me now." I squeeze my eyes shut as the ache between my legs gets even sharper.

I can feel her breath on my pussy. "How? Tell me how. Tell me what you want."

She doesn't sound timid anymore. She sounds like she knows exactly how she's making me feel, but I still want to give her instructions. Hearing her ask like that makes it hard not to grab her head and pull her exactly where I want her.

"I w-want you to lick me really slow." My hands are

starting to hurt from gripping the sheets so hard. "All the way up my pussy and back again."

She sucks in a breath as I say it, and then I feel the heat of her tongue, pressed flat and firm against me. She licks me just the way I told her to, dragging the moment out until I'm shuddering.

"Like that?"

"Yes," I pant. "Just like that. Keep doing that."

She finds a drawn-out rhythm that has me dripping onto her tongue. I hiss every time she reaches my clit. I can already feel my muscles clenching and tightening.

"Now circle my clit with the tip of your tongue." I've never said anything so direct to someone before, never ordered it like that.

She does exactly what I ask, and I can't stop myself from gripping the back of her head as my hips thrust up to meet her tongue.

"That's so good. Now do it a little harder." She increases the pressure and moans against me when I cry out.

"Now fuck me with two of your fingers while you keep licking me just like that."

I throw my head back and groan when she starts hitting just the right spot inside me. The pressure of her fingers is getting me closer and closer to letting go.

"Now flick your tongue back and forth across my clit. Harder. Yes. Just like that. Oh fuck, just like that. Keep fucking me, Hope."

The way her actions follow my words is addictive. I can't stop. I can't stop any of this, and I don't want to.

"I'm gonna come for you. I'm gonna come in your mouth."

She mutters something low and guttural I can't make out and then clamps her free hand down on the underside of my thigh. Her nails dig into my skin, and the pain feels so good. Too good. I can't hold out.

"Fuck me harder. Fuck me as hard as you can."

She's slamming into me now, thrusting again and again as her tongue criss-crosses over my clit, every stroke tightening something deep inside me.

"I'm going to...to..."

My body arches so hard I fly forward until I'm sitting with my hands still tangled in her hair. Bright white light streaks the backs of my lids as I squeeze my eyes shut to shudder and gasp my way through the release. For a few seconds, I can't hear anything. I can barely feel her fingers still working me, making the pleasure roll through me in wave after wave. I'm floating somewhere beyond reality until I fall back on the bed and come crashing into myself.

When Hope lays down beside me, I'm shaking. She covers my body with hers and lays her head on my chest without saying a word.

I don't need words. I just need this. I just need her.

14

Becca

"So why this song?"

Hope runs one of her fingertips along the tattoo on my upper back. We're both sitting on my bed, her kneeling behind me while she braids my hair. I have my cardigan spread over my lap, and she's wearing her hoodie with the zipper undone, but other than that, we're still naked. It must be almost two in the morning, but I'm not tired yet.

I can't be tired yet. If I'm tired, the night will end, and I don't want to think about what will happen when it does.

"I've been a Ben Howard fan for a really long time," I answer, "and that song meant a lot to me when I was a teenager. It still does."

"It fits you. You do keep your head up and your heart strong." A soft, tingly feeling spreads along my scalp as she reaches for more pieces of hair to braid. "You always seem so strong. I noticed that about you from the start."

"I guess I try to be. I don't know if I always succeed."

She makes a skeptical sound as she combs her fingers through a tangle. "What did the song mean to you in high school?"

"It was...hard growing up the way I did."

I don't know how to go on. I don't have words for that kind of loneliness, that kind of doubt about myself. Those feelings carved out a hole in me I'm not sure I'll ever fill.

"I think I mentioned it before, but my mom was really...in and out," I begin. "They finally got divorced when I was thirteen, but they didn't really seem married for a long time before that. I don't know if they ever really loved each other. I guess they must have, at some point, but I'm not sure."

Hope traces my tattoo again. "I'm sorry."

I shrug. "I guess I got used to it, and it wasn't *that* bad. Other people have it worse. We didn't have much, but I always had a house and food to eat. After the divorce, my dad moved us in with his sister. I already stayed with her a lot when he was away working, but we were never close. Her house never felt like home, even after I didn't have anywhere else to call home."

"That's so sad. I can't imagine not being able to feel at home in the place you live, especially when you were so young."

I pick at a patch of pilled fabric on my cardigan. "I feel like I'm whining. We can talk about something else."

"You're not whining. I asked. I want to know about you."

My heart speeds up.

"Why?" I ask before I can stop myself.

"Because..." Her hands go still. She trails off, hesitating, but when she speaks again, there's a forced casualness in her tone. "Because I'm interested. So answer my questions and stop whining about whining when you're not even whining."

I laugh as she smacks my shoulder. "Okay, okay. What else do you want to know?"

She starts braiding again. "So you said you weren't close with your aunt. How about your dad?"

I nod and then go still when I accidentally tug a piece of hair out of her grip. "My dad and I were always pretty close, or as close as we could be with him away working so much. We're still pretty close. He was a fairly serious hockey player when he was young, so he loves that I'm really into a sport too. It's a big part of our bond. Being on the team here makes me feel close to him even though we're far apart, and I know he's really proud of me being captain. We used to spend hours doing lacrosse drills in the evenings during the summer."

I smile as I think back on warm, dry Alberta nights when we'd wait until the temperature dropped enough for us to exercise without overheating. We'd stay out tossing the ball back and forth until the moths started flocking around the floodlight in my aunt's driveway.

"That sounds amazing," Hope says. "I used to pay my brother with rolls of pennies to practice with me when I was a kid. He was terrible at it. Eventually my parents got me a rebounder so I would stop bugging everybody all the time. I was pretty...insistent."

"You don't say," I joke.

"Hey now!" She gives my hair a tug. "Watch it."

I pretend to wince, but really, I'm just trying not to get turned on all over again. I don't think I'll ever be able to forget the feeling of her hands in my hair when she came.

"Was there anyone else in your family you were close to?" she asks.

That helps cool me down. There's really only one other person I can think of.

"I was close with my dad's mom too, but she died when I was ten." I run one of my hands over the quilt she made me. "She always used to tell me and my dad to keep our heads held high. It was kind of her thing. That's part of why I like the song so much."

I can feel Hope's fingers working down to the tips of my hair. "That's beautiful."

"Yeah, she was pretty great. She was, like, a master quilter. All the old ladies would come to her for quilting advice."

I jump when Hope lets out a sudden shriek.

"Oh my god! We totally desecrated your grandma's quilt! We had very explicit, sensual lesbian sex on it! Oh my god, what have we done?"

I burst out laughing and twist around so I can face her. "I'm sure she'd approve of you if she was around. She wouldn't need to know about the...what did you just call it? Explicit, sensual lesbian sex?"

Hope covers her face with her hands. "Okay, fine. I deserve to be mocked for that."

"Who says I'm mocking you? It *was* sensual, and *very* explicit."

I drop my gaze to her mouth.

Her mouth that made me come so hard I temporarily went deaf and blind.

She leans forward, and I meet her halfway to press my lips to hers. I still don't think I could ever get enough of kissing her. I'm just about to turn all the way around and climb on top of her when she pulls back.

"Wait! Your hair! I didn't put the elastic in yet." She pushes on my shoulder to urge me to turn back around and then fiddles with my hair for a moment. "There we go!"

"How does it look?"

She snorts. "Terrible. I'm so shitty at braiding hair."

I reach back and grab the braid, pulling it forward so I can see what she's talking about. "It looks all right to me."

"You can only see the end part. That part's all right. The top is, uh, not good."

"Guess we'll be sticking to Jane doing our hair on game days."

She laughs. "Yeah, Jane is the braid master."

Something shifts between us. A tension slips into the room as I turn myself around so we're face to face. There's no sound in the house, but it suddenly feels like we aren't as alone as before.

There's a world out there, a world we're part of.

A world with rules and expectations.

A world where I have a past and we both have futures.

We don't just live in a perfect little box made of her and me and my bed, no matter how much I wish that were true.

"I should probably go home, right?" she murmurs. "I should probably get there before anyone wakes up?"

This is what I wanted to avoid: the sneaking around, the lying, the risk.

The pain.

I feel panic start to loop around my chest and squeeze me so tight my lungs burn for air.

"I know the team is important to you." She slides her hand closer to mine, but then she hesitates. Our pinkies are an inch apart on the quilt. "I'm not going to do anything to mess that up. It's important to me too."

I want to tell her *she's* important. I want to tell her tonight wasn't some distraction or fluke. I want to grab her hand and place it over my heart and tell her she's already got a piece of it, no matter how crazy that sounds.

She deserves all that and more, but instead I just sit there like a statue, pulling further and further into myself to keep from spinning out.

I can still see Lisa, her face twisted into something I

didn't recognize as she threw the photos of Kala and I down on the floor of the locker room. The whole team went silent. Her shouts echoed off the walls and filled the room. The old stack of disposable camera shots I kept in my dresser scattered at her feet. I still don't know when she took them, whether she hunted around for something to use against me while I was sleeping or snuck into my room when I wasn't there.

Most of the photos were completely innocent, just out of focus shots of the U19 team or typical high school girl group mirror selfies and failed artistic depictions of feet. There were a lot of Kala and I, some with her arm slung around me while we smiled in our lacrosse uniforms, some of her making dumb faces at the camera in our school cafeteria.

They all confirmed exactly what I told Lisa: that Kala and I came out around the same time, dated for a few months because it seemed like the obvious next step to two teenagers who didn't know any other queer people, and then ended things and went right back to being best friends when we realized that's all we were meant to be.

I didn't know how to make Lisa understand when she seemed so bent on doing the opposite. I *really* didn't know how to make her understand why there were a few blurry selfies of Kala and I kissing. I didn't keep them because I still had feelings for her; I kept them because they were a reminder of that rare, brief innocence when fear and wonder were all wrapped up in one, when a new world was opening up in front of me—a new way of being myself, of being whole and complete and defiant in the face of anyone who told me what made me *me* was wrong.

Lisa could never see it that way. She was always suspicious, even at the beginning when things were good between us. After she proved to the entire team that I had photos of teenage Kala and I kissing stashed in my drawer along with a whole stack of pictures of us hanging out, a lot of them got suspicious too.

That's when we started losing games. That's also when I started losing Kala's friendship. She had her own stuff going on, and I let it all get pulled into my mess. It felt like the situation was getting doused with splash after splash of gasoline, and when the match finally dropped a few weeks later, everything exploded.

"Becca?" I look up from where I've been staring down at the cardigan still draped over my lap and find Hope blinking at me from behind her glasses, two creases deepening between her eyebrows. "Is something wrong?"

"I, um..." I have to stop and clear my throat. "Sorry. I think I'm just tired."

I see the hurt flash across her face before she turns away to hide it.

"Right. Of course." She gets up off the bed and starts pulling the rest of her clothes on. "It's late."

I need to say something. I need her to know that being with her took me somewhere I've never been before, that even now, I haven't quite come back. I don't know if I will come back.

Maybe there's no coming back from her.

"Okay, I guess I'll just...go now?" She's dressed now, her hood thrown over her head and her hands tucked into her pockets as she hovers beside the door.

I still can't move. I can't get any words out. She stares at me, searching, and then I see her eyes start to get watery. She turns around. Her shoulders are set in a tight line as she reaches for the handle.

"Hope, wait!"

I can't let her cry. I can't let her walk out of here

crying, not after what we did. Not after what we shared together.

I grab her arm, and she turns around, one tear sliding down her cheek. "What is it?"

"I'm sorry." I lace my fingers through hers and squeeze. "I got really, really scared. I'm so scared, but you mean so much to me."

Her eyes are wide and still spilling tears. "I—I do?"

I nod. I didn't plan on saying that, but it's out now, and it's true.

"You do. Maybe it's a little crazy of me, but you do." My voice cracks, and my vision starts to get blurry. I force a chuckle. "Shit, now I'm crying too."

"Becca, hey, it's okay." She frees her hand from mine so she can throw her arms around my neck. "It's okay. We'll figure it out."

I sag against her and take a deep, shuddering breath.

"We will."

We have to. This isn't just a crush on some girl. I don't know exactly what this is, but it's already stronger than any rule I've ever made for myself.

She holds me for a few moments and then pulls back to swipe at her eyes, grinning. I start to smile too. It's hard not to smile when she's smiling.

"I really should go now. We'll figure the team stuff out, but not tonight, so I should get back."

"Right. Yeah. Are you okay to walk alone?"

She slips her hands into her pockets again. "Yeah, it's only a couple streets."

"Text me when you get there, okay? I want to know you're safe."

She nods, her mouth lifted in a dorky smile, and then hesitates for a second before she leans in to kiss my cheek. I feel the warmth of her lips through my whole body.

"Goodnight, Becca."

"Goodnight," I whisper.

She heads out, and I drop onto my bed as soon as I hear the door to our unit close. I crawl under my quilt and shut off my bedside lamp without even bothering to brush my teeth. The exhaustion is immediate, turning my thoughts sluggish and my limbs heavy as I lay there and wait for her text.

We'll figure it out.

I hold onto her words like they're a talisman warding off all the ways this probably *won't* work out. I'll deal with the details later. Tonight, I just need to hold on.

15

Becca

The details become a persistent whine over the next couple days, like a mosquito trapped in my head. Hope and I text a bit but don't make plans to see each other. We have two days off from practice, so we don't have any lacrosse-related contact either.

The break from being around her has two very opposing effects. One is that I can't stop craving another night with her—or another coffee date, or another dinner in the park, or even just another smile. It's almost not even worth going to my lectures; I just sit there thinking about her.

The other effect is that I can't stop thinking about how truly, deeply fucked up this all is. Hope deserves to know everything, but I can't tell her everything without pulling Kala into my mess.

Again.

Then there's the team to contend with. We've only just started the season, and we're aimed at our first real shot at the title. I know far too well how much team drama can throw us off, and I also know exactly what this will look like: like I'm the spoiled scholarship girl who won a big donation for the team and now thinks she can do whatever —and whoever—she wants, no matter the cost. It's even worse now that I'm captain. I've drilled the no-dating policy into the team almost as hard as I've drilled it into myself, and now I'm out here doing the complete opposite.

Hope doesn't even know *I'm* the reason we have the policy in the first place.

By the time I meet up with Kala for the Tuesday dinner we have planned, I'm a twitchy, nervous wreck. I almost give into the temptation to 'forget' about dry season and accept the wine she offers me in her studio apartment. I pull it together enough to ask for water instead; there has to be at least one team rule I can follow.

"Right. I forgot about dry season," Kala calls from behind the half wall that separates her tiny kitchen from the rest of the room.

She comes out with a water glass for me and a wine glass for her. The glass top of her coffee table tings as she sets them down and settles herself beside me on the faux-leather couch. She's made the apartment look way nicer and fresher than the rest of the old, slightly decrepit building. Her two dozen house plants and giant, fluffy pink area rug really spruce the place up, along with the warm orange and red prints of three Hindu deities that take up most of the wall behind the couch.

"The quiche still needs twenty minutes."

I drop my head back and groan. "Worth the wait. I can't believe you made quiche. I feel spoiled."

She laughs. "Yeah, turns out not being on the lacrosse team gives me time to cook things besides scrambled eggs and instant noodles."

"I eat more than instant noodles!" I protest.

"Yeah, but you're an obsessive athlete who prioritizes

making detailed nutrition plans. The rest of us don't get up before six in the morning every day."

"I mean...fair enough."

We both laugh as we clink our glasses together and take a sip.

"How are your classes going?" I ask. I'm trying not to bounce my knees or pick at her throw pillows or do anything else to let her know I've been freaking out for forty-eight hours straight.

She doesn't need me to monopolize our friendship with my problems again.

"They're great. Tough, but great. Seems like I'm actually going to graduate on time."

I finish off a frantic swig of water. "That's so exciting. You'll be, like, *done*. It's crazy that we're already in fourth year."

"Mhmm." She's giving me the side-eye like she knows something's up, but I just keep trudging through the conversation.

"And how are your parents?"

"Still good." Now she's really giving me a weird look, but she keeps indulging me. "Still probably not interested in having a bisexual daughter, but what else is new? My brother's probably going to get engaged soon, so my mom is really pushing the whole 'when are you going to start a family thing?' with me. It just sucks because we're so close otherwise, and I wish I could share my whole self with them."

"That does really suck." I give her arm a squeeze. "You know I'm here for you."

She nods and smiles. "Thanks. That means a lot."

We sip our drinks in silence for a moment. I look down and realize I've started bouncing my heels on the ground in a manic rhythm. Kala notices too.

"Okay, *what* is up with you, Becca?"

I drum my fingers on the side of my water glass. "Um, nothing. Just stressed about school I guess."

"Bullshit."

I force myself to stop fidgeting and sit completely still. Kala sighs.

"Becca, come on. You don't have to worry about atoning for your sins or whatever it is you think you have to do in this friendship. This is about that girl on the team, isn't it? You can talk to me about it. I'm not going to be mad."

"Shouldn't you be?" I set my water down and put one of the throw cushions on my lap so I can keep my hands busy by squeezing it. "Shouldn't you be mad I'm doing this again?"

"Beccaaaaaaa!" She throws her hands in the air. "You just like a girl who happens to be on your team. It's not a war crime. I feel like you think dating Lisa caused this cataclysmic apocalypse that made everyone hate you. Like yes, some people were pissed, but that was mostly because Lisa was acting freaking insane."

"I hurt you," I point out. I make myself hold her gaze as I say it.

"And you apologized, and I accepted," she answers. "I was only ever hurt because it felt like you were choosing this person who treated me horribly, who treated *you* horribly, and I couldn't understand why. I know now it was more complicated than that. You really trusted her, and she was your first *real* girlfriend."

We chuckle at the memory of our fumbling attempt at dating. Even those photographed kisses were awkward.

"I haven't gotten to have that yet," she continues, "and I'd probably fight for it just as hard as you did. It was just really hard to see that with everything I had going on…"

"Kala, don't ever say that." I inch closer to her and take her hand in mine. "You were going through one of the hardest things a person can go through, and I never should have put you in a position where that felt like a problem."

She squeezes my hand. "Thank you. Sometimes I still need to hear that."

"I'll say that as many times as you need. What you went through was never a problem, and I shouldn't have let it get caught up in mine."

She rests her head on my shoulder and sighs. "I still think about going to the clinic, you know. Sometimes I feel so ashamed, and sometimes I feel so fucking *tired* of being ashamed. I believe it was the right choice, but that doesn't mean I can just forget about it."

I remember sitting in the waiting room with her just like this, with her head on my shoulder. A Celine Dion album was playing through the room's speakers. I remember wondering who the hell decided Celine Dion should be the soundtrack for an abortion clinic waiting room.

"It was the right choice. I'm proud of you. You were brave and strong. There's nothing to be ashamed of."

It definitely *felt* like there was something to be ashamed of when we got back to my place afterwards and Lisa was hanging around, waiting to ask me why I wasn't studying at the library like I said. I had no answer for her, other than to say Kala needed me and that it wasn't up for discussion.

That's the only answer I had when she told the whole team what happened.

"You're the best." Kala sits up and reaches for her wine again. "Let's talk about happier things. Tell me how things are going with this girl."

"I don't know if I would call that a happy situation..."

She makes a face. "Oh, come on, you're clearly crazy about her. You haven't even said anything, and I can already tell." She wags her eyebrows. "Have you done the nasty yet?"

I burst out laughing. "I can't believe you still call it *doing the nasty*. What are you, ten years old?"

"Well have you?" she urges.

I glance down at the floor.

"Oh my god, you have! When? Tell me everything!"

"It was, uh...a couple nights ago. After the game."

"So much scoring in one day!"

I laugh again, but I trail off into silence after. We aren't just chatting about some girl I met at the library who has no connection to the team, and I can't keep ignoring reality.

"Becca," Kala says in a soft voice, "I know you probably won't believe me, but I think this might all be a lot less complicated than you realize. People weren't mad that you and Lisa dated. They were mad that things exploded the way they did and cost you guys the league qualifiers. That wasn't your fault. That was Lisa's, and anyone who believed otherwise left the team with her."

I stay quiet, waiting for her to realize those weren't the only people who left the team.

"And me," she adds after a moment, "but I left because my life was better without the team. I needed to focus on myself and get my grades back up. Did things with Lisa spur that decision on? Yes, but I know I would have left eventually anyway."

I want to believe her. I really do. I want to believe this is all simpler than I realize, that I could just date Hope and have it all be fine, but I still remember the whispers. I remember the dirty looks. I remember the disappointment and anger all aimed at me every time we lost, and I can't help thinking I deserved it. I got involved with Lisa in the first place after all.

How I feel with Hope is so different from how I felt with Lisa. I can't even compare the two, but that doesn't mean things with Hope couldn't go wrong in their own way. I made it through nearly losing the team once, but I don't know if I could make it through losing the team *and* Hope.

"I know the team is special to you," Kala says, displaying her knack for reading my mind, "but you need relationships too, of all kinds, and this seems like it could be a really good one."

"If I don't fuck it up," I mumble. "I'm already so nervous about all this that I don't know how I'm going to get through our next practice, never mind our next game. We're not even actually dating, and it's already having an impact on the team. She doesn't even know anything about *us* yet. I feel like I'm wrecking it already."

"Okay, back up the bus." She brandishes her wine glass at me. "How about we take this one step at a time? You only did the nasty for the first time two nights ago."

She smirks and wiggles her eyebrows again, so of course I have to laugh.

"Your game is next weekend, right?" she asks. I nod. "So why don't you just focus on getting through that? You're always kind of...tense leading up to games anyway, so there's no point trying to face every single complication when you're already stressed. Maybe after you guys get back from Montreal, you, me, and her could have lunch or something."

"Really?"

She chuckles at how incredulous I sound. "Yeah, of course. I'm not saying I would have been down to get friendly with Lisa, but I think it might help for you to be like, 'Want to meet my best friend? We randomly dated for a few months in high school and it was so awkward we went right back to being besties. I would love for us to hang out!' Lisa only found out we dated, like, what? Two months into your relationship?"

Kala was still in the process of coming out around campus back then, and I didn't want to tell Lisa about our history before she was ready to be out to the whole team.

Yet another way in which I messed up and made Kala feel like a burden.

"Only if you're comfortable with that," I tell her. "I'd love for you to meet her, but it's totally up to you."

She grins. "I'd like that too. It's pretty nice to see you interested in something other than lacrosse, to be honest. She must have really nice boobs or something."

I laugh and then tip my head back to rest on the top of the couch. "Ugh, she does. *So* nice. I can't mess this up, Kala."

She pats me on the knee. "You won't. Just get through this game, and take it from there."

16

Hope

"Okay, lax rats!" Coach Jamal paces in front of the team. He has us all lined up at the end of practice, braced for one of his impromptu speeches. "We're just a few days out from our Montreal match. We're looking good. We're moving fast. We have everything we need to win and beat McGill so hard they won't even know what hit them. There is only room for one red jersey team in the league, after all!"

I thump the end of my stick on the ground and whoop along with everyone else. I shiver a little as a gust of wind sweeps over the field and hits the dried sweat stuck to my body. We're into the first week of October now, and morning practices are getting fresh as fuck. The tips of my ears are burning from running around in the chilly air.

The temperature doesn't stop me from getting fired up by the speech. Everyone is jumping around and cheering as CJ keeps stalking up and down in front of us, his aviators sitting on the bridge of his nose and his hands clasped behind his back.

"I need you all to keep your focus. We haven't won the

battle yet. Get some sleep this week. Eat well. We all need to be in top condition, especially with a long journey ahead of us. When we get off that bus in Montreal, I want the ground to shake. I want everyone in the city to stop what they're doing and realize something has changed. Maybe they won't know what. Maybe they won't know why, but they'll know. They'll feel our power, and they will quake before us!"

His voice grows into a hoarse bellow as he raises one fist in the air. Sometimes I can't tell if he's trolling us or not. He does keep a straight face as we all lift our sticks in a salute.

I touch mine to Jane's beside me, and we laugh as the team splits up and heads for the edge of the field or down the path to the locker room.

"You ready for this?" she shouts, doing her best impression of a testosterone-fueled football player.

I flip my stick over and grip it with both hands before hoisting it in the air. "SO READY!"

I hear someone chuckle behind me, and I glance over my shoulder to find Becca grinning at me. She's talking to Coach, and he smiles at me too before waving for me to come join them.

"I'm being summoned," I tell Jane before jogging over.

I should probably be more subtle about it, but I'm sure my face is stretched in the biggest dork smile ever as I get closer to her. It's been over a week since the night I went to her place, and I still haven't fully come down from the high. The way she sounded, the way she felt, the way she came on my tongue—it's hard to imagine a day when that won't play in my head in a constant loop.

We haven't had much time together outside of practice since then, but we text most days, and we've grabbed coffee from the Lobster Trap once. She told me she wants

Catch and Cradle

to take things slow, especially with the big trip to Montreal coming up, and that's fine with me.

I don't even know what we're doing, but for now, I've decided not to care. I just like being with her, and if it takes some time for us to figure out how to do more of that, then so be it. I do wish I could kiss her more. We haven't even held hands since that night, but I understand why she wants to keep things on the down low. I'm trying my best to stop myself from spinning out and taking it as a sign something's wrong.

"What's up, C—I mean, Coach Jamal?"

I see Becca's lips twitch as she tries to hide a smirk. Being near her makes it hard to remember a lot of important things, like the fact that I'm not supposed to call Coach 'CJ' to his face.

He might actually like it. It's hard to tell with him. He *is* pretty insistent that we always call him Coach.

"I'm running an idea past Becca, and I thought we could include you too," he answers. "Your picks for the new recruits have worked out great. I really took your suggestions to heart, and it paid off in that first game. I think there are a couple newbies who could use a little more work on the basics, however. Just to get them up to speed with the rest of the team."

I nod. "Makes sense."

"I was just asking Becca if she'd be okay facilitating an extra hour of practice for them before we head to Montreal, and I think you two should run it together."

I glance between the two of them. "Uh, really?"

They both bob their heads.

"You're great with leading drills, especially for the newer players," Becca says. "What they really need is confidence, and you're so good at bringing it out in them. I bet you could run the whole practice yourself, but I told

Coach that would be a lot to spring on you last minute." She gives him the side-eye. "I guess he was fine springing it on *me* last minute."

He lifts his hands in surrender. "I only had the idea today! We only need to do it if you two can fit it in. I can send an email to the girls and find a time that works and all that. My household has only just found its rhythm as a well-oiled baby schedule machine, and I'm already throwing it off with the Montreal trip, so I'm unfortunately not able to be here for it myself."

"We'll do it!" I say before I can give myself a chance to hesitate.

I'm done listening to the little nagging voice that tells me I'm not cut out for responsibilities like this. I'm done questioning the compliments I get and wondering if I'm really responsible or just a fraud.

I loved running tryouts, and I was good at it. I want to do more with the team, and I'm not going to turn the opportunity down just because I need to put in more effort than other people to balance my school work with the rest of my life.

"Great!" Coach claps me on the shoulder. "I'll send an email tonight."

He heads over to his bag so he can make a note in his phone about it. Most of the team is gone now. I turn to face Becca and nudge her foot with my stick.

"Look at us! The dynamic duo!"

She smiles and shakes her head. "You are such a dork."

"You like it."

Her eyes flash, and once again, I'm thinking about being naked and on top of her.

"I do."

We stand there staring at each other long enough that my fingers are twitching with the need to touch her. I'm seconds away from forgetting everything else and just lunging for her when Coach's shouted goodbye snaps the magnetism between us.

"We should head in," Becca says after we've answered him.

We walk back to the athletics centre together and head to the locker room. A few of our teammates are still sitting around chatting, and I can hear some of the showers going.

"I'm gonna rinse off," Becca announces before walking over to her locker.

I get caught up in a conversation with a few of the girls about things to do in Montreal. I've been a bunch of times to visit my brother, so they're all eager for suggestions. By the time we wrap up, I realize I'm the only one who hasn't changed yet. I haven't even put my stick away.

"Go ahead," I tell the group when they ask if they should wait for me. "I have to study after this, so I'm going straight to the library."

I decide the library probably won't appreciate me smelling like a sweaty jock and pull out my stuff to take a shower. I can still hear water running, and it's more than a little distracting to know Becca is literally wet and naked just a few meters away from where I'm standing. My footsteps echo as I pad around the locker room, checking if there's anyone else here.

I don't know if Becca would be down for some illicit fun, but it's worth scoping out the area to see if that would even be possible.

I'm out of sight in one the locker bays when I hear two of my teammates leaving the showers and walking back over to the bay that houses the lacrosse lockers. It's hard to be sure, but I'm pretty sure they're two of the older girls on the team who I don't talk to very much.

"Okay, so tell me if I'm imagining this, but do you get, like, a vibe between Cap and Hope?"

The question carries over the lockers to where I'm standing. I freeze. I can hear them shuffling their stuff around, and I strain my ears to pick up on the other girl's answer.

"Cap and Hope? Huh. What makes you say that?"

"I don't know. Just a feeling. I noticed them sharing this, like, blazing look at practice the other day, and they just seem way closer than they used to be."

"You really think Becca would be involved in something like that?"

A locker bangs shut.

"Yeah, that's the thing. Becca's the one who started the whole 'don't date your teammates' rule."

I almost blow my cover by staggering back a few steps and bumping into the locker behind me. Thankfully the impact isn't very loud; I don't know how I would explain creepily listening into their conversation.

I also don't know how to explain their conversation itself. I knew the 'no dating' thing was important to Becca, but she's never mentioned *starting* the rule herself. It's been a thing the whole time I've been at UNS. I never questioned it. It seemed like a logical-if-a-little-strict part of the team's culture, especially since there'd been drama in the past.

When people said 'drama in the past,' I always assumed *ancient* past.

"Well, if they're gonna date, I just hope they come out with it. I don't care if people on the team date. I just care if they turn it into this big secretive, dramatic thing, you know?"

"Yeah, for sure."

Another locker shuts.

"You ready to go?"

"All good! I'm starving. Can we stop at Subway?"

Their voices trail off into silence as the door swings open and then closes with a thud. My heart starts pounding like a jackhammer tunneling into my ears as a chant I can't switch off fills my head.

Stupid. Stupid. Stupid. You are so stupid, Hope.

I squeeze my eyes shut to block it out, but it continues.

So stupid.

I ball my hands into fists, ordering the voice to stop.

"I am not stupid," I whisper.

I must look like a crazy person, but it helps.

I am not stupid.

Nobody is trying to hide anything from me. Nobody is taking advantage of me. I haven't made a mistake. I overheard one small part of a confusing conversation, and I'm going to ask Becca to clear it up. That's all.

I step out of the locker bay and pause instead of continuing to the showers. All of my sexy fantasies about slipping into a stall with Becca have faded. I want to talk to her, but not here. Not like this. I have too much dread curling in my stomach to have this conversation while she's wrapped in a towel and dripping wet.

So I walk back to my locker instead and change out of my gear before leaving the room without saying anything at all.

THE WEEK IS SO PACKED with schoolwork and preparations for the Montreal trip that I don't see Becca again until the extra training session two days later. I texted to let her know I wanted to hang out, but we didn't manage to fit anything into our schedules.

That also means I didn't get a chance to ask her about what I heard in the locker room.

I jog down the halls of the athletics centre on my way to meet her at the lacrosse supply closet. I'm already late. All my brainpower today has been exerted on a huge assigned reading, and I lost track of time. That doesn't do anything to help the nerves twisting my stomach in knots.

I've gone back and forth on the conversation I overheard so many times I'm starting to lose my grip on what was actually said. Everyone knows Becca has always been more militant about the 'no dating' thing than anyone else, but she's more militant about *everything* than anyone else. In the weeks we've been texting, I've realized what a huge part of her life the team really is. She plans her class schedule around lacrosse. She plans what she eats around lacrosse. Of course she'd take what might have been a generally acknowledged guideline and turn it into a core part of the team's culture, especially if she thought it was protecting the team from harm.

When I think about it that way, it's a very Becca thing to do, and it explains what I heard in the locker room without the need for any other motives.

I pick up my pace as I turn down another hallway and pass a group of guys in basketball uniforms. I try to keep my nose from wrinkling as I pass them. Girl sweat smells so much better than guy sweat.

I can feel my shoulders getting tighter and tighter the closer I get to the supply closet, my muscles bunching up with stress and anticipation. At this point, I don't even know if I should bring the conversation up at all. I'm literally using the word *motive* in my head like this is some sort of crime investigation. Becca doesn't deserve to be interrogated, and I don't know how to tell her I overheard something while hiding in the locker room from our teammates without sounding like a crazy person.

I don't want to hear somebody I care about call me crazy. Not again.

By the time I turn the final corner and find Becca standing outside the closet with an armload of practice gear, I'm on the verge of developing an eye twitch. I force myself to let out a long exhale before she notices me and try to smooth my expression into something passably normal.

The first thing she does when she sees me is frown and ask what's wrong.

Clearly I didn't do enough face smoothing.

"Sorry I'm late!" I say instead of answering. "I got caught up with schoolwork and lost track of time. Won't happen again."

"Hope." She tilts her head to the side, her eyebrows furrowed. "Is something up? I'm not going to, like, play the hardass captain card and yell at you. Plus you're only..." She shifts the gear around so she can check her phone. "Four minutes late. Everything is totally fine."

She takes a step closer, watching me with concern. Even now, I can't help getting distracted by how gorgeous she is. Her hair is pulled back into a high ponytail that emphasizes the strong features of her face, and she's wearing casual practice clothes like me. If 'hot and kind of intimidating sporty girl' was a yearbook category, she'd be the only nominee.

"Okay. Thanks." I blow out another long breath. "Sorry. I just got stressed."

"No need to apologize." She smiles, but her eyes are still searching my face. "The rest of the stuff is on the floor in the closet. Do you mind grabbing it?"

"Aye aye, Captain." I try to lighten things up, but my voice comes out strained and stilted.

The tension just keeps growing as we carry the gear out to the field. The walk is a few minutes long, and the prolonged silence feels like a sheet of sandpaper grating against my skull.

I just want this to be normal again. I want to go back to joking and laughing and feeling like we're locked in our own little world. I want her to kiss me again. We've barely even touched since that night at her place.

Maybe I was terrible in bed.

It's not the first time I've thought it over the past couple days. I know I can't have imagined how intense the night was, and there's no way that was all one-sided, but maybe I was just really bad at eating her out.

Maybe she's trying to figure out how to end this—whatever *this* is.

By the time we reach the middle of the field, I've spiralled so much that my attempt to gently set the gear down turns into me dropping it all with a clatter. The ball sack's drawstring catches on one of my fingers, releasing a volley of lacrosse balls that scatter across the field around me.

"Fuck!" I shout, all of my nerves and frustrations making their way into the word.

I crouch down and start grabbing whatever gear I can reach, but I freeze when the tips of Becca's shoes appear in front my eyes.

"Hope," she says softly before crouching down. I keep staring at her shoes. "Hope, look at me. What's wrong?"

I hesitate for a few seconds and then shift my gaze up to meet hers. "You still want to do this, right?"

She's resting on her knees, our faces just a couple feet apart. "By this, you mean...?"

"I mean this." I gesture between us. "It's okay if you don't, but I'd like to know."

"Of course I do." She inches a little closer. "You...I can't stop thinking about you. I don't want to stop thinking about you."

"Really?" I whisper.

She nods, the corners of her mouth lifting. "Really. I'm...I like you a lot."

Something in me releases at the words, like a spring that was waiting for just the right trigger. The whole world seems to take on a golden tint as my chest floods with warmth.

"I like you too," I murmur. "A lot."

She nods, her smile getting bigger and bigger. "That's good."

"So, that night at your house..." I can't help adding. "It was...I mean...I got worried that I wasn't very good at—"

"Hope, oh my god." She grabs one of my hands and takes it in hers. "I haven't stopped thinking about it for a second. That was...I've never felt anything like that. Why would you think it wasn't good?"

I drop my eyes to our hands and mumble, "It's just...we haven't even held hands since then."

"Oh, Hope." She squeezes my fingers. "I'm so sorry. That's my fault. I've been stressed and kind of paranoid about the team. I want to make this work. I promise I will. I just need a little time to figure it out, but I shouldn't have let that make you feel unwanted. You are *very* wanted."

I look up just in time to see her eyes flash as her tongue darts out to wet her lips.

"I want you so bad," I whisper before I can stop myself. "I wish I could kiss you right here."

She freezes, and my cheeks flush at my mistake. Our

teammates haven't arrived yet, but we're not exactly hidden out here in the middle of all the sports fields.

"I know we can't," I rush to add. "I just—"

I don't get time to finish my sentence before her mouth crashes into mine. For a second, I'm stunned, but then her lips shift and mine respond, starting the first step of a dance that leaves us breathless. Her fingers are still laced with mine, squeezing hard as her other hand cups the back of my neck.

My backs of my eyelids are streaked with gold. Everything is gold when I'm kissing her. She makes the whole world melt down into nothing but precious metals.

When we finally break apart, we're both panting. Her neck is flushed the prettiest pink, and her eyes are shining with need.

"Hope," she says, her voice heavy with intention, "I promise I'm going to fix things so I can kiss you whenever I want. I need that so bad."

I can't stop looking at her lips. "Me too."

She slides her hand off my neck and runs her fingers through my hair before dropping her arm back to her side. "Is there anything else I can help with?"

"Uh..." I can think of quite a few things, but they really aren't appropriate for a sports field. "I guess, um..."

The more she looks at me like that, the harder it is to believe she'd try to hurt me. I know my head is still clouded with the kiss, but I don't want to launch an accusation at her, not after a moment like this.

"I just...If there was something you needed to tell me, you'd tell me, right?"

She tilts her head to the side, and I realize that wasn't exactly the clearest question ever.

"Like, you wouldn't keep stuff from me just because you think I can't handle it?" I ask. "I'm really worried about people doing that. Ethan did that. He just stopped telling me things because he thought it would be too much. He didn't even *ask* me what too much was. He just decided for me, and it made me feel stupid."

"You're one of the smartest people I know." She pauses for a second, holding my gaze. "I'm not going to decide what you get to know and what you don't. I'm not going to decide what you can handle."

"Okay, good."

I take a deep breath and let that sink in. If I want this with her, I'm going to have to trust her. I won't let the past stop me from having a future.

"So..." Becca rocks back on her heels and glances around us. "Do you want to grab some balls with me?"

I burst out laughing, and she joins in. By the time we've got all the scattered gear gathered up, our teammates have arrived. I catch Becca's eye as I welcome them, and she flashes me a thumbs up.

The world is still coated in gold.

17

Becca

"Focus, Moore!"

Coach Jamal's shout carries over the triumphant roar of the crowd in the stands and the groaning of my teammates. I just lost possession of the ball for what feels like the millionth time this game.

It's probably more like the third time, but that doesn't make the situation much better. We're down by two in our Montreal match with less than half the game left.

I watch our defenders spring into action as the McGill players make their way up the field. A few good blocks slow them down, but a surprise pass sends the ball arcing through the air and straight into the basket of an opposition attacker who's in a perfect position to score.

I hold my breath along with what feels like every other player on the field. Our goalie dives like there's no tomorrow, but it's not enough to stop the perfect angle of the ball as it whips past her stick and slams into the back of the net.

The stands erupt before the point is even officially called. McGill is a massive school compared to UNS, and even on a cloudy October day like this, their bleachers are full enough to make an ear-splitting amount of noise as they cheer for our demise.

Focus, Moore.

I repeat Coach's words to myself as the ref sets up for the face-off, even though I'm pissed enough I want to snap and tell him he's not being helpful.

I'm not really mad at *him*. I'm mad at myself. I've been off the whole game, and it's starting to affect my teammates as they all begin to wonder what's wrong with me and whether or not I can be trusted to catch a pass. We're no longer a single, many-armed machine. We've split off into mismatched fragments with wires that don't connect.

This is exactly how it felt after things started going bad with me and Lisa.

I shouldn't be thinking about that. I shouldn't be thinking about any of it. I'm creating a self-fulfilling prophecy with my constant stress, and it's costing us the game. I realized my whole 'wait until after the game to tell Hope everything' plan was possibly not the best idea ever when I spent the whole twelve hour bus ride here as wide awake and jittery as someone who'd just downed two pots of coffee.

We got into the rented McGill dorms we're staying in late last night, and everyone crashed right away to be prepared for our game at noon today. I'm not sure if I even slept. I spent most of the night listening to Bailey snoring in the bed across the room and replaying every conversation I've had with Hope this week.

I promised her I'd find a way to make this work, and I meant it. I just haven't been able to *find* that way, no matter how many hours I spend lying awake at night thinking it over. I don't want to pull Hope into the mess of my past without being able to offer her some glimpse of a solution.

It all comes back to the same thing: if I mess this up or

if things between Hope and I don't work out, it will have an impact on the team. That part is inevitable. It may not have as big of an impact as I think it will, like Kala pointed out, but there's no denying there will be *some* impact.

No matter what, there's a chance I'll lose the team. I'll lose my captaincy and my scholarship, but more than that, I'll lose the most important thing in my life: my place on this team.

But is it?

A little part of my brain that's been getting louder and louder these past few days speaks up as I stand tensed and ready for the result of the face-off.

Is it the most important thing in your life, or the only *thing in your life?*

It hit me during one of my late-night worry sessions: maybe those aren't the same thing.

The team is my home. It gives me something I never had growing up: a place that's really *mine*. Lacrosse is even the thing that bonded me and my dad when our idea of home fell apart, but when have I ever tried looking for a home somewhere else? When have I ever looked beyond the walls I've boxed myself inside?

I only have another year left before I'll be forced to look beyond lacrosse whether I want to or not. I haven't even thought much about my career, or where I want to live, or who I want to be when I'm no longer captain of the UNS lacrosse team.

"Becca! MOVE!"

Paulina, one of our midfielders, shouts the command around her mouth guard as she swerves past me with the ball in her basket. A flurry of players from both teams follows in her wake, closing in to block her or spreading out to vie for a pass.

"Shit, shit, shit," I mutter around the edges of my own

mouth guard as I scramble to get into a more helpful position. The McGill defender who's marking me is good at her job, and after my delayed start, I can't get close enough to help Paulina.

I edge my way forward, unable to do anything but watch as Paulina passes to Bailey, who passes to Hope, who aims at the net and just manages to clear the goalie's reach by a fraction of an inch. The ball whacks the back of the net and drops to the ground.

"YES!" I scream as the groans from the crowd fill the air. "YES!"

We're still down by two and closing in on the end of the game, but the goal is just what we need. It's just what *I* need. I glance over at Coach, and we use the personal sign language we've developed over the years to debate whether or not we should call a time out. He agrees, and a couple minutes later, we're all crowded around him on the side of the field.

He whips off his aviators—a true sign that things are getting serious.

"Okay, lax rats." He scans all our faces. "I know things look bad, but we've been in worse trouble before. We've still got fifteen minutes left, and you've had some great goals in this game already. You can do this. When you guys are on, you're *on*. You're unstoppable. We just need to get you back there."

A moment of silence passes, and everyone starts shifting around while trying not to stare at me. I feel their eyes anyway. We all know I'm the reason we're off.

I need to own it.

"I haven't been playing my best," I announce. "I know that. I've cost us a couple goals."

I glance at Hope on the other end of the semicircle of players. Most of her face is obscured by her goggles, but I can still see her watching me. I don't look away as I continue.

"You deserve all my focus, and you have it. I promise. Let's win this thing!"

"Fuck yeah!" a few people shout. Half the team still has their mouth guards in, so the agreement is a garbled mix of words and grunts.

Hope nods at me and then punches the air before leading the team back onto the field.

I'm still not at peak performance, but I'm no longer a menace to the game when it picks up again. We orchestrate another goal within a couple minutes, and our defence keeps the McGill players from getting anywhere near our net. By the time we're down to four minutes on the clock, we've tied the game.

The air is thick with anticipation now, tension obscuring the atmosphere like cloudy breaths on a cold day. My muscles are burning, my heart a constant thumping in my ears as I strain my body to give its all to these last few minutes.

We can score. I know we can.

We lose the face-off after our tying goal, and the McGill team gets the ball all the way down to our net just to have their shot blocked by our goalie. Two minutes tick by without either team scoring.

"Come on, come on, come on," I chant around the plastic in my mouth as one of our midfielders takes possession and clears a few metres up the field, cradling the ball as she searches for someone to pass to.

Another midfielder gains some ground ahead of her, and she sends the ball flying into their basket. A defender is on her immediately, keeping her locked in place, and I see my chance.

I sprint into position and see her attention lock on me.

The pass is almost botched by the defender, but I manage to catch the ball before the girl marking me realizes what's happening. I'm out of there before she can catch up, tearing towards the goal at full speed as half a dozen players charge at me. My wrist whips back and forth in a frenzy, the rhythmic movement of cradling as instinctive as breathing, as living, as *wanting*.

A deep, guttural sound bursts out of me as I launch the ball at the net. The goalie dives but misses by at least half a foot.

I just scored.

I scored with less than a minute left in the game.

Everything rushes back into focus. I can hear my teammates cheering, see Coach doing a very dad-like happy dance on the side of the field, feel the sweat trickle down my back as my lungs burn for air.

I scored.

"YES, BECCA!" Bailey slams into me from behind. "OH MY GOD!"

We still have to get through the last forty seconds, but they pass by in a rapid blur that leaves our score intact. Everyone piles into a group hug with me at the centre when our win gets announced. I laugh and cheer and whoop with everyone else, but part of me feels distant, detached, separate from the thrill of the moment.

We won, but it was far too close.

I can't let this happen again.

I STAND outside Hope's room in the McGill dorms, urging myself to knock while my arms stay glued to my sides.

I *think* this is Hope's room. It's going to be an awkward encounter if I'm wrong.

The whole team is planning on getting a late dinner tonight, but for now, everyone is taking a few hours to chill or explore the city. My plan is to ask Hope if she'd like to hang out and somehow segue that into giving her a primer about what happened in my freshman year. I still don't know if a team-wide trip to a city a twelve hour bus ride away from Halifax is the best time to do this, but the more I wait, the more this starts to feel just like it did with Lisa: like bracing for a match to drop and set off an inevitable explosion.

I don't want to be in that position again, and now that we've made it through the game, I need to at least tell her *something*.

My arm finally obeys my order to lift itself. I'm just about to knock when the door opens and Hope nearly runs straight into me as she charges into the hall.

"Oh! Becca!" She pauses with her arm halfway through the sleeve of a denim jacket. Her purse is slipping off her shoulder, and her glasses are slightly askew. "What's up?"

"Um...are you going somewhere?" I ask in a complete statement of the obvious.

"I had a nap and slept through my alarm." She gets the jacket on and straightens her glasses. "I'm meeting up with my brother and his girlfriend for a few hours."

"Oh, cool." I slide my hands into my pockets. "That sounds fun."

"Did you need something?"

I don't know why I didn't text first like a normal person.

"No, no. I just uh—I was gonna ask if you wanted to hang out."

"Oh." A grin spreads over her face. We stand there for

a few seconds, me shifting my weight from side to side and her adjusting and readjusting her purse.

"He was at the game," she says, breaking the silence. "My brother. I was gonna ask if you wanted to meet him, but you seemed busy, and I didn't know..."

I can guess what she's thinking: we don't even know what to call what's going on between us, never mind how to take it to the meeting family stage.

Besides Kala—who doesn't really count, since we've been friends since childhood—I've never met the family of anyone I've dated. I've never introduced anyone to mine, such as it is.

"Do you want to come with me?"

"Huh?"

Hope starts fiddling with the edge of her jacket. "I mean, it's not a big formal thing. You can just come along as my teammate. They'll love it. We're going to the Biodome."

"The Biodome?"

"Yeah, it's like this big, uh, dome thing, and it has a bunch of wildlife exhibits and aquariums and these cool overhead walkway things that make it feel like you're walking through the top of the jungle looking down at all the animals. They have a bunch of different ecosystems set up. At least I think they call them ecosystems. You would know better than me with all your environmental science." She presses her lips together and breathes deep through her nose. "Wow, I'm rambling, but yeah. You can come if you want. It would be nice to have you there."

I do want to go, not just because it sounds freaking amazing, but because I've started to treasure every new experience with her like it's a new jewel in a necklace. I want more, in every colour I can find. I want to know what life with her is like.

Since it doesn't seem like we'll get a chance to talk on our own today, I'd rather be near her than pacing away the hours until dinner in my room.

"You're sure your brother and his girlfriend won't mind?"

"Not at all! Zach is a sweetheart, and DeeDee loves people. She's gonna go crazy over your hair. She's studying to be a hairdresser. She did my ombre for me, actually. Just brace yourself. I'm sure she's going to want to touch yours and ask you over and over again if that really is your natural colour."

I laugh and reach up to touch my ponytail. The ends are still damp from my post-game shower. "I think I can live with that."

Hope beams. "Okay, great! Do you need to get anything before we leave?"

We stop by my room so I can grab a jacket and my bag. Hope is all dressed up in grey skinny jeans and a slouchy black t-shirt—practically formalwear compared to the sweatpants, leggings, and various lacrosse-branded tops the whole team seems to wear every day at UNS—so I take a minute to change into some skinny jeans of my own and throw on a bomber jacket.

"Where are you off to?" Bailey asks, looking up from where she's lying in bed with a book.

"Something called the Biodome. It's some kind of wildlife exhibit thing."

She nods. "Sounds like something you would like. Who are you going with?"

"I, uh, ran into Hope in the hall. Her brother lives here and she was going to go with him, so she asked if I wanted to join."

I realize just how far from casual that sounds as soon as it leaves my mouth and rush to correct things. "Do you want to come too? I can ask if they'd be okay with another person coming. It would be fun."

She yawns and sets her book down on her chest. "Thanks, but I think I'll hang back. I'm wiped, and I want to rest up before dinner. Wouldn't want to crash you and Hope's date anyway."

She laughs, but I go completely still as the bottom of my stomach drops.

"Becca? I'm kidding."

I force a chuckle. "Ha. Yeah. Sorry. I'm super tired too. I hope I make it through this."

She squints at me. "Mhmm."

"I better head out now. Enjoy your book."

"Enjoy your afternoon!"

I might be going crazy, but the word *enjoy* sounds extra loaded in the goodbye she calls out as I leave the room. I suck in a breath and force myself to believe I'm imagining it.

"Oooh, fancy jacket!" Hope gives me an appreciative once-over as soon as I'm back in the hall. "I don't think I've ever seen that before."

My stress starts to seep away as I watch her watch me. I grin and do a twirl.

"Gotta look good for Montreal. People are supposed to be stylish here, right?"

"Ha. Wait until you see my brother's dork beard. I think he grew it to be more *hip*,"—she puts the word in air quotes—"but he just looks like a farmer."

She leads the way down the hall, and I fall into step beside her. We talk more about her brother and his girlfriend, and as we make our way outside and up the busy city street to the metro station, all my nerves fade away. Everything fades away.

There are no rules, no roles to fill. We're not lacrosse

players. We're not even UNS students. We're just two girls exploring a new city, and for the very first time with her, I feel like I can take a breath, stretch out my arms, and fill myself with the possibility of everything we could be—of everything *I* could be.

I feel limitless.

"There they are!" Hope points up the crowded sidewalk to a set of metal doors with the metro's blue and white logo jutting out above them. Just under it, a girl with bright pink hair is standing next to a guy in a green jacket while the two of them peer around the street.

The closer we get, the more clear it is he can't be anyone but Hope's brother. Aside from his sandy blond hair and beard—and the fact that he's a guy—he's basically Hope's carbon copy.

"Brother dearest!" she shouts when we're a couple metres away. She jogs over to hug him.

I follow along behind with my hands in my pockets and nod at the girl while Zach and Hope finish up their hug. She beams at me.

"*Ma belle*, you brought a friend!" she says to Hope in a French-Canadian accent.

Hope turns to me after stepping back from Zach. "Guys, this is Becca. She's my team's captain. Becca, this is DeeDee and my weirdo brother Zach."

"Nice to meet you." Zach offers me his hand. "You guys played great today."

"I wish I could have come!" Deedee adds. She has a throaty voice that matches her smokey eye makeup and pink lipstick. "It is good to meet you, my dear. By the way, I must ask, is that your natural colour?"

Hope and I burst out laughing, and she glances between the two of us.

"I told her you would ask that," Hope explains. "I knew you'd go crazy over hair like that."

"It is gorgeous!" DeeDee steps to the side to get a better look at my ponytail. "And so thick! You'll have to take it down for me later. Do you have layers? That would look so good with some nice, bouncy layers, especially with your face. *Très belle.*"

She lifts her hands like she's itching to get a hold of my hair. Zach leans over to grab her arm.

"Okay there, haircutter lady. You just met the girl. Let's not scare Hope's friend away."

I laugh. "No problem. I don't really *have* a haircut because I never know what to do with it. I'd love some professional suggestions."

DeeDee's eyes light up.

"Let's talk about it on the way there," Zach says. "You guys have to be back in time for a team dinner, right?"

"Yeah, we actually don't have that long," Hope answers.

We head into the cavernous metro station, and the smell of damp concrete mixed with something metallic is so foreign in my nose. I haven't smelt a subway system since our match in Toronto last year. Endless streams of people rush around us as Zach walks Hope and I through the process of buying tickets from one of the machines. I can hear the whoosh of departing trains and the ding-dong sound they make when they arrive.

Everything is so big and loud and alive. I feel like I'm standing on the edge of a vast, dense jungle, but instead of being afraid to step inside, I'm thrilled by the possibilities, by the sheer space in which to grow and explore and become.

"What are you smiling at?" Hope asks once we're standing on the platform waiting for our train. Zach and

DeeDee are busy looking at a big advertisement on the wall a few feet away.

"Oh, I just..." I try to wipe what I'm sure is an idiotic smile off my face, but it stays firmly in place. "It's just exciting, isn't it? Being out in the city like this. Sometimes I forget how small Halifax really is. Sometimes I even forget there's a city beyond the UNS campus."

Hope laughs. "Yeah, sometimes a whole week will go by, and I'll realize I haven't left the same five kilometre radius."

That's not going to be my life for much longer. By the middle of next year, I'll be looking for jobs and internships. I might even end up here in Montreal. I could go anywhere. It's the first time I've really, truly realized what that means, and the thought wipes the whole start of the day away. I'm not thinking about the game. I can barely even remember it. I'm thinking about this city and this girl and how much I want to take her hand and explore with her.

Hope tilts her head to the side and grins. "You're smiling again."

I shrug, still beaming. "I can't help it. I'm happy."

She moves a few inches closer and lowers her voice. "I'm always happy when you're happy."

I want to kiss her. I want to kiss her right here.

I nearly jump when Zach calls out, "That's us!"

Hope and I step apart as a train zooms out of the dark tunnel and slows to a stop beside the platform. We manage to get four empty seats. Hope takes the one next to me with Zach and DeeDee across the aisle from us. Her thigh and calf are pressed against mine, but she doesn't seem to mind that everyone can see, and neither do I. I've never had this feeling with a girl before: like I need everyone to know what she means to me, like I want to scream it out for the whole city to hear.

I've always had to keep quiet. Whether it was Lisa or Kala, there were always complications that meant I had to stifle my most important relationships. Even with Hope, I've been so muted and cautious, stealing moments where I can and always looking over my shoulder. I've been out as a lesbian since I was seventeen, but I've never loved out loud.

I glance at Hope as she hunches over her knees to chat with DeeDee. Her glasses slip an inch down her nose, and my hand twitches with the urge to push them back up.

It's way too soon to call this love, but I can't help wondering what that would be like: just taking it slow, getting to know her and watching this thing between us grow without the constant pressure of the situation bearing down on it like a load of rocks.

What if we could just *be*? What would it take to get there?

"Becca, you have to let me see your hair down!" DeeDee's voice calls me back to the present. Her accent makes my name sound like *Bee-cah*.

I look over and find her gesturing for me to take my ponytail out. Hope is laughing, and both of them seem oblivious to the way I was staring at her, but I catch Zach stroking his short, barely-there beard with a knowing grin on his face.

I brace for the nerves to hit, but instead, I just feel warm inside. I feel right. I smile back at him as I reach up to let my hair down.

By the time we reach the Biodome, DeeDee has demanded I switch seats with Zach and spent the rest of the ride holding different pieces of my hair up around my face. I make a mental note of a few of her suggestions. I really am clueless when it comes to haircuts.

There's a bit of a line to get tickets, but eventually we head in with the throngs of people spending their Saturday afternoon getting acquainted with the wonders of the natural world. The place is huge, and just like Hope said, they have several full-size ecosystems set up with special overhead pathways for visitors to walk through them without disturbing the animals.

"Do you like it?" Hope asks as the four of us stand waiting for our turn to get a good look at some penguins.

"It's amazing!" I answer. "I love all the conservation aspects. I'm a little iffy about zoos, to be honest, but this is really incredible."

"So it's up to your environmental science standards?"

I chuckle. "Yes, I would say it is."

Zach turns to me. "So that's what you're studying? Cool!"

"Oh, it's just my minor," I explain. "I'm a kinesiology major."

"But it *could* be her major," Hope adds. "She knows so much about it. She's like an oracle of environmental knowledge. Like here, watch this!"

She heads a few feet to our left, where there's an information sign with a 'pop quiz' question and answer section.

"Becca, what are the five major biomes?" she calls back to us.

"They want five? Hmm." I cross my arms and think. "I mean, a lot of people disagree on what a major biome is. Some people say there are up to nine, but if they want five, it's probably...aquatic, grassland, forest, desert, and tundra?"

"Damn!" Hope bounds back over to us. "Five for five!"

Zach and DeeDee clap.

"You sure that's only your minor?" Zach asks.

It's only a high school science level question, but I smile at the compliment anyway. I have to work to drill kinesiology terms into my head, but something about environmental science has always just stuck for me. It's effortless, like cradling a lacrosse ball up the field.

We get a look at the penguins and then continue making our way through the exhibits, with Hope throwing out pop quiz questions at me off the signs every now and then. I get them all right.

"Oh my god, *capybaras*!" she shouts when we're up on one of the walkways, looking down on a grassy landscape dominated by a big pond and a small forested area. "I *love* capybaras!"

There's a herd of capybaras swimming and laying on the shore of the pond. They look like long-legged guinea pigs, but they're all as big as sheep dogs.

Zach groans. "We'll never get her out of here now."

Hope glares at him. "Do not mock my adoration of the world's largest rodent!"

She makes her way to the edge of the path and rests her chin on her hands to stare dreamily down at the animals. The rest of us join her. Zach and DeeDee move on after a couple minutes, but Hope insists she'll catch up later.

"I just love them!" she gushes while I lean against the rail next to her.

"They *are* very cute," I say without looking away from her.

She squeals every time one of them does something new. It's adorable.

"I'm so glad you came with us," she says after another few minutes, glancing at me before going back to watching the capybaras like her life depends on it.

"Me too."

Our hands are only a few inches apart on the rail. The longer we stand there, the closer her pinkie gets to mine.

"It's really cool that you know so much about nature. I love hearing you talk about it."

I love talking about it. I've never realized quite how much until today. I've never been anywhere like this, and I can't help thinking about all the people who keep this place going, all the jobs it must take to create something that makes everyone who visits care a little more about the world around them.

That could be my job. If I could miraculously find the time to switch to a double major, I could end up working somewhere just like this.

"That means a lot."

The side of her pinkie brushes mine. I take a breath in through my nose and cover her hand with mine. I hear her inhale too, and for a second we both stand frozen and tense, but then she shifts her hand so our fingers are woven together. My heart feels like it's too big for my chest.

I want this. I want her. I want more—of everything. I'm starting to realize just how small my world really is, how much I've shrunk it down and limited myself to make sure I'm safe.

"Hope."

We turn to meet each other's eyes, hands still linked on the rail.

"I, um, I really like you. I've really liked doing this. I want you...I want you to be in more of my life."

She blinks and whispers, "Really?"

I nod, biting my lip. Just because I want it, doesn't mean it isn't terrifying. I still don't know exactly how this will work, but I'm starting to see a path, and it leads straight to her.

"I was thinking, um, you know my best friend Kala who I've told you about?" I pause, and she nods. "I've been wanting to ask you if you'd like to hang out, just the three of us. I'd love for you to meet her."

Her whole face lights up. "Really? I would love that too. So much."

I can do this. I can introduce her to Kala and show her our friendship really is just that. I can stop compartmentalizing and sectioning off at least one part of my life. I can let Hope in, and maybe together, we can figure out the rest.

We're surrounded by people, but when she leans in to kiss me, I meet her halfway. Her lips press against mine just for a second, but it's enough to make every colour in this miniature paradise gleam brighter and bolder when I open my eyes.

I don't want to hide her away and kiss her in corners anymore. I want the real thing.

18

Hope

Jane is the only twenty year-old I know who can cook a turkey with the skill and precision of a wizened housewife. She's even wearing the frilly gingham apron she only busts out for special culinary occasions.

Since Thanksgiving happens so early in Canada and falls during a pretty inconvenient time in our lacrosse schedule this year, the four of us decided to do a Babe Cave Friendsgiving. We've only been back from Montreal for a week, and we have a home game next weekend, so it just made the most sense.

"How's the bird?" Iz asks, coming into the kitchen to join me at the table while I watch Jane work her domestic magic.

"She's a comin'," Jane answers as she peers through the oven door. "Gonna be right juicy."

Iz and I have to look away from each other so we don't burst out laughing. Jane is very serious about her turkey.

I thought about inviting Becca over tonight. She's in Halifax for the holiday too. We're finally getting a chance to hang out with her friend Kala tomorrow, but I figured

Thanksgiving might be overkill. I also didn't know if my housemates would find me inviting our captain over for an intimate Friendsgiving gathering to be normal or suspiciously weird. The only guest we planned on having was Jane's boyfriend.

"Can we help with anything, Jane?" I ask.

I need the distraction. My head's been spinning since the trip to Montreal. I know Becca wants more, but it's hard to see how we'll get that if she keeps on believing the whole team will fall apart if we date. I can't imagine growing up the way she did, and I totally get the lacrosse team being a family for her. It's a family for me too, and I just wish she knew families aren't supposed to be conditional.

Sure, some of the team might be a little pissed at first, but I can't imagine all the people who care about us turning their backs just because we care about each other.

"You can start on the cranberry sauce," Jane answers, "and Iz, you can finish up those turnips I started mashing."

We get to work. It's cramped in here with the three of us all chopping, mashing, and mixing. It only gets worse when Paulina returns from a last-minute trip to the corner store to grab some milk Jane needed, but we turn on some music and start joking and grooving our way through all the bumping into each other.

It doesn't take long for the room to get warm enough that my hair is sticking to my forehead. I lift it up to fan the back of my neck and find myself grinning when the song coming out of Paulina's phone switches to an acoustic guitar intro I recognize.

"This is Becca's favourite song," I blurt before I think better of it.

I expect a few curious looks about why I know Becca's favourite song, or maybe just some nods like it's understandable information to have. I'm even braced for suspicion and questions.

What I don't expect is for everyone in the kitchen to freeze and exchange nervous glances while the tension creeps in like an ominous shadow even Ben Howard's optimistic lyrics can't block out.

"What?" I ask when it becomes clear no one else is going to speak.

"Uh, nothing," Paulina answers. "It's, uh, a good song."

"Seriously, what's up?"

I know my friends. This isn't how they would react if they only thought I had a crush on Becca, or even if they thought we may be involved.

They're giving me serious we-have-bad-news-we-don't-want-to-talk-about vibes.

"Wait, is something wrong with Becca?" I demand. "Is she okay?"

It doesn't make any sense for them to know something about her being hurt without me knowing too, but I can't think of anything else that would make them react this way. They all look like somebody died.

"Oh, Hope, of course not." Jane leans against the single foot of free counter space left. "Becca is fine. I mean, as far as I know."

"Then why are you all acting so weird?"

"I don't know if we could call her *fine*," Iz mutters.

Jane shoots them a withering glare. "Iz, come on!"

I give up on mashing cranberries and stand with my hands on my hips. I'm sweating bullets now, and it's not just from the heat of the room.

"You guys, spit it out. What the hell is going on? You know I hate when people don't tell me things."

They do their exchanging of glances thing again, and then Jane sighs.

"I'm sorry, Hope. We just...we only found out yesterday, and we didn't want to ruin Friendsgiving for you. We've all been working so hard this year, and we figured it was better to just have a nice holiday and then deal with stuff. I mean, we don't even know what's actually true."

My heart is pounding so loud I can barely hear her, and my gut is twisting itself in knots so tight I have to clutch my stomach.

I hate this. I hate people keeping things from me 'for my own good.' They *know* I hate this.

"I need somebody to tell me what the hell is happening right now," I get out through my clenched jaw.

Jane looks down at the floor. "Of course. It was wrong not to tell you right away."

I can feel a vein pulsing somewhere in my forehead. "Tell me *what?*"

Paulina sets down the salad tongs she's been holding in mid-air for the past minute and drums her nails against the countertop, taking over for Jane.

"So...we all kind of thought there was something up with you and Becca, and I just want you to know we don't care if there is. I mean, I get the team's no dating policy, but it's a little extreme, and it's not like you can help who you have feelings for, so if you do have feelings for her...we're there for you, you know? We figured you'd tell us when you were ready. I think the whole team feels the same."

Great. The whole team. It was bad enough when I thought a couple of the older girls might be onto us, but all of my closest friends talking about this behind my back makes me feel so small. I don't know how I was so oblivious.

So stupid.

"Could someone shut that off?" I snap.

The Ben Howard song is still playing in the background. Paulina reaches for her phone, and silence pushes its way in the overcrowded, sweltering kitchen.

"So if you do—" Paulina tries to continue, but I cut her off.

"Fine. Yes. I do. I wanted to tell you when I was ready, but I guess we're past that. Becca and I have a thing."

They all look at each other again, and I press my arms even harder over my stomach.

"I really want you to know we don't have a problem with that," Jane says after a moment of strained silence. "Just like Paulina said, you don't decide who you have feelings for, and we support you. I really don't want you to think we're trying to, like, undermine your happiness, Hope. You have to know that."

I just stare at her, waiting for the rest. She takes a deep breath in.

"Has Becca...told you about her past?"

"What past?"

I really wish they would all stop looking at each other like that.

"About...the team?" Jane prompts.

Again, I just stand there. Again, she breathes in like she's gearing herself up to deal a death blow.

"Okay, so you know Kelsey?"

I nod. She's one of the older players on the team—and one of the girls I thought I heard in the locker room that day. A chill creeps up my spine, making the dampness on the back of my neck feel like it's turned to ice.

"So, the other day when you were at the library, the three of us were hanging out on the stoop, and she happened to walk by on her way home from campus. We asked her to join us, and we all talked for a while. Then she said she had a question for us and that we didn't have to answer since it wasn't really her business. She said some people on the team have been talking, and...she wanted to know if we thought you might be involved with Becca."

I lean against the table as the nausea flipping my stomach gets worse and worse.

"We wouldn't have said anything even if we did know," Jane rushes to add. "I told her no, and she made some weird comment about thinking history was repeating itself. We...we asked her what she meant."

The conversation in the locker room echoes back to me —the conversation I wrote off as a misunderstanding on my part.

"What did she say?" I sound calm. Too calm. My voice is somehow the only part of me not on the verge of shaking. My words are flat and hollow.

"We've all heard that people on the team dating each other has caused drama in the past. I always thought it was, like, the *distant* past," Jane continues, voicing what I've thought myself since freshman year. "Kelsey was surprised we didn't know. I guess just the year before we started at UNS, Becca...She started dating a girl on the team. It got ugly. Kelsey said most people were on Becca's side, even after...after what happened, but it still tore the team up pretty bad. A lot of people left. It didn't help that there were some people who thought Becca was unfairly guaranteed a spot on the team because of that big donation for the program she got with her scholarship."

Becca's mentioned that last part to me, at least. It's still crazy to me that there are people who've questioned whether or not she's here because of her talent. She was freaking scouted by American schools, for fuck's sake. She's a powerhouse on the field.

I hold onto that thought—of Becca running up the field with her thick, red braid streaming behind her, of the way I'm always the first person she looks at after we score a goal.

I need something to hold onto.

"Becca had this friend on the team. Kala."

"Wait, what?" My eyes flare wide as my brain starts doing rapid calculations and playbacks.

She never mentioned Kala being on the team. She's brought her up a few times during our texting, but she's never said that. I would have remembered.

"Yeah." Jane's eyes search my face, her forehead creased with concern. "This girl, Kala, was Becca's friend from high school, and Becca's girlfriend was always really jealous of that. I guess they, like, had a thing in high school, and the girlfriend couldn't accept they went back to being just friends. Kelsey said she went a little nuts getting all suspicious."

"Wait." I'm still getting past the second sentence. "Wait, wait, wait. Becca *dated* Kala? Kala is her *ex*?"

Kala—the girl I'm supposed to meet and hang out with tomorrow.

Just how many fucking people aren't telling me things lately?

"Supposedly," Jane says, her tone edged with caution. "That's what Kelsey said, at least. This girlfriend of Becca's...she found all these pictures of Kala that Becca still had and dumped them on the floor in front of the whole team. She sounds like a right piece of work. Somehow, the two of them kept dating after that, but it was really straining the team, and then...then one day, Becca was supposed to be alone studying, but the girlfriend caught her going somewhere with Kala."

"Where?" I croak. I'm really shaking now. I have one

arm wrapped around my stomach and the other braced against the table for support.

"That was...the problem," Jane answers. She's practically wincing as she says it. "Becca didn't explain it or try to justify herself. She just said Kala needed her and that she wasn't going to talk about it. The whole situation blew up. The team lost the ECULL qualifiers, and then a bunch of players left. It was a big deal. I still can't believe we've never heard about any of it."

"Seems like Becca's been pretty good about keeping it quiet," Iz says in a low voice.

Paulina elbows them. "Iz!"

"I'm sorry, but it's true." Iz looks at me with a pained expression. "We really care about you, Hope, and I hate thinking she kept this from you when you clearly care about her."

"*You guys* kept this from me!" I can't stop myself from shouting as the storm inside me explodes out into the room. "You were going to keep it from me for two whole days, or maybe even longer! You were just *fine* with me continuing along with Becca like an idiot for two days? You were fine knowing she was possibly lying to me? You were fine not doing anything about it? I mean, fuck, she asked me to *meet Kala* tomorrow, and I didn't even know they dated until just now. You were really going to keep this from me? Why?"

"Hope." Jane's face has crumpled. She looks like she's about to cry. "Hope, it wasn't like that. We just wanted to let you have a nice weekend and then—"

"You think this is *nice*?" I hurl the words at all three of them. I'm out of control and I know it, but I can't stop. "You think it's *nice* to keep things from me so I can be happy and dumb? It's not nice. You know how much that shit bothers me. You especially, Jane. You seriously listened to me cry to you on the phone all summer about Ethan doing exactly the same thing just to turn around and do this?"

It's not a fair comparison. I know that as soon as I say it, but I can't take it back. I'm too angry, so angry I can barely see. Everything is blurred. I don't know if it's from tears or fury, but I can't see anything except the hazy outlines of the room around me as I leave the kitchen and stumble my way through the living room to get to the entryway.

"Hope, wait!"

Jane is the first to come after me. She catches my arm as I'm hunting around for my Keds. I shake her off and regret it as soon as I glance back to see the pain streaking her face. She really is crying now, but all I can do is turn away and keep chucking shoes aside to find mine.

It's like someone else has taken over my body. I can sense my emotions, but I'm separate from them. They're too much to take on. I don't want to feel. I want to move.

"Where are you going?" she asks, her voice cracked.

I finally find the fucking Keds and stoop to pull them on. When I straighten up, Paulina and Iz are standing beside Jane, each with a hand on her shoulders as they watch me.

"I need to get out of here. I need to go see her. I need...I need to know what the fuck is going on."

"Hope." Jane lifts a hand like she wants to reach for me again, but she hesitates. "Hope, please. I'm so sorry. I fucked up. I really fucked up, but can we please talk about it instead? I'm worried about you."

"No." I shake my head. "I really can't talk about it right now. I need to see her."

"I'll go with you. I don't want you to be alone. We can—"

"Jane, *no*."

A sob bursts out of her, and I force myself to take a shuddering breath. My hands are balled into fists at my sides. I'm furious, but she's still my best friend.

"I need to do this, okay? We'll talk after. I...I know you care about me."

"I'm so sorry. I—"

I hold up a hand to stop her. That's all I can take.

"I'm going now."

Turning my back on them all, I step outside and pull the door shut behind me. I try my best not to slam it. The whole way up the street, I focus on the simple action of one foot in front of the other.

One step at a time. First things first.

A steady rhythm. Something to count on, just like the thump of a lacrosse ball in my stick's basket and the flick of my wrist as I cradle.

I can do this. Maybe no one else believes I can handle whatever is going on, but I know I can.

I can do anything.

When I reach the giant old house Becca lives in, my heartbeat has stabilized. My vision has cleared. It's nearly dinnertime and already semi-dark out. The big tree in the yard casts creepy shadows across the lawn, the shape of its bare branches stretching like gnarled fingers. They flit across my skin as I walk to the door.

I still don't know which doorbell is for Becca's unit, so I ring them all. I don't think I could focus on the little letters on my phone screen enough to call her or send a text.

I wait almost a whole minute before I hear footsteps on the other side. The lock clicks, and then the big, old-fashioned handle turns. Becca is revealed inch by inch. Her face goes from surprised to elated to concerned in a couple of seconds.

"Hope." She steps forward and reaches for me. I go rigid. "What's wrong?"

"I—I—"

I try to summon up some deathly calm to put in my voice again, but none comes. There's a lump in my throat I can't swallow, and all I manage to do is stutter.

"Hope, hey. It's okay. Whatever it is, it's okay."

She folds me into a hug but lets go when I keep standing there like a statue, my arms glued to my sides. When she pulls back, I can see the traces of panic in her face, the widening eyes and trembling lips that are starting to look more and more like guilt.

"Hope..."

"Did you date somebody on the team before me?" I wish I sounded stronger, less desperate. My voice is hoarse and uneven, almost squeaky. It's pathetic.

Becca blinks—one, twice, and then she presses her lips into a tight line and closes her eyes for a second.

"Yes," she whispers.

"And did you date Kala? In high school? She's your ex?"

Her chin starts to shake. "Yes, but—"

Now it's me squeezing my eyes shut. I just want to erase this moment. I want it all to fade like a dream.

"I really don't want to hear the *but* right now, Becca," I interrupt. "Just tell me it's true. Tell me you've dated a teammate before and that Kala is your ex."

I look at her again. Her already pale skin has turned a pasty white.

"Yes, that's true," she says, so low I almost have to read her lips.

"And you didn't think I needed to know any of that?"

"Hope, I wanted to tell you. I've been figuring out how to tell you. I wanted to make everything okay first. I wanted to make sure it wasn't going to be like last time. I wanted to make sure I didn't lose—"

"The team," I cut in. "Yeah, I get it. The team is important, I know, but what about *me*, Becca? Where exactly did I fit into all this for you?"

"I wasn't going to say the team."

Her eyes bore into mine, and my traitor heart skips a beat, but that look is not enough to change anything.

"If you were concerned about losing me, did it ever occur to you to just tell me the truth? To let me be part of figuring it out? Or did you just not think I was capable of that?"

"Hope, that is not it at all."

I don't give her a chance to continue. "How did you think this was going to go? Were you even going to tell me about Kala before I met her? Were you really just going to let me walk into that blind? Do you know how stupid it makes me feel that I had to hear all this from someone else? Everyone's been talking about us. Everyone suspected something was going on, and somehow, I'm the last person to find out you've dated a teammate before, and that you're the whole reason we can't date teammates now. I don't even care all that much about your history, Becca. I really don't, but I do fucking care that you didn't tell me about it, and I want to know why."

When I finally stop, I'm panting. My shoulders are so tense they're shaking from the strain. Becca isn't moving at all. She doesn't even blink as she watches me with the frozen horror of somebody staring at a ghost. I almost want to ask her if she's okay. Almost.

"I—I—" She starts to stammer after a moment. Her voice is just a whisper. "I didn't want it to happen again. I was s-scared."

"And you thought hiding everything from me was the

answer?" I'm not shouting anymore. Now I just sound cold.

Part of me wants to throw my arms around her and tell her it's all going to be okay, but I don't know that. I don't know how we're going to make any of this okay, especially when she can barely talk to me about it, even now.

"I was going to tell you. About Kala. Before you met her. I promise." Her sentences come out in stilted chunks. "I just...I kept trying, but—but that's when everything went wrong last time. I didn't want it to get like that again."

"Becca." My arms twitch with how bad they want to reach for her when I see a pain deeper than any part of her I've witnessed before darken her face. "Did you really think I would let it get like that? Do you really not know me well enough?"

Everything Jane said back in the kitchen is still a blur, but there are parts I can pick out about what *before* must have been like: the suspicion, the jealousy, the stolen photos getting thrown in the faces of the whole team.

Even now, I can't imagine doing anything like that. Even with a million reasons to be angry, I can't see myself airing out the situation in front of the entire team and publicly dragging Becca's name through the mud.

It's really not my style, and it hurts to know she could be so afraid of that happening she'd keep this from me even after what we've shared.

"I was just—I couldn't—I—" Her hands clutch at the air like she's trying to pluck the right words from the atmosphere, but she just keeps stammering. Her voice gets more and more breathless. I start to worry she's going to do something extreme like tip over and pass out on the porch, but then a creak from inside the house makes us both peer into the entryway behind her.

"Becca?" a voice calls.

More creaking follows. Someone is coming down the stairs.

"Becca, is everything okay?"

A dark-haired girl wearing jeans and a yellow sweater steps into the entryway and comes to stand next to Becca. She glances between the two of us, and if our stock-still body language and the thick, choking tension in the air weren't enough to clue her in that something's up, the fact that neither of us bothers to speak must.

"Um, hey." She lifts her hand in a wave but drops it back to her side after a second. "You must be Hope? I'm Kala."

I guessed who she was as soon as I heard her voice. Something in my gut just knew.

"Hey," I bite out.

The tension takes over again. Kala opens and closes her mouth a few times.

"Um, should I go back upstairs? Is this a bad time?"

It's a *very* bad time for Kala to be here at all. This morning when I asked Becca about her Thanksgiving plans, she wasn't sure what she was doing. She didn't mention Kala. I'm trying to cling to the belief that there's a reasonable explanation for all of this, but my capacity for the benefit of the doubt is getting smaller by the second.

I need Becca to talk to me, but all she does is stare with that same wide-eyed horror.

"You guys are having Thanksgiving dinner together?" I'm trying so hard to keep my voice even I sort of sound like I'm possessed.

"Just takeout." Kala says when Becca remains silent. "There was a big deal on Chinese. We have a shit ton of food."

She laughs, but neither of us joins in.

"Okay, I think I'm gonna head back up." She tries and

fails to catch Becca's eye before looking back at me. "It was nice to meet you, Hope."

I jerk my chin down in a single, sharp nod. The stairs fire off a series of creaks when she leaves.

"Becca, I am really trying here," I say as soon as she's gone, "but you're going to have to give me *something*. Is it...is it true that your ex caught you and Kala together, and you refused to explain it?"

She opens her mouth, but no sound comes out.

"Is that true?" I ask again. I'm fighting not to sound shrill.

"Yes," she finally rasps, "but I...It wasn't...It's not like that."

We both wince at the cliché.

"So what's it like?"

She keeps staring at me, her hands fluttering in the air, grabbing at words that won't come. That's when I start to accept it: I'm not going to get what I need from her. I've been asking and asking, but she can't find it and give it to me.

That's what really makes me crumble.

My eyes start to burn and my throat gets thick, but I swipe the gathering tears away.

"I can't do this, Becca. I can't."

I turn and bound down the porch steps as the first sob claws its way up out of me. She doesn't call out or chase after me as I stumble blindly up the street. She doesn't do anything at all.

19

Becca

"This is really what you want?"

Coach Jamal's eyes look like they're in danger of popping out of his head. He's even taken his aviators off for the occasion. We're sitting at one of the picnic tables on campus, both of us wearing jackets and gloves. Even with all the funding I won for the program, there's still no office for the lacrosse coach, so we hold all our meetings outside or in coffee shops. We were heading for a Starbucks when we decided the day was nice enough to just sit down here.

Khadija thinks her dad is making faces at her and giggles. She's all bundled up in her carrier on top of the table and has spent most of the meeting staring at the orange leaves drifting off the tree branches.

"It's really what I want." I nod, and his eyes only get wider.

I take a shaky breath of crisp, autumn air. I just did it. I just told Coach Jamal I won't be on the UNS lacrosse team next year.

"Becca, I just want to be sure...this is about *you*, right?

Not the game? It was one game, and it doesn't reflect on your captaincy."

I wince. Our home match this past weekend was a disaster, and it certainly *did* reflect on my captaincy. Everything I wanted to avoid has turned into a reality: the team is tense and dysfunctional, there are endless whispers about what's going on, and we lost zero to four on our own turf. We're not knocked out of the running yet, but it was a hit to our pride and morale. Even Coach is having a tough time getting the team to bounce back. All our practices this week have been filled with sloppy plays and dejected drills.

That's not the worst part.

As far as I can tell, I've lost Hope. After that disaster of a Thanksgiving night, I tried to get in touch with her. I spent hours drafting gigantic speeches before I sent a text asking if we could talk, but she told me she needed time.

So I've been waiting. It's been almost two weeks, and I've been dragging myself through every practice where she avoids even looking at me, but nothing seems to be changing. Every day, it feels like another piece of her is gone from me, like the links between us are snapping off one by one.

"It's about me," I answer Coach. "I need to start thinking about more than lacrosse, as crazy as that sounds. It's been my life, but maybe that's the problem. I don't really know what I want to do after I finish school. It's only started occurring to me this year that I haven't even thought about it much."

He nods but stays silent. Coach always seems to know when I need a chance to just talk it out.

"I've had a good run," I continue. "I've played for UNS for four years, and that's an honor, but I need space for other things. I've talked to an academic advisor, and if I really work hard and switch some things around, there's a chance I can graduate with a double major instead of just a minor in environmental science. I wouldn't have time to keep playing next year, though, let alone keep being captain. I'll need a part-time job too, since I'll be giving up my scholarship."

Coach starts to rock Khadija's carrier. She laughs her little baby laugh and kicks her feet under her blanket.

"Becca," he says, "I don't want to make you uncomfortable, so say the word and I'll let it go, but if you need help with tuition—"

"I couldn't," I cut in, shaking my head even as my heart twinges at him offering. "I couldn't accept that from you."

"I'd be happy to talk to the department so everything is aboveboard, and you wouldn't be on the team anymore, so there wouldn't be any favoritism concerns," he insists. "You've done so much for this team. You know I couldn't have run it without you. I…okay, so maybe Coach is getting a little soft here, but I've always kind of thought of you as, you know, a daughter. It would mean a lot to make sure you can finish your degree. It would mean a lot to my wife too. Sometimes I think she's more grateful for you than me, considering how many times you've saved me during all these baby scheduling issues."

I try and fail to clear the lump in my throat. I have to look away and blink a few times before I can face him again.

This is what I mean when I tell people the team is a family to me. As much as I know I'm making the right decision, leaving still hurts like hell.

"Thank you, Coach," I choke out. "That's…You don't even know what that means. I still can't accept it, but thank you."

I pause as he chuckles and shakes his head.

"I think if I work full time all summer," I add, "and move into a smaller apartment, *and* work part-time next semester and the whole next school year, I should be able to scrape things together. It...it really helps to know you're there, though."

"Always. You know you don't just *stop* being a Lobster, right?" The side of his mouth pulls up into a grin. He lifts one of his hands and makes a claw snapping motion. "Claws out! What's the dance you weirdos are always doing?"

He jumps to his feet and starts doing a terribly uncoordinated version of the Lobster dance while I double over laughing and slapping my thighs.

"Oh my god," I gasp when he sits back down. "Why didn't I film that?"

He puts on his stern coaching voice. "That was a once in a lifetime experience for your eyes only, Moore."

"Right. Of course."

He reaches over to bop Khadija's nose, which kind of defeats the whole intimidating lacrosse coach act.

"If you're looking for a job next semester, I can see if my sports connections have anything," he tells me. "I know some people who run intramurals leagues for the city. I can't see the pay being all that spectacular, but running around a gym has got to be more fun than flipping burgers."

"Or customer service," I add with a shudder, thinking back to my last summer job coordinating kayaking bookings for demanding tourists.

"I'll ask around," Coach assures me.

"Thank you so much. That would be amazing."

It never occurred to me to look for a job in sports. That just seems too good to be true. Even a paper-pushing position for a city sports centre would be better than being stuck in another cramped booking office. Running intramurals games would be a dream, and I know the sting of leaving lacrosse behind won't hurt as bad if I still have athletics in my life. Maybe I'd even get the chance to play some casual lacrosse myself.

"I don't know how we're going to replace you as captain, Moore." Coach's voice calls me back from where I've been staring out at the lawn dotted with students, fantasizing about my as yet non-existent job. "Got any suggestions in mind?"

I only have one. She's the clear choice. I'm sure he sees it too, but when I go to say her name, I can't make a sound. I don't know how much he's heard about what happened. He knows the gist of what went on with Lisa, and he can't be oblivious to what I'm sure everyone is whispering about now.

"Hastings," he says for me, and the concern he puts into that one word turns it into something between a question and a reassurance.

I don't know which I need more.

"Yeah." I nod. "She'd be incredible. She's a natural."

"Does she want to be captain?" he asks.

"I..." I squeeze my hands into fists to ward off the pain. "I think it's something she's thought about, at least a little, but we...we aren't really talking right now."

Or possibly ever.

My nails dig into the heels of my palms so hard I'm sure they'll leave marks.

"She's a good person, that Hope Hastings. One of the best."

I nod. It hurts too much to speak. It hurts too much to hear about her being a good captain and a good person and know I lost my shot at a place in her life. I fucking *choked* when I needed to speak—over and over and over again. I did the one thing she told me not to: I kept things from her because I thought it would make both our lives easier, even if just for a little while, just until I figured it out.

She didn't deserve that. She deserved everything, right from the beginning.

Coach props one of his elbows on the table. "What I mean by that is that she's not like Lisa."

I jolt at the mention of Lisa. Coach gives me a cautious look.

"I hope that's all right to say. I just mean that...Look, I really shouldn't say this, but considering you only have a few games left on the team...I'm glad Lisa left. I'm glad all those girls left with her. She was a bully, Becca. At first, it was never enough for me to justify asking her to leave the team, but I saw it, and a lot of other people saw it too. She had a way of controlling people, and it's not your fault you got roped into that. I just wish I'd known everything at the time. I would have done more. I wouldn't have let it go so far. I'm the coach. It's my job to make sure all my players feel safe and respected. I let you all down, and I'm sorry."

"Coach." My voice cracks, and I force myself to slow down and take a deep breath. "You didn't let us down, and it wasn't that simple. I messed up too. Lisa...she *was* a bully. She did some really not okay things, but I...I mean, especially with Hope, I...God, I fucked up so bad. I just didn't want it to be like that again."

Now I really am crying. Coach waits for me to let it all go. I pull myself together after a couple minutes and stare down at my hands in my lap.

"You're tough, you know that?" he says once I'm no longer a sniffling mess. "And tenacious. You make your world into what you want it to be. It's what makes you shine on the field. If you don't like something in the game, you just...fix it. Sometimes I can't even figure out how you've done it, even if I've been standing there watching the whole thing."

I grin down at my lap. It's pretty common to hear him standing on the sidelines shouting '*I don't know how you did that, Moore, but do it again!*'

"Even your choice to leave the team and pursue a double major is impressive," he continues, "as much as it encumbers me to have to replace the team captain."

I make a face at him. "Did you just say *encumbers*?"

He shrugs. "I learned it from my wife yesterday. I'm trying it out. The point is, when you want something, you rearrange your whole life just to get it. That's the kind of person you are, and I think you need to remember that. That's all I'm saying."

He lifts both his hands in an 'okay, I'm done' gesture.

I smile at him. "Thanks. Maybe I did need to hear that."

Khadija coos at a leaf as it drifts down to land beside her carrier. Coach gazes at her like he's crazy in love before he starts patting down his pockets to find his phone.

"Oh shit. I think I'm late. I'm supposed to meet the wife for baby music class."

I hide my snort with a cough. Coach may have some soft spots, but imagining him in a room full of babies listening to some woman in a floral dress play 'Twinkle Twinkle Little Star' on an acoustic guitar is still a hilarious contrast. I wonder if he wears his aviators in the class.

"Oh yeah, we gotta go," he says after swiping at his phone screen. "You gonna be all right?"

I nod. I'm still not sure which parts of me are okay and which aren't, but after our talk, I feel more equipped to handle them all.

We say goodbye, and I shoulder my backpack to head

to the library. The campus is buzzing with activity as people head to classes and meet up to hang out on the lawns despite the chill in the air. It's only late October, but in just a few weeks, we'll all be locked up inside to face the looming threat of exams.

At the last minute, I switch paths and steer myself away from the library. I'm not sure where I'm going until I see the lacrosse field come into view up ahead. After so many treks out to practice, my feet seem to carry me here by default.

There's a football practice happening on one of the other fields, but I ignore how weird I must look as I walk all the way out to the centre line. I drop my backpack on the turf and then sit down beside it. I close my eyes and breathe deep, the cold, clear air stinging my nose as I listen to the shouts from the football field. After a couple minutes, I tip onto my back and lay spread out with my arms stretching as wide as they can. My eyes open, and I stare up at the cloud-streaked sky.

There's so much to see. There's an endless blue dome curving high above me, always changing and shifting. There's a new sky every day, every minute. Just when we think we've got nature figured out, sitting there all smug with our calculations and predictions, something happens to throw them all off course.

We can panic, or we can take a moment to watch in wonder and awe.

I want to choose more wonder. I want to stop holding onto one way of being so tightly I forget the beauty of change. There's fear in change, of course—even terror, and I feel that with every step away from the path I've protected for so long, but I was built to handle change. I am the latest link in a chain that stretches back millennia, just one incarnation in an eternal process of adaptation.

I can do this.

I can do anything.

Still lying on my back, I reach for my bag and dig around until I find my phone. I don't even realize why I've picked it up until I'm scrolling through my contacts list and stop on that name.

I press dial and bring the phone to my ear. It rings once, twice, and then halfway through the third ring, he picks up.

"Hey, Becky Boo! Haven't heard from you in a while."

I grin up at the sky and shake my head. "Dad, when are you going to stop calling me Becky Boo?"

"Hmm." He pretends to think. "How about never? Does that sound good to you?"

I laugh. "Actually, that sounds pretty perfect."

I rest my free arm behind my head, nestling onto it like a pillow as I keep watching the clouds shifting and twisting into endless new shapes.

"What's up?" he asks. His voice always reminds me of wooden matches and logs piled on a fire. Everything he says sounds warm. "I can already tell you've got something on your mind."

"Sorry I haven't called much," I reply, dodging the question for now. I just want to lay here and revel in some small talk for a few minutes. "I'm hitting that mid-semester workload."

"Don't you worry about that. I know how it is. I'm so proud of how well you do in all those crazy courses—almost as proud as I am of you being team captain. Again!"

"Aww, Dad. Thanks."

He's not usually this sentimental. He tells me he's proud, sure, but our phone calls usually ease their way into all the mushy parent stuff instead of heading there straight off the bat. I must *really* sound like something's up with me.

"I mean it," he continues. "You're a rock star. With you doing an extra year, you're going to take that team straight to the title two years in a row!"

I force myself to chuckle and ward off the ominous silence, but it doesn't take long for it to creep in. So much for a few minutes of small talk.

"Um, Dad, I actually have some news for you."

I can hear the note of wariness in his voice even though he tries to disguise it. "Oh?"

I take a deep breath as I work up the nerve to speak. Lacrosse wasn't just *my* thing growing up; it was *our* thing. Even when he came home exhausted from his two week stints on the oil fields, he was never too tired to run through some drills with me after school. He had to miss most of my games growing up, but he always called and had me walk him through the entire match while he did terrible impersonations of a sports commentator.

I'm sure he probably had dreams of teaching his kid to play hockey just like him, but he never once tried to change my mind after I got hooked on lacrosse. We turned it into something that bonded us together, something steady we could count on even when our family seemed to be falling apart.

Now I'm taking that away from him. I'm taking that away from *me*.

"Becky Boo?" he says when all my efforts to keep my emotions in check result in a loud and embarrassing sniffle. "You know you can tell me anything, right? I know I'm far away. I know I've been far away for a lot of things in your life, but I'm always your old man. You don't have to be afraid."

"I'm so afraid," I murmur. "Dad, I'm really scared."

Underneath all the dramatic revelations and drastic changes I've been making lately, that's what I am: terrified. I don't know what comes next, and it makes me feel like a little girl huddled under my grandma's quilt in my room back in Alberta, waiting to find out who was coming back and who wasn't. I could never keep track of which of my parents was supposed to be home. My bed was a tiny boat in a bottomless ocean, and I had no way to steer.

"You're safe, Becca." My dad somehow sounds fierce and gentle at the same time. "Whatever it is, you're safe. I'll make sure of it."

I don't know if he can. I don't know if anyone can; what I'm really scared of is *life*, and there's never a guarantee that will be safe. Maybe that's all we have, though: our promises to defend one another, to count on each other, to always remember we don't have to do it alone, even if we've been hurt or let down before.

"Dad, I'm not going to be on the lacrosse team next year."

He starts to say something, but I talk over him. I have to get this all out in one go.

"I'm changing some stuff around with my major, and I'm not going to have time, but that's not the only reason. It just hit me that I don't even know what I want to do when I graduate, and I'm already in my fourth year. Lacrosse has been everything to me. *Everything*. I shaped my whole life around it. Sometimes I think I don't even know who I *am* without it, but I want to find out. I have to. I have a whole life to live, and I...I...I'm sorry, Dad. I know it makes you proud of me, but I can't do it next year."

The line stays silent for a few seconds, and my whole body tenses up, bracing for his confusion or disappointment or even anger.

"Becca, I will *always* be proud of you." His voice is

shaking with sincerity, and it makes a lump form in my throat. "I'm proud of how you play lacrosse, sure, but what I'm really proud of is your dedication, your passion, your courage, your leadership. You go after what you want, and you always get it. You have those things whether you're on the field or not. You always will. I know you feel like you don't know yourself, kiddo, but I do, and you're amazing."

I reach up to rub my eyes and realize my cheeks are already streaked with tears.

"Thank you, Dad," I say, my voice thick. "Thank you."

"You'll always be my girl, Becca. We'll always be a family, you and me. You don't have to be on a lacrosse team to be sure of that."

I nod and then mumble into the phone when I remember he can't see me. For a few seconds, I'm beyond words. I don't know how he knew, but he said exactly what I needed to hear.

He's my dad, and nothing is changing that.

"There's something else," I say once I've pulled myself back together. "But don't worry. I have it figured out. I'm just bringing it up so you know I have a plan. I won't be eligible for my scholarship next year since I'm leaving the team, but I'm going to start working next semester and—"

"We'll figure it out," he interrupts. "I'll talk to your aunt, and we'll all make a plan together. You won't be in this alone."

I might need him to say it a few more times, but I'm starting to believe it. I'm not losing everything and everyone by leaving the team. Even Coach Jamal wanted me to know that.

I'm going to be okay.

"Thank you, Dad," I say again.

We stay on the phone for almost half an hour after that. My fingers and toes start to go numb from lying on the cold ground for so long, but I don't care. We talk about life in Alberta, what my aunt is up to, and how my classes are going. By the time we hang up, I'm back to laughing and smiling at the sky.

I lay there for another few minutes after I tuck my phone back in my bag. The muffled shouts and crashes from the football field are still going strong, but they don't disturb the moment of peace that's settled over me.

The only thing that keeps me from slipping fully into that peace is how much I miss her. Even with the reassurance that I have people on my side no matter what, I still feel her absence as a constant ache. I started carving out a place for her in my life before I realized what I was doing. Now that space is collapsing in on itself, and it *hurts*.

I want her back. I want to at least *try* getting her back, and maybe it's time to start figuring out how.

20

Hope

Halloween is on a weeknight this year, but that hasn't stopped the whole campus from turning into a giant party. I'm sitting on the edge of a saggy couch in some sketchy rental house a few streets over from ours. The room is packed with drunk UNS students in costumes that range from elaborate creations to cowboy hats and bunny ears worn over normal clothes.

We're still in the team's no-drinking season, so I'm stone-cold sober while I sit here watching the party get sloppier and sloppier as the night goes on. The music is loud enough that it feels like it's rattling my skull, and every part of the couch except for the tiny square of cushion I've claimed is taken up by a couple whose make-out session looks like it's about to reach the ripping-off-clothes phase.

I shift another half-inch away from them and glare as I sip my ginger ale. They don't notice. The guy is now fully on top of the girl.

"*Why* is there no furniture in this room besides this couch?" I ask the room at large. It's too loud for anyone to hear me.

We've been party-hopping for a while now so I can't be sure, but I think this house belongs to some guys on the football team. The typical 'jock college boys who don't know how to furnish or decorate their house' vibe fits. There aren't even real curtains, but I guess I'm not one to talk. We've been known to use UNS flags as window coverings in the Babe Cave.

I still shoot a judgemental look at the fleece blanket tacked over the front window anyway. I shoot a judgemental look at the whole party. The room smells like sweat and cheap beer, I have no idea where my friends are, and I've now got some girl's foot in my lap while her boyfriend dry humps her on the cushions.

"Fine! I give up! You can have the couch."

I remove the offending foot, and the two of them seem to notice me for the first time. They blink at me like I'm some kind of alcohol-induced mirage as I get up off the couch. Then they go back to making out.

I clutch my ginger ale can to my chest and edge my way through the tightly packed crowd, dodging sloshing Solo cups and waving arms. Normally I'd be in the thick of it all, shaking my ass with my friends and living our best college lives, but I'm not exactly in a partying mood.

I haven't been in what I'd call a 'good' mood since Thanksgiving. It's been over two weeks since that fiasco, and every day that goes by just leaves me staring at my phone for longer and longer, looking at the few texts and missed calls I've gotten from Becca since then.

All I've told her is that I'm not ready to talk. I don't even know if that's true. I *want* to talk to her—so badly I even dream about it most nights—but I'm scared she won't say what I need to hear. I'm scared to feel like I did that night: like I was asking and asking, and she just stood there giving me nothing. If I don't face her, I don't have to face the possibility that she might not be who I thought she was.

If I don't face her, I don't have to face the possibility of losing her.

That's what it will come to. I've spent the past two weeks realizing I'm never going to be with someone who makes me feel small ever again. I want someone who makes me feel equal in every way, who makes me feel like I'm worth trusting and relying on. I'm not going to be treated like the stupid girl who can't handle things.

That's not who I am. It doesn't matter how much I like Becca or how much I miss her; if she can't convince me I'm enough for her to trust me, I'll end this for good.

That doesn't mean I *want* to, and that's why I've been putting things off way longer than I should. The whole team is suffering. Even my friendships are suffering. I forgave my housemates for keeping things from me. Forgiveness seemed like the only way to get some normalcy in the house, but there's still tension lurking in every room I walk into. There's still something pulled so tight it feels like it could snap at any second, and I think that thing might be *me*.

Things can't go on like this forever. They just can't.

"Whoa, a turtle!"

A super drunk guy in a cowboy hat and a plaid shirt steps in front of me and blocks my path when I'm only a few feet from the front door.

I almost forgot I was dressed like a ninja turtle—a sexy ninja turtle. The Babe Cave is famous for our group costumes every year, and this time we settled on slutty Teenage Mutant Ninja Turtles. I wanted to be Mikey, but Iz called dibs, so I ended up with Leonardo to match the teal ends of my hair. I have a blue bandana with eye holes cut in it tied around my head and a matching blue bustier top on, along with elbow and knee pads. Jane went full craft mom on us and made four papier-mâché turtle shells with backpack-style straps attached to them. Mine has two plastic swords tucked behind it.

"A *hot* turtle!" the guy slurs. "With swords!"

He's teetering on his feet and squinting at me. I might be bothered if I thought he could do more than that, but instead I roll my eyes and step past him.

"Turtle, waaaaait!" he calls as I yank the front door open.

"Turtle byeeeeee!" I sing-song.

Some of my grumpiness rolls off me as soon as the cool night air hits my skin. I didn't realize how boiling hot it was in there. The din of the party is still assaulting my eardrums, but it's less overwhelming now that I've got the door shut. There's a tiny front yard with a few people milling around in it, and more are gathered on the sidewalk. The whole street is a constant parade of students heading from party to party like boozed-up trick-or-treaters.

I spot a miraculously empty lawn chair a few feet away from everyone else and plop myself down on it, ignoring how decrepit it looks. The legs make an ominous creaking sound, but they still hold my weight.

I pull my phone out of my purse to send a group text to the Babe Cave chat, letting everyone know I went out for some air. I don't think they'll miss me, which is only fair. I haven't exactly been a pleasant person to be around tonight.

I look up as a half dozen people stumble their way off the sidewalk and up the path through the lawn. Most of them seem to be dressed as Game of Thrones characters. They're laughing and shouting about whatever party they were just at. I look down at my phone and start scrolling through Instagram once they reach the door.

Light from inside floods the lawn for a moment, the noise reaching maximum volume again, but I can still hear someone say, "Yeah, yeah, I'll be there in a minute." Then the door shuts and relative quiet takes over.

I hear footsteps coming to my side of the lawn, but I only look up when someone says, "Hey. You're Hope, right?"

"No, I'm—"

The rest of my sentence gets stuck in my throat when I look up and see Kala—dressed in a Daenerys Targaryen costume consisting of a long blonde wig and a toga-like dress that seems to be made out of a twisted-up bed sheet —standing in front of me.

"I'm Leonardo," I finish. It comes out all squeaky, and I hope my bandana hides some of my cringe at my own voice.

I don't want to sound scared of her.

"Oh of course, yeah. I see it now. Teenage Mutant Ninja Turtles." She laughs, but I don't join in. "I'm, uh, I'm Kala."

"I remember."

I deepen my voice to avoid the squeak and end up overcompensating. I sound like a pre-pubescent boy trying to do Christian Bale's Batman voice.

Kala gives me a confused look. "Are you, uh, okay?"

She probably thinks I'm drunk out of my mind. I would too.

"Perfectly fine." That at least sounds like it was said by a normal human.

"Look, I get why you might be pissed at me—"

"I'm not pissed at you."

I *feel* pissed at her, but right now, I'm pissed at everyone.

I don't really have a reason to be mad at her—as far as I can tell. Becca couldn't even bring herself to give me enough information to know if I *should* be mad Kala.

"Hope, I...Look. Do you mind if I sit down?"

I was getting pretty into scrolling through Instagram over here in the dark by myself like a true angsty teenage reptile, but she seems like she's got something to say. I might be grumpy, but I'm still curious.

"Uh, sure," I answer as I look around the yard. "I'm not sure you should sit on the ground, though. It's too dark to tell what might be going on down there."

It seems like a dangerous choice considering the state of the house. I can only imagine what people may have wandered out to this lawn to do.

"This will work." Kala walks over to the tiny front porch and reaches under the edge to retrieve a neon green inner tube. She drops it onto the ground beside me and plops into the middle like she's floating around in a pool. "Comfy."

I raise my eyebrows. "Is it?"

She laughs and shakes her head. "No, not really, but it will do."

We fall silent for a moment. I reach for my ginger ale and finish it off. Kala drums her fingers on the sides of the inner tube.

"I really do feel like you're pissed at me, and I can see why," she announces. "I'd probably be pissed at me too, if I were in your position."

"Why would I be pissed? You're Becca's friend. You guys were hanging out. Nothing to be pissed about there." There's a challenge in my tone, like I'm waiting for her to contradict me.

She doesn't say anything for a while. The inner tube squeaks as she resettles herself. We both watch a big group of girls dressed as sexy Disney princesses walk by on the sidewalk, shivering and clutching their arms.

I'm shivering too. I wish I had more than papier-mâché and a bustier covering my upper body. I was planning on spending minimal time outside tonight.

"There's some stuff I'd like to tell you about Becca," Kala says once the girls are gone. "If you want to hear it. You two haven't talked since Thanksgiving, right?"

I nod. We've exchanged a few necessary words during practices and games, but nothing more than that. Just being near her makes me feel this searing combination of anger, pain, and tenderness. I want to hold her as much as I want to yell at her, and it feels like it's splitting me in two whenever I see her, never mind talk to her.

"Becca and I met when we were kids," Kala begins. "We played on the same lacrosse team in our city, and we started going to the same high school a few years later. We went all the way to the U-nineteen team together. She's my best friend. I've known her longer than almost any other friend I have. Becca is...She's intensely loyal. She's *fiercely* loyal. She's quiet about it, so I don't think most people even notice, but if she chooses to let you in—*really* let you in—you become one of the most important things in her life."

I've noticed that about her. She's loyal to the team, yes, but it's different from that. The way she talks about the people who matter to her is like nothing else. She loves just like Kala said: fiercely.

"It's true that we got together in high school," Kala continues, "but it was more about finding ourselves than finding each other. We both started realizing we were queer around the same time. I think dating each other was a way to make it real. I knew I couldn't come out to my family. I still haven't, and Becca was there for me through all of that. I mean, we were teenagers. We just felt so much about everything, and so of course we ended up directing that at each other. It only lasted a few months, and it was really awkward the whole time. We kissed like...four times, and by the fourth, we just laughed and decided we never needed to do that again. I'm still glad we shared that, though. She made me feel safe when I needed it. She's good at that."

She made me feel safe too. Whether we were in her bed or wandering around Montreal, she made me feel like she was there for me. I knew there was so much she was scared of, but she still always came through and told me what I needed to hear.

Until Thanksgiving, when she was silent.

About Kala.

"When we came to UNS, Becca fell hard and fast for this older girl on the team, Lisa. At first it was sweet, and I was happy for her, but it got ugly fast. All that loyalty Becca has, all those worries about holding onto the people she cares about...Lisa just seemed to know how to use it against her. She used *me* against her. It's taken me a while to realize just how hard Lisa was trying to pit us against each other. At the time, I thought Becca was pulling away from me, but really, she was getting pulled in half."

Kala's getting more and more worked up as she speaks. Her wig has slipped a little, and her lopsided hairline would be funny if the conversation weren't so serious.

I know what it's like to have your insecurities thrown in your face by someone you care about. Ethan did it to me in front of the whole team, and I'm starting to realize Becca must have gone through pretty much the same thing.

"Becca may have messed up by waiting so long to tell Lisa about our history, but Lisa did some totally unacceptable things when she found out. She stole pictures out of

Becca's room. She hung around her house just to see if she was home. She got...scary. I didn't even see it for what it was at the time. I was...I was having a pretty bad year myself." She goes quiet for a few seconds, staring down at her hands in her lap. "Even with everything she had going on, Becca still supported me. At the time, I thought she was leaving me behind, but now I see she was just doing the best she could under the circumstances."

I nod, waiting for her to go on. This sounds like the Becca I know. I'm not even sure what to trust at this point, but I want to trust this. It feels right.

"I was...kind of a mess in first year." Kala's voice is lower now, laced with a distant pain. "My family is pretty strict and conservative, and being away at college just made me feel so torn between who I am and who they want me to be. There was so much pressure coming from every direction—to get good grades, to succeed on the team, to fit in on campus, to be cool and have a social life, to start dating, to *not* date, to somehow *find myself* the middle all that...One night I was sitting in my dorm studying, and I couldn't take it anymore. I needed to get out of my head."

She scoffs at herself and lets out a dark chuckle. I'm trying to decide if I should reach over and give her hand a squeeze. There's an ominous flatness in her voice that has my heart speeding up, waiting for the rest.

"So I ended up outside the dorm of this guy I knew had a crush on me. We had sex. Once. It was my first time having sex with anyone. I'm not even sure I liked it. I definitely didn't do it for the right reasons, and...a few weeks later, there it was on the pregnancy test."

"Oh, Kala." Now I do reach over and take her hand, just for a second. She squeezes me back before I let go.

"Becca was the one who talked me out of blaming

myself. Becca was the one who sat with me while I cried for weeks. Becca was the one who talked all the options through with me, and Becca was the one who went with me to the clinic. I couldn't have done it without her. Even though our friendship hadn't been going so great, she dropped everything for me. I didn't want to be alone after, so we went to her place…and there was Lisa, waiting to ask us why Becca wasn't at the library like she said."

I can't hold back a gasp as it all clicks into place. Kala gives me a knowing look and nods.

"Yeah, that was the day. The infamous day. I'd already made Becca swear not to tell anyone. Lisa was the last person on earth I wanted hearing about it, and it fucking sucked to have that turned into a problem. Just getting an abortion made me feel so guilty I hated myself, and now suddenly it was also breaking up my best friend's relationship and our entire fucking lacrosse team. I was mad at myself. I was mad at Becca. I was furious at Lisa. Then things just built and built until everything…exploded. We lost the league qualifiers. Half the team left. My friendship with Becca almost didn't survive."

"Oh my god," I whisper.

I had no idea things were that bad. Kala just sits there nodding for a few moments before she speaks again.

"I want you to know I'm not telling you this because I feel obligated. I don't owe anyone this story, but…I've done a lot of work to stop feeling guilty about my choices. I don't hate myself. I don't feel so ashamed that I want to lock it all up and pretend it didn't happen anymore. As much as Becca probably needs you to hear this, I need to say it just as much. What I went through wasn't the problem then, and it isn't the problem now. Telling you all this helps me believe that, and I hope…I hope it helps you believe some stuff too—namely that Becca really cares about you and was never trying to hurt you. She just didn't want any of that to happen again."

At first, I don't have words. My heart is hammering against my chest like it's trying to break free of my ribcage so it can go find Becca right now, but the rest of me stays motionless in my chair.

"I know she still made some mistakes," Kala adds. "I just...I overheard some of your conversation that night, and I've been wanting to talk to you ever since. You mean a lot to her."

She means a lot to me.

I'm still hurt. I'm still frustrated. There's still a lot I need to hear from Becca herself, but I'm ready to hear it now. I'm ready to believe she wasn't trying to hurt me.

I've become so ready to assume people want to hurt me: Becca, my roommates, the team. It's like I swung from naive to hyper-vigilant when what I really needed was to land somewhere in the middle. I don't want to be the kind of person who questions my friends' motives all the time. I don't want to be skeptical of love, in any shape or form.

"Thank you," I say after a moment. "Thanks for telling me that."

"Thanks for listening."

A shiver runs through my body, and Kala rubs hers hands along her bare arms. I was so caught up in the conversation I forgot about the cold, but now I can't ignore my goose bumps and chattering teeth.

"You want to head inside?" Kala asks.

"I think we better."

I stand up, and Kala goes to do the same, but the inner tube is so low to the ground she only raises herself a few inches before falling back inside. We both burst out laughing, letting all the tension drain from the moment as we clutch our stomachs and make everyone in the yard turn to stare at the noise we're making. I get myself under control enough to help pull her up, and we walk into the party side by side.

Daenerys Targaryen and Leonardo the Ninja Turtle: an unlikely alliance, but an alliance nonetheless.

"Those are my friends!" I shout over the noise when I spot the three of them in the crowd. "Come dance with us!"

I pull Kala along behind me as I weave and dart my way through all the people in the room. Iz, Paulina, and Jane cheer when they spot me. It's too loud for me to introduce Kala, so I just start dancing, and everyone follows my lead. We've only been going for about a minute when Little Mix's 'Wasabi' comes on and the four of us scream while Kala laughs and looks slightly afraid at the same time.

"IT'S OUR JAM!" Paulina shrieks.

We break out our most exuberant dance moves, our turtle shells shaking and sliding around as we drop it low. It's the first time I've felt like myself in weeks. It's the first time things between the four of us have felt right.

Later tonight, I'll give them an apology—a better one than I did after Thanksgiving. I don't want them keeping things from me, but I also believe they were only trying to have a nice Friendsgiving dinner. None of us deserves to have almost two and half years of friendship jeopardized over that.

For now, we dance. We dance until my feet hurt and my cheeks are strained from smiling, and I can't do anything but believe this will all turn out all right.

21

Becca

"Okay, does everyone know where they're going?"

I scan the faces of the team where they're standing in a semi-circle in front of me. Coach is right there with them. We're all dressed for practice and holding sticks, but we won't actually be playing today.

The only person missing from the field is Hope.

"Aye aye, Captain!" Jane shouts, raising her stick in the air. Everyone follows suit, and I find myself beaming at them even as my stomach continues to churn like it's been doing all day.

I spent Halloween night alone in my room drafting up plans for this moment. It took a week to pull it all together —and to work up the nerve—but now everything is ready. There's no stopping this. Hope will already be getting close to the locker room, where she'll find a set of instructions.

The team heads out to their designated spots all spaced a couple metres apart along the path between the field and the athletics centre. A few of them are stationed inside too, forming a chain of lacrosse players that leads all the way to the locker room. Even Coach has taken a spot in line.

Each of them has part of a letter I wrote to Hope stored in their pockets. The first section is waiting for her along with a lacrosse ball on one of the locker room benches, and the final section is clutched in my shaking hands.

I've been writing a lot of letters lately. I wrote one to the whole team, minus Hope, and sent it out as an email to announce I'd be stepping down as captain and leaving lacrosse at the end of the season. I explained my reasoning, and for the first time, I really let myself open up and explain to everyone just how much it's meant to have my UNS family. I wanted to respect Hope's privacy, so I didn't go into detail about the two of us, but I did apologize for letting my personal life affect everyone's playing. I said sorry for choosing fear over trust in the people who've always had my back.

Then I let them know I had a nomination for our new captain and needed help making the announcement. Part of me expected everyone to say no. Part of me expected a few 'good riddance' emails in reply. I would have deserved it, but like always, the Lobsters came through. I've even gotten a bunch of thank-you's for all I've done as captain, and a few people went out of their way to assure me we all bring our personal issues onto the field sometimes.

Even more of them echoed what Coach told me when I made the announcement to him: I'll always be a Lobster.

"I think she's coming!" one of the girls down the line shouts.

My first reaction is to gulp like a cartoon character as a fresh wave of nerves shoots through my body. I smooth the front of my already smooth red lacrosse sweater and strain my eyes to catch the first glimpse of Hope coming around the corner of the distant building.

A few seconds pass. Then a full minute goes by.

"Hmm. False alarm!" my teammate shouts back to me.

It doesn't bring me any relief. I start shifting from foot to foot, clutching the letter in my hands and coming dangerously close to shredding it in a nervous fit.

Having the team back me on this meant the world, but the only reaction I've really been waiting for is Hope's. I've lain awake in bed the past few nights, staring straight up at the ceiling and imagining all the ways this moment could go.

She might turn around and go home as soon as she sees the first letter, vowing never to speak to me again for the rest of her life. That would probably be the worst case scenario, and the longer I stand here fidgeting and waiting for her to arrive, the harder it gets to convince myself that's not exactly what's happening.

My stick is lying on the ground at my feet, and I narrowly avoid tripping over it as I shuffle around. I order myself to stay still; falling on my face and greeting Hope with a bloody nose would also be pretty high up there in the worst case scenario list.

Staying still doesn't go very well, so I distract myself by unfolding the papers in my hand and reading over the words I've already memorized. I have the full document here, including the part I left for Hope in the locker room:

Dear Hope,

I've been staring at my computer screen for over half an hour, watching the cursor blink and wondering how to start this. It feels like there's a long chain of words coiled up inside me, and I'm searching and searching for the loose end that will let me begin unwinding it all.

That's what these weeks with you have been like: an unwinding. Spending time with you made me aware of all the knots that were keeping me from being the best person I can be. You made me want to undo them for the very first time. It's been messy. I mean, fuck, has it ever been messy, but it's also been exactly what I needed.

I know I haven't always been exactly what you needed. I've been afraid. I've been silent when I should have been loud. I thought I was playing it safe, but really, all I did was hurt people. I hurt you.

I'm so sorry, Hope. I was so scared of the past repeating itself I stopped paying attention to all the signs telling me just how different and amazing the present is. You didn't deserve that. You deserved to have me take your hand and share it all with you: the good and the bad, the fear and the joy.

I have never seen you as anything other than amazing, capable, and strong. You shine in every part of your life, and I'm sorry for handling things in a way that made you doubt how much I respect you. I want to untangle all the knots in this chain and make everything clear.

So here's how this works: we're going to do a new lacrosse drill I've come up with—a catch and cradle chain, specifically. If you're up for it, you can take this ball and cradle it out of the locker room to your first partner. They'll give you the next part of this letter and cradle the ball while you read, or they can read it out loud to you. I've told them all that's okay. I want this to work whatever way is best for you. Then they'll pass back to you, and you'll continue up the chain.

I've thought about you at least once a minute every day, Hope. You've changed so much for me in such a short amount of time, and I want you to see that. Whatever else happens, you deserve to see just how wonderful you are.

Bye for now,
Becca

"*Now* she's coming!" A shout from down the line makes me snap my head up, but there's still no sign of Hope. "She's still in the building, but she's started!"

I didn't think my heart could manage to climb any higher up my throat, but it does. My breath is coming in short little spurts now, and I force myself to shut my eyes and slow everything down.

All I can do is my best. All I can do is present her with the truth and make peace with whatever happens next.

Head up. Heart strong.

I still don't have the patience to just stand here waiting for her to arrive, so I keep myself busy by reading through the rest of the master copy of the letter Hope will be receiving bit by bit.

You deserve an explanation for everything that's happened, but I can't do that without first telling you exactly what you mean to me. The absolute worst part of this mess is that it's made you feel looked down on. Hope, you are one of the most looked up to people I know—not just by me, but by the whole team. Some people shine in a way that makes everything around them go dim, but not you. You light the world up. Cheesy? Maybe, but it's absolutely true.

I noticed you the first time I saw you. You have that effect on people. I'm not going to lie and say a big part of that wasn't your kickass lacrosse skills (yes, I've always thought you were a star player, even when I was calling you a troll). I'm also not going to lie and say a big part of that wasn't how gorgeous you are and how dangerously cute you look in your glasses (yes, I was very into you even when I thought there was a zero chance probability of it coming to anything). Neither of those were the main reason, though. When I looked at you, even from the very start, it was like I felt this nudge at my back urging me towards something different. It was like I could sense my course shifting inch by inch every day until I finally collided with you.

I'd been pretty set in my course for a long time before I met you. I did everything I could to bring security to what was a pretty insecure life. I wanted things and people I could count on, and I see now I tried to achieve that through control instead of the one thing it really takes to rely on others: trust.

I scan through the next few paragraphs, wincing as I wonder what she'll think when she reads them. I wrote out the story of my history with Kala, the disaster that was my first year, and the way things blew up with Lisa and the team. Every words was like pulling teeth, but when I had it all down on paper, I realized how much better I felt with it all out of me.

Hope deserved that from the start, but at least she has it now. There's still no sign of her on the field, so I keep making my way through the pages in my hands.

I know you probably still have questions, and I'm happy to answer them, but when it comes to that day with Kala, I still have the same answer: I was helping a friend when she needed me. It wasn't right to lie to Lisa about being busy studying, and I won't be doing that to anyone again, but I will always protect Kala's privacy. I understand if that isn't enough of an explanation for you, but I hope you can believe it.

After that, I doubled down on living my life with the tightest control I could manage. I held onto the few things that hadn't been blown to bits and told myself nothing would make me let go.

That's not a life, though. That's not living, and every minute I've spent with you has made me see that more and more. Life changes. It's always moving and shifting, just like the sea or the sky. The world grows and evolves, and we have to grow and evolve right along with it. Counting on people isn't about asking them not to change; it's about trusting them to keep being there for you even when they do change.

Hope, just by being you, you've shown me how narrow the life I was living was, how stuck I was. I kept my head down, but you lifted it up. I'm ready to change, and I realized so much of that just by being around you.

The thud and clatter of a lacrosse ball hitting someone's basket reaches my ears just before I get to the final few paragraphs—the ones I plan to read to Hope out loud. I follow the sound down to the end of the field and gasp when I see her. She's just made it around the corner of the athletics centre, and she's got her head bent over a piece of paper while Paulina stands grinning at her and cradling the ball.

Her glasses are missing; she must have already put her contacts in for practice. Her teal-tipped hair is pulled back in a ponytail, and she's wearing leggings and a baggy UNS sweater. Even now, I can't stop myself from getting a little dazed by how sexy the whole ensemble is on her.

She finishes reading and stuffs the paper in the front pocket of her sweater. I watch, frozen in place, as she catches a pass from Paulina and starts cradling in turn. I expect her to run to the next girl in line, but instead, she stays right where she is and peers across the field.

She's looking right at me.

I gasp again.

She's too far for me to read the details of her expression. I can at least tell she's not glaring at me, which I take as a good sign, but she's not smiling either. From where I'm standing, her face looks oddly blank, like she hasn't worked out what she's feeling yet, or like she's trying to hide it.

We're locked in place for a few seconds. I notice the team members on the field all looking back and forth between us, but all I have eyes for is Hope. For those few seconds, it's just us on this field. It's just us in this world.

She's made it this far. Something sparks and flares to life in my chest as I start to believe there might still be a chance.

The moment breaks, and Hope continues making her way up the line. She gets closer and closer, passing off with each teammate and reading the note they've been given or listening to a few as they read out loud. She doesn't look at me again, but now that she's only a few metres away, I can watch the shifts in her features as she reads. I see her eyebrows draw together and her forehead crease at times, but I also see the corners of her mouth lift and the way she raises her hand to her lips every once in a while.

I'm so focused on every miniscule detail and what it

might mean that I don't register how close she's gotten until she only has one note left before mine. Jane is positioned a couple metres ahead of me, and before I have time to turn into a crumbling pile of nerves, Hope is taking the ball from her and turning to me.

I don't hear her feet on the grass. I don't hear the click of the ball pinging between the edges of her basket as she cradles. I don't even hear my own breath. Everything is silent as I watch her. She hasn't met my eye in weeks, but now she doesn't look away even for a second.

I can't think. Everything has faded to black—everything except her.

She's the beginning.

The words come from the same part of me that recognized her before I even really knew what I was recognizing. Hope is the beginning of so much for me, and if we make it through this moment, it might be the beginning of us.

My muscle memory kicks in as she prepares to toss me the ball. I'm still clutching the letter, but I manoeuvre things around to grip my stick with both hands and catch the ball like I've done thousands of times. I feel the impact travel down the stick into my hands. I start cradling on instinct, but after a moment, I lower my stick so it's crossing my body and then bend to set it down with the ball still in my basket.

I look down to settle the stick on the turf, and when I stand back up, I notice Hope's eyes are shining. She's opening and closing her mouth like she wants to speak, and for a second, I almost let her. I'm aching to hear what she has to say, but I need to finish this letter first.

She needs to hear everything.

I straighten out the papers in my hands and flip to the right page. The typed black letters are jumping around, too blurry for me to read, and it takes me a moment to realize it's because my hands are shaking.

I try to start, but my jaw is clamped shut. A wave of icy panic hits, freezing my muscles even more. This is exactly how I felt when she was standing on my porch that night, demanding an answer I couldn't find the words to give.

Not again. Not again. Not again.

I stare down at the trembling paper, but the words are still shaking too much for me to read, like I'm trying to decipher a billboard I'm flying past on a highway. I'm going to crash.

"Becca."

Hope's hand is warm where it grips mine, steadying me. The paper stops shaking. I still can't look up from the words.

"Becca, it's okay."

I shake my head. It's not okay. My jaw is still locked tight, and I'm breathing so fast through my nose I doubt I could talk even with my mouth open. The tips of her shoes are only a few inches from mine. Her thumb brushes my wrist, and all I want is to look at her, pull her closer, tell her everything, but I don't. I can't.

"It's okay," Hope murmurs. "One step at a time. Just breathe with me. In. Out. In. Out."

I do what she says, and it only takes a few rounds before we're both chuckling even as I cling to her instructions like a lifeline.

"There we go," she says. "Much better."

"I..." I stop to swallow down the hoarseness in my voice and force myself to go on. "I have more to read to you."

"You do?"

I nod. I'm still staring at the paper. "I just...I don't know why I'm such a wreck right now. I—I—"

I cut myself off and focus on breathing again. Hope's grip on me tightens.

"It's okay," she says again. "Kala...Kala talked to me. On Halloween. She told me what happened."

That makes me look up. Hope's eyes get wide at what I'm sure must be the extreme shock written all over my face, but she softens and lifts the corner of her mouth after a second.

"Yeah. I've been...I've been trying to figure out what to say to you ever since."

I blink several times. "O-oh?"

I don't know if that's a good thing.

"Yes." Her smile gets wider. "Looks like you beat me to it. I definitely wasn't planning anything as impressive as this."

"I just—I just—"

In. Out. In. Out.

I focus on her eyes and nothing else.

"I just need you to hear this, Hope. I want you to know."

I drop my eyes to the paper again, finally ready to read. Hope squeezes my hand a final time before stepping back to give me some space. She doesn't go far, and she still has that soft smile on her face.

In. Out. In. Out.

Just like the ocean.

"There's so much I haven't given myself a chance to explore yet," I begin reading, "and even though it's scary, it's time to start. I've decided to switch my courses around next year so I can graduate with a double major. It's occurred to me that I might not even want to work in kinesiology at all, and I'm excited to make environmental science a bigger part of my life and give myself more options. Of course, that's going to mean spending a crazy amount of time on school work. That's part of the reason I've made this next decision, but mostly, I'm doing it because I want to get to know *me*. I want to be everything I can be, for myself and also for the people I—I care about."

My voice trembles, and I look up at her, hoping she'll see everything else I typed out and then deleted because I wasn't sure how this moment would go: I want to be all these things for *her* too, if she's willing to stick around while I become them.

I don't know how much she understands from the glance we share, but her eyes are shining again. She dips her chin in a nod.

"This will be my last season on the lacrosse team, as captain and as a player."

Hope gasps. "Becca, you don't have to—"

I look up again and see her face is creased with distress.

"I want to," I tell her. "I need to."

She looks like she wants to say more, but she stays quiet so I can start reading again.

"I'll always be grateful for lacrosse and what it's given me. It will always be a big part of who I am, but I'm ready to be other things now too. I don't...I don't know if I can ask you for a second chance, Hope. I don't know if that's fair, and the last thing I want to do is keep being unfair to you, but I will say this."

I look up, just to be sure everyone is in position. Hope has been so focused on me she hasn't noticed the whole team gathering behind her. Jane flashes me a thumbs up from her spot at the head of the group.

Jane has been a big part of pulling this day together, especially when it came to making sure Hope came to practice alone without getting suspicious. After I sent the email to the team announcing I was giving up my captaincy, I asked Jane to meet up with me.

I know how much a best friend's support means, and I wanted Jane to hear the truth and believe it as much as I wanted the same for Hope. We talked for a long, long time, and by the end of it, she was even more ready to make this plan happen than me.

I bite the inside of my cheek to keep from smiling at her. I don't want Hope turning around just yet.

"Hope, you are an incredible combination of so many things. You're a hilarious goof who can turn anything into a good time, but you're also focused, responsible, and always ready to get serious when it counts. You lead by example, not force, and that's what makes your leadership so inspiring. I know there have been things in your life that have made you doubt yourself, but no one on this team has ever doubted you, and despite what the past few weeks might indicate, I've never doubted you either. You have what it takes to do anything you want, and if this is something that you want, then I..."

Now I do stare past Hope and grin at the team. They all look like they're holding their breath, and even Coach is on his tiptoes, leaning forward to catch every word I say.

"I nominate Hope Hastings to be the next UNS lacrosse captain!" I shout in the loudest, most authoritative captain voice I can manage.

The team breaks into roaring applause, jumping around and waving their sticks as they start chanting Hope's name. She whirls around, and when she looks back over her shoulder at me, her face has gone slack with shock. I'd laugh if I wasn't still so nervous. My stomach is so twisted I don't know if it will ever straighten out.

I move to stand beside Hope. She keeps looking between me and the team like she's waiting for something to click into place. Her mouth opens and closes as a few times while the team keeps carrying on with their celebrating. They've started doing the Lobster dance now. Even Coach is getting in on it, to everyone's delight and mockery.

"Hope?" I say, moving in even closer so she can hear me. Our arms are just a few centimetres away from brushing. "You don't have to accept if you don't want to."

I expected her to say something by now, and the longer her silence goes on, the more dread seeps into my system.

"I...I just..." She turns from watching the team to blink at me. "You want *me* to do it? *They* want me to do it? *Me*?"

I risk a grin. "In case you couldn't tell, they're in unanimous agreement over my choice."

Her eyes are so wide. "But I...*Me*?"

"Yeah, you. I really meant all those things I said. You'd be perfect at it."

"And we think you'd be perfect at it too!"

Hope turns around to face Jane, who's crept up behind us. I watch as Jane pulls a piece of paper out of her sweater's front pocket and makes a big show of clearing her throat.

"We have some letters for you too, Hopey. When Becca told us all she was nominating you for captain, we wanted to make sure you knew you're everyone's top pick."

She heads back to the team, who are all lining themselves up in front of us and pulling out papers of their own. Hope glances at me, her eyes getting rounder by the second.

"Did you know about this part?"

I shake my head, just as shocked and overjoyed as she is. "I had no idea."

"Hear ye, hear ye!" Jane is first in line. She holds up her slip of paper and starts to read. "I accept this nomination with my whole heart. Hope, you are one in a million, and I know you'll be my best friend for all of this life and probably the next. You can handle *anything*. I've seen you do it again and again. You're going to be a right fine captain, and I can't wait to see where you take our team. I love you."

She lowers the paper and beams at us before trudging to the back of the line. Paulina steps up next.

"I accept this nomination too. Hope, you are so inspiring. I've never met anyone who can light up a party like you and still be one of the most responsible and hardworking people I know. We can always count on you, and you can count on us to follow you wherever you lead us, Cap!"

Iz takes their turn next. "I accept this nomination hands down! You're a badass motherfucker, Hope, and I'm lucky to call you one of my best friends. I'll be lucky to call you my captain too. Claws out, *chica*! We love you."

The praise goes on and on. Even Coach Jamal has prepared a little something. Hope stays next to me the whole time, tears streaking her face. She doesn't bother to hide them or wipe them away. She smiles through all the crying, and when the last speech has been made, she turns to me and nods before facing the group.

"I-I-I..." She stutters for a moment and takes a deep breath. "I really don't know what to say, guys, other than...I accept."

Another ear-splitting round of cheering takes over, and as we stand laughing at all the commotion going on in front of us, the side of Hope's arm presses into mine, and then her pinky curls around mine too. My breath catches in my throat. All the cheering dims. I can hear my heartbeat. I know it's impossible, but I feel like I can hear her heartbeat too, pulsing in the veins of her little finger that's wrapped around mine like a promise.

"You meant all of it?"

I nod.

"You said...you said you didn't think you could ask for a second chance," she says.

I nod again. I've stopped breathing. She's so close now. I've been craving to have her this close for weeks, and I don't care who might be watching.

I don't care about any of that anymore.

"I think you should ask for one."

The corners of my eyes start to sting, but I can't cry. Not now. Not yet.

"Hope...I want to be with you. I want to be with you for real. You mean so much to me, and I want to do this. The right way. I promise to give you my best. I'm not hiding anymore. Can we...can we give this another shot?"

She cups one of my cheeks in her hand as her whole face stretches into one huge, beaming smile brighter than any sun I've ever seen.

And then she kisses me. She kisses me, and I kiss her back, and maybe it's only our lacrosse team going crazy, but it feels like the whole world cheers just for us.

22

Hope

I don't think I've ever been this sweaty in my life. We're playing an outdoor game in November, but my jersey is damper than it's ever been during a humid summer practice. Even my lacrosse socks are soaked.

It's a super sexy look.

Despite the cold, the sweat makes sense. In all my years of lacrosse, I don't think I've ever played this hard. Lacrosse's nickname of 'the fastest game on two feet' feels like an understatement for our game today. The ball has to have travelled up and down the field a record-breaking number of times.

We're down to the last ten minutes of the game—the game that will determine who takes home the title this year. We've been tied two to two with the University of Toronto for almost half an hour. I can feel the tension radiating off the crowd as they wait for the next goal like sharks hungry for blood.

We're all hungry. We're all starving for victory. Toronto might have the home field advantage, but they haven't worked like UNS has just to be in this league in the first place. We're here to prove ourselves, and we're fighting for it like gladiators to the death.

Or something equally dramatic and violent.

"COME ON! COME ON! COME ON!" I scream around my mouth guard as our defenders spring into action.

I'm like a caveman flooded with an overdose of testosterone as I stalk the field's midline. As an attacker, I'm not allowed to go past it, so I focus on keeping my eyes trained to the ball, anticipating where it will go next so I can set myself up in the best position.

I catch sight of Becca doing the same thing. Her hair shines like a flame in the chilly afternoon sunlight. A cloud of condensation forms in front of her face every time she breathes out.

We don't acknowledge each other, but we don't need to. Our teamwork is fluid and flawless. We're like one machine negotiating the field. The two goals we've scored this game came from Becca and I's passes to each other. We're in sync, linked together in a way I'm not even sure I understand.

It's been three weeks since I walked into an empty locker room to find a note from Becca sitting on the bench. The whole thing still feels like a dream, like one of those moments you replay for the rest of your life and wonder, 'Did that really happen?'

But it did happen. Becca did that for me. Becca did that for herself too, and that's really what convinced me to give this another shot. She didn't just say sorry; she realized we both needed her to make changes, and that's what has made these past three weeks so incredible.

That's what has me looking forward to an incredible future.

With her.

We haven't had the girlfriend talk yet, but we're definitely dating now—real dates to real places where we don't have to look over our shoulders all the time and sneak back in the house when we go home. I won't lie; a little sneaking around was fun and even sexy at times, but I think I've maxed out on sneak appeal for possibly the rest of my life.

And I have all the sexiness I could ever ask for. I really am going to have to start sneaking back into the house again if I spend any more nights with Becca this week. My friends are not subtle with all their jokes about how often I've been 'banging the captain.'

I will admit that accidentally showing up to practice in a shirt with Becca's name on the back instead of mine was asking for it.

I watch Becca jog a few feet up the field, her attention fixed on the action still happening down near our goalie, and even amidst all the tension of the game, I still feel my throat go dry as I watch the flex of her leg muscles.

I had those legs wrapped around my waist just two nights ago. I had them over my shoulders too.

I bite my lip and catch myself smirking. Becca and I have been very creative about 'making up' and 'getting to know each other more.'

"HASTINGS! MOVE!"

CJ's bellow from the sidelines makes me jump. I focus back on the game and find the action has started moving up the turf, way on the other side of the field from me.

"Fuckity fuck fuck!" I mumble around the plastic in my mouth as I sprint so fast my legs burn and a fresh layer of sweat coats my body.

I force my way into the chaos surrounding the Toronto player who has the ball. The defender who's assigned to mark me springs into action, obscuring my view as she mirrors my every movement. I do my best to lose her, ducking and weaving around the action until a lightning-fast interception sends the ball whipping up to Bailey's waiting basket.

A surge of adrenaline sears through my system, giving my fatiguing legs the boost they need to get up the field faster than anyone else.

Almost anyone else.

A shadow and flash of movement in my peripheral vision makes me turn my head even as I keep pounding up the turf at full speed. Becca is only a few steps behind me. She cuts away to my left as we approach the net, setting ourselves up to help Bailey.

I can feel the rush of an impending goal building and building like a drug pumping into my veins. We're going to score. There can't be more than a few minutes left. This could be the goal that wins us the championship for the first time in UNS history.

I can hear the crowd getting rowdier, but it's muffled. All my senses are tuned into the game and hyper-focused on the ball.

I can see it all in my mind before it even happens. Bailey ducks around the girl blocking her, scanning the field for someone to pass to. I move closer. Her attention locks on me. The ball arcs through the air, avoiding all the sticks of the Toronto players diving for it to land with a thump in my basket.

I turn to the net, but the defender I thought I ditched appears out of nowhere, blocking my shot and nearly making me trip from the shock of her appearance. I catch my footing just in time for two midfielders to show up behind me, boxing me in.

I'm surrounded. There's nowhere for the ball to go. The only gap I could make a pass through is closing, and I can't see any of my teammates on the other side.

I glance over both my shoulders. I'm trapped. Both teams are closing in, but there's no one to help me. They're all in the wrong places.

"HOPE!"

Most people wouldn't recognize the garbled shout as my name, but I've been playing lacrosse long enough to recognize full sentences spoken with a mouth guard in. I twist to look back at the only gap in the players so fast my neck twinges in protest.

I ignore the pain. Becca is right where I need her to be.

The pass is perfect. Her shot at the net is perfect. I don't see what happens after she aims and launches the ball, but the split second of dead silence followed by an explosive mix of cheering and groaning from the crowd makes it clear.

She scored. The Lobsters scored.

"YES!" I scream as everyone backs off from where they're still caging me in. "YES!"

"TWO MORE MINUTES, LOBSTERS!" I hear Coach thundering from the sidelines. "JUST KEEP THAT LEAD FOR TWO MORE MINUTES!"

Two minutes. We can keep them from scoring for two minutes. We could do it in our sleep.

This championship is ours.

Iz charges past me, shaking their fist and shouting something I only just make out as, "NO RAGRETS!"

I whoop and shake my stick in reply, following after them to set up for the face-off.

When we toasted to our reunion on my first night back at the Babe Cave, I told my friends I wanted this year to be something special, something to remember. I wanted to take chances and make everything count.

All things considered, I'd say I'm off to a pretty—as Jane would say—friggin' great start.

We win the face-off, and as soon as the ball is in play, I'm flying around the field, pushing and straining through the burn and fatigue to give these last two minutes my all. Toronto's team is playing as hard as we are, but I know we want it more. *I* want it more. Everything in me is screaming for victory.

The ball changes possession so fast and so many times I'm sure we must be just a blur to the audience. As the seconds tick by, I can feel the desperation in the stands grow like it's a storm cloud gathering over the field, waiting for the chance to split open and streak the sky with thunder.

We're close. We're so close.

I catch a pass from one of our midfielders and start tearing up towards the goal. I've lost all sense of time, but we can't have more than a few seconds left. The end of the field is swamped with players. There's almost no chance I'll score, but I only need to keep *them* from scoring until our win is called.

I search for someone to pass to, and then I see it.

My shot.

It's another crazy, potentially impossible opportunity no player in their mind would risk taking—just like that winning goal I scored during our first home game.

Maybe I *am* crazy sometimes. Maybe I have reckless moments that seem irresponsible, but maybe that's okay. Maybe sometimes you just need to take the damn shot and stop worrying about what everyone else will say.

So I take it. I take the shot, and we win the title.

Everything after the ball hits the back of the net is a blur. I think we even have to go through another face-off and finish out the last few seconds of the game, but I don't remember any of it. I'm in an adrenaline and endorphin-fueled haze, and I only come back to myself when I'm squished into a dog pile in the middle of the field with all my screaming friends surrounding me.

We're pure joy, all of us somewhere between sobbing, laughing, and shouting at the top of our lungs.

This is what we've worked for.

This is why we do it.

This is why we've all got little lobsters tattooed on our ankles: because nothing beats the feeling of being a team.

I squeeze the players closest to me and make a promise to all these people right here and now.

I'm going to be the best captain I can be. I'm going to be the leader you deserve.

It's a tall order. It's an order that still terrifies me with its immense, demanding tallness, but I'm ready, and I know I'll have all the help I need.

I extricate myself from the pile so I can head to the sidelines and grab some much-needed water, lifting up my goggles so I can swipe away the dampness on my cheeks as I do. I'm not sure what's sweat and what's tears. I'm going to need the longest shower of my life after this.

"There she is! Our shooting star!"

Coach comes over from where he's been alternating between hugging his wife and hoisting Khadija up in the air like she's a trophy. He's taken his aviators off, and his whole face is lit up brighter than I've ever seen it. He's practically bouncing on the turf, and I beam right back at him.

"I don't even know what to say, Hastings! That was brilliant."

I finish slurping down my water and grin. "Thanks, Coach."

"I'd expect nothing less from our future captain."

I feel my smile falter as my stomach flips at the word. I

know I'm ready to be captain. It's exactly what I want, but that fear of not being enough still creeps in sometimes.

"You really think I can do it?" I ask, quiet enough that he has to lean closer to hear.

He pulls back and stares at me for a moment, his face pursed like he's thinking something over.

"Hope," he finally says, "I think you can do anything you want, and if you don't believe me, you can just ask her."

He nods over my shoulder, and I turn to find Becca standing a few feet away from our pile of teammates. She's looking right at me. Her goggles are slung around her neck. Her sweaty jersey is clinging to the front of her body. Her hair is a mess, and she's somehow gotten dirt streaked across one of her cheeks.

And she's beautiful.

She's so fucking beautiful.

I don't even answer Coach. I just run to her. I crash into her arms and almost take us both down, and as soon as we've caught our balance, I kiss her.

I kiss her just like I've wanted to all along: without fear, without worry, right where everyone can see just how hard I've fallen for this gorgeous, determined, stubborn, strong, sweet, and beautiful girl.

"HOW ARE YOU THIS BEAUTIFUL?" Becca pulls my face down to hers and tangles her hands in my hair. "Seriously, how?"

I'm straddling her lap wearing nothing but my bra and underwear. Becca is completely topless but still has her sparkly red celebration shorts on. The rough material feels surprisingly good against my thighs, and I can't help grinding into her. She swears, giving up waiting for an answer to her question, and starts kissing my neck instead. I moan, thrusting my hips even harder against hers.

Sometimes I think she must be taking notes about my body. She knows exactly how to drive me crazy. Her lips always find just the right spot. She adds a scrape of her teeth that makes me shiver and throw my head back, giving her access to more of my skin.

I always want to give her more of me.

"I want to see your tits," she murmurs, reaching around for the clasp of my bra.

I hiss. "I love when you say things like that."

"Oh yeah?" She glances up and catches my eye. "You like it when I tell you that you have the best fucking tits and I need my mouth on them right now?"

"I...yes."

She chuckles at my stammering and helps me pull my bra off. The cool air of the room makes goose bumps rise on my bare chest. The University of Toronto dorms we're staying in have some kind of heating problem, but I'm too focused on Becca to care.

We ditched the post-championship party at a nearby bar and did our best to make a subtle exit. Half the team still cat-called us on our way out, but I know they all think we're cute together. My housemates are all fully on board the Becca train now, and we've even had her over for a couple of our Babe Cave dinners.

Of course, they also have plenty of jokes about me eating Becca for dinner.

"Oh my god, Becca, that feels so good."

I gasp and dig my nails into her shoulders as she flicks her tongue over one of my nipples. She sucks and bites and teases me for so long I can feel how wet I am every time I move.

"I need you," I say between moans. "Please."

She flips me onto my back on the tiny dorm bed in one fluid motion. After shimmying out of her shorts, she spreads my legs and climbs on top of me. We only have two thin layers of fabric between us now. She's surrounding me: the warmth of her skin on mine, her hot breath in my ear, the thump of her heart where our chests press together. Even just the smell of her hair is enough to make me lose it. I pull her mouth to mine, and we kiss like we're starving. My legs wrap around her waist, and she starts to rock against me.

She breaks the kiss and rests her forehead against mine. Her eyes are squeezed shut, and her mouth has gone slack with desire. Sometimes she just looks so stunning and totally lost in the moment all I can do is stare at her in awe.

I make her feel like that. She wants me this much. Sometimes I still can't quite believe it.

She shifts around so she can slip one of her thighs between mine. I thrust onto it, needing the pressure. We both gasp, and her eyes fly open to stare into mine.

"Fuck, Hope. You're so wet."

I couldn't look away from her if I tried. "You make me so wet."

She leans even harder into me, and I squirm. I need her fingers. I need her tongue. I need her to make me fall apart, and then I need to do the same to her.

Over and over again.

"Becca, please. I need you. I need you so much."

She closes her eyes again, and her expression shifts into something I can't read.

"Hope..."

She rolls off me after a second and flops down on her back, dragging a hand down her face.

"You okay?" I ask. I'm still so turned on everything

feels spacey, but a flash of worry starts bringing me out of the fog.

"Yeah." The corner of her mouth lifts, and she flips onto her side to face me. "I'm *very* okay. I...I've just been meaning to ask you something for a while now. I wanted to do it after we won today, right there on the field, but it didn't seem quite right. I've been waiting for us to have a moment on our own all night."

"Well we're definitely on our own now." I make a show of glancing around the room Jane and I are sharing. "Unless Jane is hiding under the other bed. Yo Jane, you here?"

Becca laughs as I cup a hand to my ear.

"Huh, nothing." I say. "Guess we really are alone."

"Guess we are." She's still laughing, and she takes a deep breath once she's got herself back under control. "Hope, these past couple weeks have been *so* amazing. Today was amazing. I'm so proud of every single thing you do. I can tell you have this incredible future ahead of you, and I...I want to be there for it."

I scooch in closer to her. Our faces are just a couple inches apart on the pillow. Her voice has dropped to a murmur.

"You will be, Becca."

She chews on her lip for a moment. "I mean I want to be there...officially. I want to be part of each other's lives. I want...I want you to be my girlfriend, and I want to be yours."

My heart starts clanging against my ribcage like a butterfly on speed, and maybe it's not the coolest or most chill response, but I sit straight up in bed and squeal.

"You do?!"

Becca starts laughing, somewhere between shocked and amused. "Of course I do."

"I—I—I—Wow. I just—I've wanted that *so* much, but I didn't want to rush you after everything we've been through. I just—*Wow*. Oh my god."

She sits up beside me. "So...is that a yes?"

I throw my arms around her neck. "Of course it's a yes. Yes, I want to be your girlfriend. Yes, I want you to be my girlfriend."

She hugs me back and buries her face in my hair. I squeeze her tight, and we hold each other for a long, long time, letting the weight of the moment sink in. I feel like we've been building something for months, and now we've finally gotten the chance to step back and take a look at our work.

We've made something beautiful.

"We're girlfriends," I whisper.

"Yeah, we are," Becca whispers back, her voice thick. "We're girlfriends."

We pull back enough to look at each other. Becca's eyes are shining, and mine are stinging like I'm about to cry too.

I've never had a girlfriend before, and I've somehow lucked out and got the one of my actual dreams.

We just stare for a few moments, not saying anything as the tears dry and we slowly start to remember that not only are we girlfriends, but we're also girlfriends who are currently almost naked in bed together.

"So..." I say as I twist a strand of that gorgeous red hair around my finger. "Do I get any special girlfriend privileges now?"

Becca grins. It's that one grin of hers that always tells me I'm about to get it in the best way possible.

"Several," she answers. "Let me show you a few."

She tackles me and pushes me onto my back again before pinning my wrists above my head. My chest heaves, and hers does the same above me as her fingers close even tighter around my wrists.

"You ready?" she asks.

I nod.

I am so ready for all of this.

23

Becca

"See you later, Tina!"

I wave to my boss as I head past her desk on my way out of work. I've been at my new job for about a month now. Working as an admin assistant in the city's recreation department hasn't exactly been thrilling, but it's been easy to fit around my school schedule, and they've promised me a full time job as an assistant coach for a youth intramurals league in the summer.

Coach Jamal came through with his connections.

"Any plans for the afternoon?" Tina asks, looking up from her ancient desktop computer screen and tucking her silver bob behind her ears.

I can't help smiling like an idiot. "I'm heading over to pick up my girlfriend from the airport right now actually. She's coming back from winter break."

I already came out to Tina when Hope stopped by to see the office one day. She smiles and nods. "Oh fun! Well, I hope she's had a good flight."

I thank her and head for the door. I knew I'd be cutting things close with my shift today, so I decide to splurge on an Uber instead of taking the bus. My ride takes me through the hilly streets of downtown Halifax and then out to the small airport. It's a typical coastal, overcast day in late December, but even the dull grey gloom looks like warm, glowing sunshine to me.

I haven't seen Hope since she left for Christmas. I went back to Alberta but flew into Halifax a couple days ago so I wouldn't miss too much work. This is the longest we've gone without seeing each other since we started dating.

Which isn't saying much, considering we've only been dating since November, but it doesn't stop me from bouncing my knees in the Uber like an overexcited child.

I get dropped off at the arrivals area and head inside to wait. The Uber bought me more time than I thought, so after checking Hope's flight status on the board, I find a bench to sit down and wait. After a few more minutes of knee bouncing and people watching, I pull out my phone to distract me. I have a few texts from Kala about a dinner at her place we have planned for later this week.

Somehow, me dating Hope has made my friendship with Kala even stronger. Whatever lingering tension and guilt I had left is gone now that it's clear I really can have a girlfriend without messing things up for us.

Kala's been making a lot of changes in her life too. She came out to her parents a few weeks ago, and while their reaction wasn't exactly a dream come true, they're all finding their way through things. I've made sure to be there every step of the way and to let her know she'll always have me.

We're family too.

I answer her texts and then get lost in the void of Instagram until a message from Hope pops up on my screen.

Just landed! See you soon.

It's followed by a string of alternating peach and heart-eye emojis. I grin down at my phone. She's such a dork.

By the time she finally walks through the doors, I've been pacing up and down in front of them for so long people have started giving me weird looks. I freeze as soon as I see her. I don't know when she's going to stop having that effect on me.

Hopefully never.

Her teal-tipped hair is loose over her shoulders, and her winter coat is hanging open over a UNS t-shirt. She's carting a carry-on size suitcase behind her, and her free hand is clutching a small bouquet of pink tulips.

"MY GIRLFRIEND!" she shouts when she spots me, her voice echoing through the room.

We run at each other like we've been separated for years, not a couple weeks. She drops the suitcase and gives me a one-armed hug, doing her best to save the flowers from getting crushed.

"Why do you have flowers?" I ask. "Aren't I supposed to do that? Oh shit, should I have done that?"

She laughs. "You're more than enough. They just had this little stand of them in the duty free area, and I had to get them because the pink ones reminded me of...um...you know."

I squint. She raises her eyebrows up and down, and I burst out laughing.

"Hope Hastings, did you seriously buy a bouquet of flowers solely because they remind you of my vagina?"

Two old, very Nova Scotian-looking ladies give us appalled looks as they walk by, but I don't care.

Hope shrugs and pretends to be coy. "Maaaaybe."

I shake my head, still laughing and holding onto her. We should probably move to a less inconvenient location for everyone, but I don't want to let go even for a second.

"They're for you, but they're also celebration flowers for me," she adds.

"Oh yeah? What are we celebrating?"

I expect another vagina-related comment, but instead she beams and whips out her phone.

"Look at this!"

I scan the email on the screen. Her hand is moving around a lot, but I manage to catch the words 'pleased to inform you,' 'accepted,' and 'internship.'

"Oh my god! Hope, you got it! Holy shit!"

We're really making a spectacle of ourselves, but that doesn't stop me from swearing more as I pull her into an extra tight hug. I knew there was no chance she wouldn't get that internship, but she was getting more and more worried as the weeks went on.

"That is amazing! You're going to be so good at it!"

"Thank you, my wonderful girlfriend." She tucks her phone away and holds the flowers out for me to take them. "May these blooms symbolize the start of our reign as UNS's leading power couple."

"Oh, so we're a power couple now?"

She rolls her eyes. "Duh."

I hold the flowers to my chest and shake my head. "I fucking love you."

We both freeze. My breath gets lodged in my throat as she stares at me.

We've never said that before. Not for real. I don't even know if I meant it for real, but as soon as it leaves my mouth, I know it's true, and there's no taking it back.

"You do?" she asks, her eyes wide.

"Yeah." I force myself to swallow. "I...I love you, Hope. I love you so much."

She jumps into my arms, and this time we do squish the flowers, but that doesn't stop her from crushing her lips against mine, over and over again in a dozen tiny kisses.

"I love you," she says between each one. "I love you so much."

I want to say it to her every night and every morning. I promise myself I will. I promise her. I pour that promise into every kiss, and I know she hears me. I know she trusts me, and I trust her right back.

She breaks away and grabs her suitcase before holding out her hand.

"Come on. Let's get out of here, huh?"

I wrap my fingers around hers, and we start walking together.

Acknowledgments

"This one is special."

We hear it a lot from authors, about pretty much every book. *This is a special story, and it's very close to my heart*. I don't think the fact that we tend to say it about every book we put out makes it any less true. Every story I write has a place of its own in my heart, but I'm going to go ahead and say it anyway:

This one is special.

I knew from the minute I decided I wanted to write romance novels that I wanted to write queer romance novels. I knew I *needed* to write about queer love and joy as much as I need to see it reflected in the world around me and in what I read myself, but it's taken me some time to feel ready to do it.

I think part of me was always waiting for Becca and Hope. I was waiting for the right story to come along—a special one, if you will. *Catch and Cradle* is the first time I've felt totally ready to share this part of myself in my work as an author, and for that reason and so many others, it fills me with more gratitude than I can contain to be sitting here at the end of this journey saying my thank you's.

My first thank you is, of course, to you. Yes, you, with this book in your hands. Thank you for taking a chance on these lacrosse ladies and following along with their love story. Thank you for making space for them and for me. That space is a gift I don't take lightly.

Thank you to my incredible team of beta readers, who

helped me polish this story into something I'm truly proud of. Your observations, honesty, and encouragement have helped make this book what it is, and as cheesy as it is to say I couldn't have done it without you, I really couldn't have done it without you. Kirsten, Farah, Teagan, and Christy: I wish I could take you all out to an elaborate thank-you brunch, but I'm sending ~grateful brunch vibes~ your way.

Thank you to the awe-inspiring team of bloggers and ARC readers helping to launch *Catch and Cradle* into the world. You are what makes the bookish world go round, and you're what creates the welcoming and uplifting community we're all so lucky to be a part of. Your generosity, enthusiasm, and general badassery are so appreciated by every author who's lucky enough to have a place on your shelves.

Thank you to all the friends and family who make doing this whole author thing possible for me and who never fail to show up with support and encouragement. While there are some of you I hope never end up reading this, I'm grateful beyond measure to have you all in my life.

Thank you to the residents of the original Babe Cave for the opportunity to be creepily inspired by your college sports escapades and to name a fictional house after your house.

And finally, thank you, Sport, for being a shining beam in my life that makes me *almost* as happy as Terrence is about beams. You are my home, Butter, and I love you.

About the Author

Katia Rose is not much of a Pina Colada person, but she does like getting caught in the rain. She loves to write romances that make her readers laugh, cry, and swoon (preferably in that order). She's rarely found without a cup of tea nearby, and she's more than a little obsessed with tiny plants. Katia is proudly bisexual and has a passion for writing about love in all its forms.

www.katiarose.com

Club Katia

Club Katia is a community that comes together to celebrate the awesomeness of romance novels and the people who read them. Joining also scores you some freebies to read!

Membership includes special updates, sneak peeks, access to Club Katia Exclusives (a collection of content available especially to members) and the opportunity to interact with fellow members in the Club Katia Facebook Group.

Joining is super easy and the club would love to have you! Visit www.katiarose.com/club-katia to get in on the good stuff.

Up Next
STOP AND STARE

Iz gets their own story in this novella available as a free download on Katia Rose's website!

Sometimes love is in the last place you look.

Iz Sanchez has looked for love just about everywhere. Granted, life as a gender non-conforming jock at a small coastal university does not exactly present a wealth of opportunity, but that hasn't stopped Iz from seizing the day.

So far their quest to find Miss Right has only resulted in heartbreak and way too many awkward run-ins with exes at the campus sports bar, but at the end of the day, Iz can always count on their friends, their glorious collection of designer sneakers, and their steadfast belief that love is out there somewhere to get them back in the game.

What they didn't expect was to have their world turned

upside down by a champagne-fueled New Year's kiss with the girl who's been their best friend since toddlerhood.

Marina Townsend has always known she and her best friend Iz were made to be more than friends. She's spent years waiting for the right moment to come along and make Iz see it too.

That moment shows up at the stroke of midnight, but instead of pulling them together, the kiss only seems to push them apart. Now that a lifelong friendship is on the line, Iz can't stop thinking about the times love has left them burned. They'll need to figure their heart out—and soon—because Marina is done waiting for Iz to realize what she's known all along:

Sometimes love comes looking for you.

Read on for an excerpt!

1

Iz

"Should we poke it with something?"

Paulina's fingers dig into my shoulders where she's trying to hide all six foot one of herself behind me. She's whispering like the raccoon might lunge at us with its fangs bared at any minute.

"Maybe we should throw a rock," I answer.

"No! Don't throw a rock at it!" She raises her voice and then yelps and goes back to whispering when the raccoon pauses the little feast he's having and looks at us. "He's too cute."

"If he's cute, why are you hiding behind me?"

"Because he might have rabies!"

I'm not an expert, but I don't think the pudgy raccoon chilling on our house's front steps is showing any signs of rabies. He's propped on his back feet as he munches his way through the contents of a shredded trash bag. He seems to have dragged it out of the knocked-over garbage bin lying next to me and Paulina on the sidewalk.

"Well I'm glad to know you're okay with me getting rabies before you."

"I have longer legs!" she protests. "If you get bit first, I can get help faster."

I burst out laughing at all the ways that doesn't make sense, which makes the raccoon look at us again, which makes Paulina scream, which makes me laugh even more as I shift around under her death grip and pull my phone out of my jacket pocket.

"What are you doing?" she asks.

"Calling Jane." I dial the number of one of our other two housemates and press the phone to my ear. "If she's in the house, maybe she can bang some pots and pans or something and scare it."

Paulina and I have been standing here in the freezing February weather for at least ten minutes. We found the front door blocked by our furry visitor after walking home from campus together. The raccoon hasn't responded to clapping, yelling, or stomping. The only thing it's done besides eat is hiss at us whenever we try to get any closer.

"Yo Jane," I say when the call connects, "you in the Babe Cave?"

It's our official name for the cramped and creaky little row house we rent a few blocks away from the UNS campus—so official we even have it printed on the welcome mat the raccoon is currently using as a dinner table.

"I am. Why?" she asks.

"Because there's a giant, super cute raccoon blocking the door, and it wants to kill us!" Paulina shouts beside my ear.

I wince. "Yeah. That."

"JUMPING JESUS!" Jane bellows, making me wince again. Her Nova Scotian accent roars to life like it always does when she gets angry.

Our fourth roommate, Hope, always says Jane has the

spirit of a little old fisherman's wife trapped inside her twenty year-old body, and I kind of believe it. I don't know any other person in their twenties who says things like 'Jumping Jesus,' but then again, Jane is the only east coast native in our friend group. The rest of us are transplants who came to Halifax for university.

"I knew we had raccoons! I just knew it!" she continues. "I knew those little buggers would go after the garbage. We're going to have to secure the bin."

"Uh, right, yeah, but in the meantime, do you have any suggestions? We're kind of stuck outside."

I can feel the tips of my ears going numb. I started growing out my shaved head a few months ago, but my shaggy little excuse for a pixie cut isn't enough to give me any warmth.

"Oh I have many suggestions for that little bugger," Jane mutters in a voice so menacing it almost makes me gulp before she ends the call.

A second later, the door swings back to reveal Jane in a pair of sweatpants with a faded red UNS v-neck on top. Her brown hair is falling out of a messy bun on the very top of her head, her eyes blazing with vengeance as she glares down at the raccoon with a broom clutched in her hands.

I can see the whole 'angry fisherman's wife' thing in moments like this.

"*Git!*" she hollers, stepping forward until her slipper-clad feet are just a few inches from the raccoon. "Git away now! Shoo! Go on! *Git*, you little bugger! Look at this mess you made!"

The raccoon shuffles away from her but doesn't leave the steps. It's clutching an empty pudding cup, and it looks straight at Jane as it slowly licks a clump of congealed chocolate off the plastic.

Jane sucks in a breath and narrows her eyes. "How dare you! This is my home! You have no business darkening my door with your insolence."

She uses the broom to try scooting the raccoon off the steps. It drops the pudding cup and turns to hiss at her. Paulina's fingers dig into my shoulders so tight I'm going to end up with bruises, and even I can feel my blood pressure rising as the raccoon tenses up like it's about to spring.

Instead of moving away, Jane drops into a crouch. My mouth falls open when she twists her face into a sneer and hisses right back.

The raccoon scrambles off the steps and lopes along the sidewalk before disappearing into a gap between two houses down the road.

Jane straightens up, brushes off her sweatpants, and beams at us. "Hey, guys!"

I blink at her. I'm sure Paulina is doing the same thing behind me.

Jane uses the broom to beckon us forward. "Well, come on in!"

"Uh, Jane," I say as I start making my way up the snow-dusted path through the little patch of dead grass we call a front lawn, "did you just *hiss* at a raccoon?"

She shrugs. "If I know anything about raccoons, it's that you've got to show them who's boss."

"You scare me sometimes, Jane," Paulina says as I reach the bottom of the steps. "In a good way. Usually."

She shrugs again. "I'll take that. Now let's get this trash cleaned up before he brings his little friends back with him."

By the time we get everything sorted out and prop a brick on top of the garbage bin to keep anything from scrambling inside, my ears are stinging and my fingers are going numb. I rub my hands together as I step inside and kick off my shoes. Jane has one of her candles going, making the whole house smell like vanilla and something spicy I can't place.

"What's the candle of the day, Jane?" I ask as she heads to the living room and flops down on the worn out, royal blue couch she has covered in textbooks, papers, and a dozen highlighters in a rainbow of colours.

"Vanilla bourbon," she answers in a dreamy voice, pausing to take a huge inhale and close her eyes as she smiles to herself.

Jane really likes candles.

"Do we have actual bourbon?" Paulina asks, stepping past me to claim an armchair. She sits sideways and drapes her model-length legs over one of the edges before running a hand through her long blonde hair. "I could use a drink."

There was a very brief time when I thought I might have a crush on Paulina back in first year. She's pretty enough to be some kind of Polish beauty queen, but she's also a complete dork in the cutest way possible. She's always tripping over stuff, and she has a knack for picking up hobbies she's not actually good at it but stays devoted to nonetheless. The collection of pots and planters coated with snow in our yard are a remnant of her annual failed attempt to grow vegetables.

I realized pretty fast that crushing on Paulina was pointless and that all we had were friendship vibes anyway. She, Jane, Hope, and I are all on the UNS lacrosse team, and the four of us got really close during first year. That combined with the team's 'don't date your teammates' code was enough to make me set my sights on other horizons.

The code wasn't enough to stop the sparks from flying between Hope and our former team captain, Becca. The drama of the century unfolded over the course of the lacrosse season last semester, and the two of them are campus's cutest couple now.

"Is Hope home?" I ask.

Jane nods and glances up at the ceiling. "Her and Becca are *watching a movie.*"

Right on cue, the rhythmic thumping of a headboard against the wall filters down from the second floor.

Paulina laughs. "They always think they're sooooo quiet."

I chuckle too. "*Dios mío*. I have to go up to my room now. I always feel like I have to be extra loud and, like, make my presence known to them, or else I don't know what I'll end up hearing."

"Good luck with that, Izzo," Jane says.

I give the two of them a salute and turn to head up there. The stairs help me out by firing off their usual series of deafening creaks as I get to the second floor. I hear some giggling and shushing coming from Hope's room as I walk up the hallway to mine.

It's past five and dark enough now that I reach for my light switch. The overhead lamp highlights how badly I need to tidy up. Textbooks are stacked in piles on the floor, desk, and bedside table, and clothes are spilling out of my laundry bin like a waterfall of button-downs and UNS sweaters. The walls are covered in a random selection of lacrosse team photos, pride flags, and the paintings and knickknacks from Colombia my dad always gets me on his trips back home.

The only part of the room that actually looks organized is the shoe rack under the window housing my collection of Jordans. My friends always make fun of me for being a lacrosse player who collects basketball shoes, but they just don't understand the glory and thrill of slipping a sick pair of vintage Jordans out of the box and trying them on.

I don't even *wear* some of the shoes; they're too divine to touch the humble soil of the earth. The rack has one shelf for Outside Shoes and one shelf for what I call Trophy Shoes—another thing my friends love to make fun of.

"But we don't need them," I whisper to the Jordans, smiling to myself like I always do when I gaze upon their multi-hued majesty. "They are not worthy of you anyway."

I might be a little obsessed.

After dropping my book-filled Jansport onto the floor next to a basket of laundry I've been meaning to put away for a week, I grab my laptop off my desk and settle onto my bed to get ready for my weekly video call with my best friend Marina.

I have about five minutes to spare, so I slip some headphones on and blast a little Kendrick, sinking into the sound and letting the day of lectures and note-taking roll off me. Even though I'm always busier during the first semester of the year when I'm balancing schoolwork and the lacrosse season, second semester seems to hit harder without the distraction of focusing on the Lobsters.

Apparently the founders of our school decided naming a coastal city's team after the mighty king of crustaceans was cool and not ridiculously stereotypical.

My professors weren't lying when they said third year was going to be tough. It's almost been enough to make me question why I decided to major in something as intense as chemistry—almost. I love chemistry even more than I love all the pick-up lines I get from being a chem major.

Let me tell you something about chemists. We like to do it on the table, periodically.

They're never *good* pick-up lines, but they're surprisingly effective.

The *beep beep* sound of an incoming call filters through my headphones, interrupting Kendrick's lyrical genius, which is way more sophisticated than my pick-up lines. I pause the song and press the accept button. Marina's face fills my laptop screen a second later.

She beams at me, just like she always does when we start our calls. Marina has the prettiest damn smile in the world, and seeing her freckled face and big brown eyes feels like home. I could pick her out of any smile line-up in the world. That cute little gap between her front teeth is a dead giveaway.

"Hey, bestie," she greets me.

"Hey, bestie," I answer, shifting so I can lay on my side to face the camera. "How's it going?"

She sighs and flops backward on her couch, holding her phone above her face. Her long brown hair fans out around her like a halo. "It's going. Is it just me, or is third year turning out to be one giant kick in the ass?"

"I was just thinking the same thing. My chem courses are turning the fuck up this year."

"Poli sci isn't any better. Now I actually look forward to writing three thousand word essays about movies for my minor. It's like a soothing break. Isn't that crazy?"

I shake my head and laugh. "You're the only person I know who would find a three thousand word film studies essay soothing."

"Sometimes it's nice to think about stories instead of diplomacy and governance."

I make my eyebrows jump up and down. "You mean it's nice to look at Audrey Hepburn."

Marina's lifelong obsession with Audey Hepburn is legendary. She's seen every single Audrey Hepburn film at least four times, and she's probably watched her favourite, *Roman Holiday*, enough to break world records. Even her phone background is a picture of Audrey Hepburn, although her lock screen is reserved for a photo of the two of us.

It's been the same one for years: an old timey, throwaway camera shot of me and Marina as kids with eyes turned demonically red by the glare. We're sitting in a laundry basket for reasons totally unknown. Marina is wearing a green turtleneck, and I'm behind her in a baseball cap with my arms wrapped around her and my cheek pressed to hers. Our faces are blurry from laughing so hard.

"We're studying the turn of the millennium!" she protests. "We just watched *The Matrix*."

"And did you sit there picturing Audrey Hepburn in a black leather trench coat?"

She wrinkles her nose and glares at me. "Do not mock Miss Audrey Hepburn. It is her god-given right to be placed on a pedestal by all of human kind. You need to respect that."

"Next thing I know you're going to be telling me Audrey Hepburn was some kind of prophet."

"I mean, if you think about it, she was kind of—"

She cuts herself off to glare at me again when I start laughing so hard I snort.

"I see you cannot take this conversation seriously. I won't say any more." She sits up and makes a show of inspecting the nails of her free hand.

I do my best to stop chuckling. "Aww, come on Marina. You know you're just too cute to handle when you're talking about *Miss* Audrey Hepburn. I love it."

She glances up from her nails, and something flashes in her eyes. My heart starts slamming against my chest in a frantic rhythm, and for a few seconds, I can't do anything except lay there blinking at her while I try to remember how to breathe.

Shit shit shit.

This has been happening more and more lately: the silence after a flirty comment I only meant as a joke. I don't know exactly when these awkward moments started, but I didn't make things any better by deciding to be the *perfecto idiota* of the century on New Year's Eve.

We were both back in Toronto for the holidays, and we decided to go to a friend of a friend's house party together. We didn't know anyone else there, but it didn't matter. We had the time of our lives downing champagne and dancing like the weirdos we are while everyone wondered what the hell we were doing there. She just looked so fucking *pretty* in her black lacy shirt and jeans with sparkly makeup glittering around her eyes. She looked more than pretty; she looked *hot*.

The more I thought about it, the more champagne I drank to try and *stop* thinking about it, but of course that plan backfired.

And then midnight hit.

It was one sloppy, drunken peck on the lips I spent the rest of the night apologizing for, but even now, I'm way too aware of Marina's bottom lip dropping open as she stares at me. I want to bite it. I want to pull my best friend's bottom lip between my teeth and thread my hands into her hair.

It's fucked up. All of it is so fucked up, and I promised myself I'd stop. I promised myself I'd be more careful. There's a place for Marina in my life, and that place is not under me.

No matter how good it feels to think about that.

Mierda.

I shake my head to clear away the pictures taking shape. It's like there's a fog drifting into my brain, obscuring what Marina means to me and turning her into something else, something soft and hot and hungry for me.

Something dangerous.

Marina has always been my safe place. I've always been hers. I don't want any danger here. I don't exactly have the best track record with things working out between me and the girls I'm into. Marina is supposed to be the person I can count on to be there when things go wrong, not the person things go wrong *with*.

"Iz?"

My head is spinning so much the screen in front of me has gone out of focus. I fix my attention on Marina again. She still staring at me with her mouth open just a bit, her eyes wide and searching.

"Sorry. Uh, just tired," I say after giving my head a final shake. My voice comes out all hoarse, and I have to clear my throat. "So many classes today."

"Right. Yeah." She glances down at her bedspread for a second and then back at me.

Double *mierda*.

She's gotta be pissed. She probably thinks I'm coming onto her. It doesn't help that she's sitting there in a v-neck shirt that shows off the perfect sliver of cleavage. She really does have the most amazing, curvy body. It's meant so much to see her discover that too, especially after how hard she was on herself in high school.

"So, um, how were your classes?" she asks.

"Uh…" I try to pull myself back to the present and scan my brain for any traces of how the day went. It's a struggle. "Well, uh…oh! Actually something good happened. One of my profs got my pronouns right!"

Her whole face lights up as she grins at me, and all the

tension fades for a moment. We're back to what we've always been: two friends who look out for each other no matter what.

This is how it's supposed to be, and I really need to get a handle on the part of my brain that's trying harder and harder to fuck it up.

"Iz, that's amazing! I'm so happy for you."

I grin right back at her. "Yeah, I was so shocked. I didn't think he'd remember. Most of them never do. He was going around talking to all the groups in the lab, and when he said something about me to our group, he called me they!"

Marina does a fist pump. "Hooray for they!"

I laugh and join in the fist pumping. "It felt really good. Honestly, I feel like the longer my hair gets, the harder I have to work to like, prove I'm non-binary or something. It's like if I'm not glaringly androgynous, it doesn't count for people."

Marina nods. "That's really shitty. People are so obsessed with gendering everything. I swear, if you put a long blonde wig on top of a lamp, everyone would be like, 'Ah yes, it is a sexy girl lamp now.' It's crazy."

I burst out laughing. "Okay, sexy girl lamp is definitely going to be my next Halloween costume."

Marina doubles over, the phone shaking in her hand as she cackles. "I need to see that. If we were doing a costume party for your birthday, I would demand you do it then."

"That would be a very memorable way to turn twenty-one." I nod like I'm considering it. "By the way, what are you guys doing for my birthday?"

Marina is coming to visit for the occasion next week. She and my roommates have been doing an annoyingly good job of keeping the 'secret theme' of the party they're planning a mystery to me.

Marina winks, and I do my best to ignore the way it makes my pulse kick up again as she speaks in a teasing tone. "Now, now, Iz, you know I can't tell you that."

"Come onnnn," I whine. "I promised to show up at the airport with your favourite Davy Jones pizza. I can retract that promise."

She shakes her head and grins. "Nah, you love me too much for that."

I raise an eyebrow to challenge her but give up after a couple seconds.

"Ugh, you're right. I do."

That's the thing: I do love her. I love her more than anyone, and I'd be an idiot to let myself lose that.

2

Marina

"What are you smiling about?"

My roommate, Alexis, throws a look at me as she heads through the living room on her way to get a snack in the kitchen. I've just put down my phone after ending my weekly call with Iz, and her question makes me realize I'm still grinning at the black screen like Iz's face is going to pop up any second and add in one last joke.

"I was just talking to Iz," I answer. I move my phone from the couch to the coffee table and pick up the cross-stitch I was working on before the call.

"Of courseeeee," Alexis drawls around the mouthful of chips she's just shoved in her face while standing in front of the open cupboard, contemplating her other food options.

She's clearly settled in for the night, with her famous raggedy bunny slippers on under her sweatpants and an equally raggedy white crop top with the words 'Band Geek' printed on it in peeling purple letters.

We're not exactly a 'party hard' kind of house. Most nights, we can be found doing exactly this: me sitting on the couch doing a cross stitch with Netflix on and Alexis wandering out of her room in search of food after a long session of oboe practice. Sometimes we even get really wild and watch an Audrey Hepburn movie together while splitting a bottle of wine.

"You tell them you're in love with them yet?"

I almost drop my needle in the middle of threading it through the next square in my embroidery hoop. "*Alexis!*"

"What?" She wanders over with the chip bag in hand, the giant pile of brown curls pulled into a messy bun on top of her head bouncing as she plops down on the couch next to me. "You *are* going to tell them, right?"

Alexis is one of the most direct people I know, which comes in handy sometimes, but also makes sharing secrets with her an extreme risk. I wouldn't have told her about New Year's Eve if I had anyone else to tell, but seeing as my go-to sounding board for any kind of confession—AKA Iz—was the reason *for* that confession, I ended up going into a rambling story about the kiss during one of Alexis and I's wine and Audrey nights a few weeks ago.

It only took about one sentence from me for her to declare she always knew I was in love with Iz. I didn't even use the word 'love' myself, but she's been ordering me to march up to Iz and tell them ever since. I had to pry my laptop out of her hands to keep her from buying me a plane ticket that very night.

Hence the extreme risk of telling her any secrets.

"No, Alexis, I'm not going to call up my best friend of almost twenty years and say I'm in love with them with absolutely no warning, especially when I'm not even sure that's how I feel, and *extra* especially when I have no idea if that's how they feel."

She rolls her eyes and points at the hoop in my hands, coming dangerously close to sprinkling chip dust on the white fabric. "Marina, level with me here. You are literally *embroidering a picture of the two of you holding hands.* You're in love, girl."

I pause and look at the blocked out design I'm only a few rows away from finishing. I'm not great at making my own cross-stitch patterns, but I'm proud of how this one turned out. It's at least discernibly me and Iz, their red button-down and matching Jordans a contrast to the green sundress I'm wearing. It's based on a photo of us from a couple summers ago. I still need to do the threaded details like the shoelaces and facial expressions, and then the whole thing will come to life.

"What?" I demand. "It's their birthday present. It's cute. Friends make each other stuff like this."

Alexis raises her eyebrows and downs another handful of chips, not even bothering to argue.

I can't blame her. If I'm honest with myself, I can admit this cross stitch is the gayest thing I've ever seen in my life.

If I'm even more honest with myself, I can admit there's no way Iz and I are just friends anymore—or at least, they're not just a friend to me.

Being with Iz feels like being myself. We just fit. When we're together, I feel like I'm wrapped up in my favourite blanket, the one that's worn and soft in all the right places and always smells like warm laundry.

That's what loving someone is supposed to feel like. I've dated a bit since I started college, but it always comes back to that: nobody feels like Iz. Nobody makes me feel that same crazy combination of safe and electrified that zings through me every time they look at me a certain way.

That's the thing: I *know* they look at me a certain way. I've seen it happen again and again. Ever since we left high school, there have been these *moments* during our visits and our calls where things between us shift. The silence stretches on a little too long. We get caught up in each other's eyes and then look away, both of us breathing hard. The looming sensation that *something* is about to happen hangs so thick in the air it gets hard to breathe at all.

But nothing ever does happen. It's always the same, just like tonight on the call when they called me cute. I know friends call each other cute all the time. We've been calling each other cute since we were kids, but *just* friends don't go quiet and stare at each other the way we did after that.

I felt it then: the weight of *something* hanging between us. I was so sure of it I couldn't move. I couldn't force out the words I wanted to say.

Do you really think I'm cute, Iz?

I don't know what they would have said, but I needed to find out. It's become clearer and clearer there's something here besides friendship.

Of course that scared me when I realized it. Of course it kept me up at night. Of course it made me feel crazy and terrified of putting one of the most important things in my life at risk, but when Iz leaned in at midnight during the New Year's Eve party we went to in Toronto a few weeks ago, it finally clicked: not going after this—whatever *this* is—would be even scarier than risking it all.

Just one sloppy, champagne-fueled peck on the lips made the whole night explode into shimmering shades of colour I'd never seen before. Iz went bright red and apologized a second later, but I didn't want an apology.

I wanted more.

Alexis keeps sitting there crunching on her chips like the embodiment of the sassiest side of my subconscious, and after completing a few more squares of the cross-stitch, I give in and sigh.

"Look, even if I *was* completely ready to tell Iz, I couldn't. They'd freak the fuck out."

"Um, I don't think so." Alexis shakes her head. "I've seen you guys together when they've visited here. They're clearly head over heels for you."

My pulse picks up at the thought of it, and I'm glad Alexis can't hear the way my heart is clanging against my ribcage.

"Even if that were true, it's...it's not that simple."

"What's not simple about it?" She shrugs. "Seems pretty simple to me. You like each other, so tell each other."

Now it's me shaking my head. "Iz...has a hard time trusting other people's feelings. They have a hard time trusting their own feelings. I don't think it would ever be a matter of just telling each other and taking it from there."

I know that better than anyone. I was there for Iz through their first heartbreak. I've been there for them through every heartbreak since. If the thought of letting our friendship shift into something more makes me nervous, that's nothing compared to the utter terror I can imagine Iz feeling.

"So, what, you're gonna bottle it all up forever because it might be hard for them? Is that fair to *you*?"

"I..." The needle goes still in my hands again, halfway through finishing the final corner of one of Iz's shoes. "Look, this is all still so new for me. I only started seriously thinking about it as a possibility at New Year's. We're talking about the person I've been best friends with since we were toddlers. Can we just leave it at that for tonight?"

"Of course, yeah." She sets the chip bag down on the table and spreads her hands in surrender. "Sorry if I pushed too hard on this. You know I just want to see you happy."

"Hmm." I glance over at the TV sitting on a cheap IKEA stand across the room. "You know what would make me happy?"

"What?"

"If you went and put on *Roman Holiday* for us to watch."

She drops her head back and groans. "Seriously? *Roman Holiday* again? How many times have you seen that movie?"

"It's my favourite!" I protest. "And you said you wanted to make me happy."

"Ugh, fine." She keeps grumbling to herself as she heads over to get my favourite Audrey Hepburn movie of all time going.

It's my favourite movie of all time, period. I've stopped counting how many times I've seen it, and I still manage to find something new to love every time I watch Miss Audrey zip around Rome on a moped as the runaway Princess Ann.

When we were kids, Iz and I used to play our own make-believe version of the movie all the time. I'd be Princess Ann, of course, and Iz would pull me around the yard in a wagon that was supposed to be our getaway vehicle. We'd imagine there were paparazzi and royal officials hiding out in the bushes trying to catch us, and we'd wedge the wagon behind the shed in my parent's yard to get 'undercover.' Sometimes we'd sit back there for hours, sharing snacks we'd packed beforehand and talking about what an amazing life we could have together in Rome if we managed to escape.

"Hey, Marina," Alexis says after settling herself back on the couch once the opening credits begin to play, "I know I'm already pushing it, but just...maybe when you're in Halifax for Iz's birthday—"

"*Alexis,*" I warn.

"Okay, okay." She waves her hands in the air. "Like I said, I just want to see you happy."

I watch the black and white images of 1950s Rome on the screen, still thinking about Iz and I in that wagon, their hand in mine as they dropped their squeaky kid's voice into a fake baritone and told me they'd show me the world, and I nod.

I just want to see us happy too.

3

Marina

There's one part of flying that always makes me feel like I'm going to puke. I'm fine for the takeoff. I'm fine for the landing. I'm fine for the part where we're cruising through the air. Not even turbulence sets off my stomach, but if I look out the window and see the plane is turning and doing that tilty thing where the ground is at a crazy angle and the sky has gone sideways, I start dry-heaving right on cue.

The lady next to me refused to switch and take the window seat, even after I told her I'm not great with flying. I can see her out of the corner of my eye, leaning forward so she can stare past me and out the round little window giving us a view of the sickening funhouse trip outside.

If you wanted to look out the window, why the hell wouldn't you sit next to it?

I bite my lip to keep from asking out loud and start rubbing little circles onto my stomach in an attempt to calm it down.

Almost there. Almost there, and then you'll see Iz.

I picture them standing in the arrivals area, and I feel the corners of my mouth lift. I haven't seen Iz in person since New Year's. We've gone way longer without a visit during our years of university, but that doesn't make it any easier to spend time apart from the person I grew up seeing nearly every day.

The fact that we kissed the last time I saw them and haven't talked about it since is, however, adding a few flips to my stomach's routine.

"Attendants, please..."

The rest of what the captain says over the speakers is too garbled for me to make out over the supposed-to-be-soothing nature sounds I have streaming through my headphones, but I look to the front of the plane and see the two flight attendants strapping themselves into their pull-down seats.

I risk a glance out the window and see the plane is parallel with the ground again. My shoulders unclench, and I sag against my seat. My stomach does one final somersault and then relaxes into merciful stillness. I pull my headphones out of my ears and watch Nova Scotia get closer and closer beneath us.

Everything is coated in white like a fine sugar dusting, and the sky is a silvery grey. We pass over streets lined with homes that look like tiny dollhouses from up here. They get bigger and bigger until we're finally zooming over the airport and gliding down onto the tarmac.

The plane is small enough that the landing makes my teeth chatter as I'm jostled around in my seat, but now that we're no longer in danger of the horizon shifting at vomit-inducing angles, my stomach is only tightening with excitement.

No matter what else we have going on, I'll always be eager for that first hug from Iz. I whip my seatbelt off as soon as the little light telling us to wear them switches off. I pull my shoulder bag out from under the seat in front of me and wiggle into my coat, doing my best not to smack the lady next to me in the face with my flailing arms, even if part of me thinks she deserves it. Then I sit there bouncing my heels up and down as I wait for the plane to empty.

I'm almost excited enough I don't feel the familiar wave of apprehension hit as I get into the aisle and reach up to grab my suitcase—almost.

I can still hear those old jeering voices in my head telling me everyone is watching and laughing at the fat girl filling the aisle. I resist the urge to tug my shirt down where it's creeping up over the edge of my jeans and focus on getting a hold of my bag's handle.

You are allowed to be here. There's nothing wrong with you.

I repeat my mantra in my head as I start wheeling the bag up the aisle. I used to try telling myself no one was laughing or staring, but that didn't work out so great on the occasions when I'd look around and find people *were* laughing or staring.

The truth is, there'll always be someone ready to get offended by the size of my thighs or the roll of skin that forms over the waistband of pretty much every pair of pants I own, since most companies are still bad at making comfy jeans for curvy girls. If I focus on what other people think, I'm always going to find a reason to feel bad, so now I focus on myself. Sometimes it works and sometimes it doesn't, but most days, I'm pretty damn proud to be me.

I wave to the flight attendants and say thank you as I pass by. The Halifax airport is tiny, and it only takes me a couple minutes of speed-walking before I'm at the door to the arrivals area. I burst through and find it busier than I expected. My first scan of the people standing around in puffy winter coats and snow boots doesn't bring any sign of Iz, but as I'm wheeling my suitcase over to a bench and pulling out my phone to text them, I hear that familiar voice calling my name.

"Yo, Mariiiiiina!"

They sing it out loud enough to make a few heads turn, rolling the *r* just like their dad always does. A second later, Iz clears the crowd, and a smile so big it makes my cheeks ache takes over my face.

They're wearing an oversized green army jacket over one of those crazy button-downs they're always finding in the dollar bin at the thrift store. This one is dark blue with a pattern of tiny oranges that matches their citrus-coloured Jordans.

I wouldn't exactly call Iz on-trend, but they always manage to look very fucking stylish.

Their hair is in the fluffy, haphazard stage of growing out a buzz cut, and the length has a cute puppy dog effect. I can't help reaching up to ruffle it as they charge the few feet of distance left between us and fling themself into my arms.

"You're so fluffy!" I say as I pull them closer.

The two of us laugh and stand there wrapped up in each other, swaying to the generic lobby music pumping through the speakers. I take a deep breath in and let out a humming sigh. Iz makes the same sound.

"I'm soooo happy you're here!" they gush. "How has it only been a month and a half? I feel like I haven't seen you in so long."

"You're right." I drop my hands to their shoulders and step back. "Let me gaze upon your glorious face."

They do an exaggerated fashion model pout and twist their head around so I can see all the angles. I laugh and call them a dumby dumb dumb—our favourite made-up insult from when we were kids—but even as I grab my suitcase and start following them out of the terminal, I can feel the heat rising in my cheeks.

Iz is hot. I don't know how six weeks made such a difference, but if I thought it was hard to ignore what their little smirk does to me during Christmas break, that's nothing compared to how distracting it is now. My whole body feels warm, and despite the fact that I've ruffled their hair more times than I can count, I can't get over how it felt to have it between my fingers with their body pressed to mine.

The bustle of the airport keeps us quiet until we're outside waiting for a bus into the city. Iz nudges a pebble along the pavement with the toe of their shoe before looking up to speak to me.

"Sorry about your pizza. The delivery guy didn't come in time, but it will be waiting when we get there, if my roommates don't eat it all first."

I blink. "Pizza?"

The concept rings a bell, but I'm still too busy recovering from the hug-induced haze to remember why I'm supposed to want pizza.

Iz chuckles and does that smirk again. It does not help with the haze-clearing.

"Remember?" they prompt. "I was supposed to bring you pizza when I picked you up. You specifically requested the chicken option from Halifax's most finest purveyor of cheesy delights: Davy Jones Pizza."

I blink again. "Ohhhh right. Wow, yeah, you really dropped the ball, Iz. I should turn around and get on a flight back right now."

I try to hide how much my head is spinning by making a show out of pretending to be offended. I turn to face the doors behind us and flick my hair over my shoulder before starting to wheel my suitcase away. Iz is laughing at me, and the sound almost cracks my fake glare to make me laugh too. I keep the charade going, and I'm about to reach for the door when I feel their hand clamp around my wrist.

My breath catches in my throat. Iz starts to say something teasing, but when I look back over my shoulder at them, their voice trails off into silence. I see their eyes get wide, and I *know* I'm not imagining it when their gaze drops to my lips for just a second before fixing on their fingers wrapped tight around my arm.

I look down too. The cuff of my jacket leaves just enough of my skin exposed for me to feel the warmth of their hand. The heat blooming from that one point of contact is enough to make my breath catch a second time.

It's like I can already see it playing out: Iz's thumb brushing over the paper-thin skin above my veins, me shivering and saying their name like it's something between a question and permission, the tense second of hesitation before they'd pull me closer, the feeling of their hot breath on my lips just before I'd finally get to find out what they taste like.

Our sloppy peck of a kiss at New Year's didn't give me a chance to do that. I've spent way too many nights since wondering what Iz would taste like, how they'd sound and move. It all feels so wrong and weird and thrilling and right. It's everything all at once, and I can't make any sense of it, but I don't think I want to.

I just want them. I want them to want *me*.

"Iz..."

My voice is so low I doubt they can hear me over the rush of cars and buses pulling up to the airport, but their eyes flick to mine, and they don't drop my hand.

I force myself to take a breath. "Iz, we—"

"That's our ride!"

A bus pulls up to the curb beside us, the brakes squeaking as the door pops open. Iz whips their head around and releases my wrist, facing away from me as they fish around in their pockets for bus tickets.

"I know I have extra ones for you somewhere..." they mumble as they pat down their coat.

Their voice sounds even—too even, like nothing happened at all. They don't look at me until they've found the tickets and stepped up to the bus, and when they glance back my way, they've got that typical Iz grin on.

And I, typically, have to stand there wondering if I imagined everything that just happened.

"You all right?" they ask.

I take a step forward and nod, even though my stomach has started doing flips again. If things between Iz and I keep shifting this quickly, I'm going to spend the whole trip nauseous.

STOMACH PROBLEMS OR NOT, I can't resist the call of Davy Jones pizza as the scent of gooey cheese, tangy barbeque chicken, and grilled red onion hits my nose. I've already had two giant pieces, but I go in for a third. Davy Jones really is a miracle. I don't know what I'm going to do if Iz moves away after university and I don't have an excuse to come to Halifax anymore.

Hope, one of Iz's housemates, raises the slice she's just taken out of the pepperoni and cheese box and holds it in the air like a substitute champagne flute. "Welcome to the Babe Cave, Marina! Let's do a pizza toast!"

We're crowded into the townhouse's little living room with all of Iz's three housemates. Pizza boxes are covering the whole top of the coffee table, and there's a pop playlist pumping out of a speaker set while the pink string lights in the front window cast a soft glow over us all.

The bond the four of them have going on is so cute it almost makes me jealous. I love living with Alexis, but we don't compare to the way Iz and their friends are all joined at the hip like a gang of besties in some idealized teen movie about what it's like to move away for college. Iz always has some crazy story about what they've all been up to, whether it's pranking their lacrosse team or shutting down a campus bar during one of their legendary nights out.

I rarely do anything more exciting than go to an art house screening with people from my film studies classes, but FOMO aside, I'm happy Iz has these girls. They've been there for them through everything I couldn't be more than a face on a screen for: their coming out as non-binary in second year, all the heartbreaks they've experienced with girls on campus, and the mundane stuff like pulling all-nighters before exams or figuring out class schedules. Iz and I tell each other everything over video, but that only goes so far when you're struggling. It helps to know these girls will always fight for Iz—almost as hard as I will.

"PIZZA TOAST!" Iz shouts, grabbing a fresh slice to hold it up like Hope.

"What exactly is a pizza toast?" I ask, dragging my attention away from the adorable flecks of tomato sauce stuck to Iz's cheek and focusing back on the discussion.

"First you gotta put your pizza in the air," Hope instructs me as she uses her free hand to adjust her glasses.

Hope is one of those girls who always looks effortlessly cool—truly effortlessly, like she really did just wake up like that. The ends of her hair are dyed in a teal ombre, a sleeve tattoo covers one of her arms, and even though I've never seen her wear anything except UNS Lobsters merch and sweatpants, she looks like she's just as ready to walk into an underground music festival as she is to show up at lacrosse practice.

I know she's closest with Jane, but when her and Iz get going, they're the wild ones of the group. The three of us went out one time two summers ago and ended up attempting to drunkenly skinny dip in the harbor at three in the morning—or at least, Iz and Hope tried to skinny dip. I stood on the dock and yelled at them while they leaned over the side and splashed me. We very narrowly avoided being caught by the police.

Whatever it is, a pizza toast at least sounds like it won't break any laws.

"Jane! Paulina! You too!" Hope orders. "We are toasting to Marina's safe arrival and to a flawless party for Iz this weekend."

"And the theme is...?" Iz pipes up, doing their best to trick us into spilling the secret.

Hope wags her finger at them. "Nuh-uh. It's a surprise. You'll find out on Saturday."

"But it's Thursday," they whine. "That's so far away."

"How do you say 'too bad' in Spanish?" Hope asks.

"Like this." Iz flips her off. Jane and Paulina burst out laughing while Hope sticks out her tongue.

"Whatever. Let's do this toast. Pizzas up, ladies and distinguished non-binary humans!"

Everyone leans forward to hold their slices in the air over the coffee table.

"To Iz and Marina!" Hope shouts.

Then they all slam their pieces of pizza together.

"Oh my god, no!" I shriek. "No way!"

Iz elbows me from their spot beside me on the couch. "You have to do it, Marina! It's a pizza toast."

"It's good luck!" Jane adds.

Jane is usually the mom-type of the group, and even she's in on this grossness.

"I don't want to waste this delicious pizza," I protest.

They're all still holding their slices together in a gooey mass.

"Oh, you won't waste it," Iz explains. "You have to eat it after. Otherwise it's bad luck."

"You guys are crazy."

"Oh, we know. Now put your pizza up." Iz laughs and pats me on the thigh.

It's just a brief touch, a couple inches above my knee, but it's enough to make me want to squeeze my legs together. I don't want anyone to spot the heat creeping up my neck, so I give in and slap my pizza to the slice pile. I wince as a glob of cheese drops onto the table.

"Atta girl!" Jane woops, her Nova Scotian accent coming out in full force.

"To Iz and Marina!" Hope shouts again, and we all echo the toast.

I glance at Iz as I pull my slice away and nibble a little bite. I am not convinced about this whole pizza toast thing, but I can't ignore how good 'Iz and Marina' sound together.

I just wish I knew Iz heard it too.

Grab your free copy on www.katiarose.com!

Also by Katia Rose

The Barflies Series

A series of dramadies centred on the lives and loves of the staff at a Montreal dive bar. Each novel can be read as a standalone.

The Bar Next Door

Glass Half Full

One For the Road

When the Lights Come On

The Sherbrooke Station Quartet

A series of steamy rock star dramadies that follow the rise of an alternative rock band in Montreal. All four volumes can be read as standalones.

Your Rhythm

Your Echo

Your Sound

Your Chorus

Standalone Novels

Stop and Stare

Falling for your best friend isn't usually the plan, but Iz and Marina are running with it. A queer novella available exclusively to Club Katia members. Visit Katia's website to grab your copy.

Catch and Cradle

Becca and Hope just broke their biggest rule: don't fall in love with your teammate. A new adult sports romance.

Thigh Highs

Modelling lingerie for her arch-nemesis was not on Christina's to-do list. Then again, nether was he. An enemies-to-lovers romantic comedy.

Latte Girl

Hot coffee is a regular fixture in Hailey Warren's life. Hot guys? Not so much. A caffeine-fuelled romantic comedy.

Printed in Great Britain
by Amazon